DOWN & DIRTY: SLADE

Dirty Angels MC, Book 6

JEANNE ST. JAMES

———

Editor: Proofreading by the Page
Cover Art: Susan Garwood of Wicked Women Designs
Beta Reader: Author Whitley Cox & Krisztina Hollo

———

www.jeannestjames.com

Sign up for my newsletter for insider information, author news, and new releases:
www.jeannestjames.com/newslettersignup

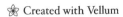 Created with Vellum

Down & Dirty 'til Dead

CHAPTER ONE

"C'mon, brother, wake the fuck up."

Slade groaned as the annoying voice disturbed his peaceful rest.

"Slade. C'mon, brother. You gotta get the fuck outta here."

For some reason, the disturbance sounded a lot like Dawg. Why the fuck would the strip-club manager be giving him an unwelcome wake-up call?

Slade popped one eye open.

Probably because he had passed out at Heaven's Angels Gentlemen's club. *Again.*

That wasn't a pillow under his head. Nope. It was a stripper's lap.

He tipped his eyes upward. Not surprised at all, she was passed out, too. Her head rested against the back of the red velour love seat, her neck bent cockeyed and her mouth wide open.

She didn't look so hot right now.

But then, he probably didn't look much better.

With a groan, he lifted his head off her fishnet-stockinged thighs. Hopefully, she didn't mind the little bit of drool that had escaped his gaping mouth during his snooze-fest.

Fuck.

He wiped the back of his hand over his mouth and groaned.

"Seriously, brother, you gotta get the fuck outta here. Wanna lock up. Take 'er with ya, if you gotta. But just get gone."

He blinked. His brain felt like a whole lot of cotton had been shoved between his ears.

He sucked in a deep breath, then grimaced.

Fuck. He wouldn't be eating that snatch any time soon.

Fuck him. That was deadly.

He pushed himself upright faster than he should have, and his head wobbled. No, that wasn't his head, that was his pickled brain.

"Want me to get one of the prospects to take you back to church?"

He blinked again, hoping his vision would clear. He turned his head to find Dawg standing about five feet away, hands planted on his hips, an unhappy expression on his bearded face. The six-foot-two biker had dark smudges under his eyes. He was probably ready to get some shuteye of his own after working all night.

Slade tried to shake his head, but that made things so much worse. "No," he finally got out, his voice croaking like a sick frog.

"Either that or Diamond. Take your fuckin' pick. If I were you, I'd take door number one. Number two might just shriek your head right off, an' then slam your dick over an' over in that door. 'Specially since your usin' one of my girls as a fuckin' pillow."

Door number one sounded like a good option. There was probably a prospect still in the club that could drag his ass home.

Slade forced out, "Where's Moose?"

"In the back, restockin'. Gonna get him to haul this passed-out bitch home in a few an' can get 'im to drop you off, too."

Slade started to nod but thought better of it.

His brain felt like soup; no point in sloshing it around more than necessary.

"Don't get why you're gettin' fuckin' plastered here every night instead of The Iron Horse. Drink free there, here you don't."

He drank here because most of the club members didn't come out to the strip club. It wasn't a typical hang-out for them. They preferred drinking in church or the public side of the bar, so they could just walk upstairs to their room to pass out.

If he had any sense he'd do the same, but after working a shift at The Iron Horse slinging drinks for Hawk, the club's VP and bar manager, and helping contain any out-of-control customers, he didn't feel like serving himself. He wanted to sit on the other side of the bar, enjoy himself, and not be bothered.

It also didn't hurt that most of Dawg's girls were easy on the eyes and came with big-ass tits.

Not to mention, soft laps to pass out on. And sometimes pussy that didn't smell like death warmed over.

But that wasn't the main reason he'd been ending up here. Fuck no, it wasn't.

The main reason was to lay low. Get his drink on without that bitch harping at him.

A bitch he hadn't even banged yet.

A bitch who had tried to get her claws in him. Take a permanent seat on the back of his sled.

He wasn't ready to have an ol' lady, for fuck's sake.

And even if he was, it certainly wouldn't be Diamond. While they had a bit of fun last summer during some of the club runs, that was all it was... fun. To an extent.

At least until she wanted to become his regular piece.

Worst part about her was the woman didn't listen. No fucking way was he putting up with backtalk and attitude.

He didn't mind claws as long as they only came out while fucking. Screw that everyday shit, though. That would give a brother a headache. Worse than the hangover he would have tomorrow.

Was the bitch hot? Fuck yeah, she was.

Long dark, dark, dark brown hair that was typical for the Dirty Angels MC women, and great for digging his fingers into. Bright blue eyes that could pierce him to his soul. Plump, red lips that would be perfect for wrapping around his cock and sucking him like a fucking Hoover vacuum. And the fucking tits on her... Damn, they'd been pressed to his back during the runs a couple times. He couldn't forget those curvy hips of hers, either. Perfect to sink his fingers into, whether he was fucking her from behind or she was riding him like a bucking bronco.

All stuff he had planned on doing with her until he found out she was fucking crazy, too. She could flip the bitch switch in an instant.

Could have something to do with Di's father, Rocky, doing time in SCI Greene for murder. She was the kind of woman who needed a firm hand and apparently didn't get it growing up with her mother, Ruby, from what he heard. The only father-figure she had was Ace and that poor man already had his hands full with his own two sons, Diesel and Hawk, as well as his nieces and nephews, Dex, Ivy and Bella.

But it wasn't like he'd had a father-figure in his life, either.

No matter what, Slade certainly wasn't going to be filling in for her "daddy" and giving her some life lessons. Especially now that she was about to turn thirty.

No. Fucking. Way.

Though... some of those so-called life lessons could be fun. Her sister, Jewel, got a lot of those from her ol' man, Diesel. It always seemed D, the club's Sergeant at Arms, was throwing his ol' lady over his shoulder and hauling her ass either home or upstairs to his room at church to "teach her a lesson."

His lips twitched. Those were the best kind.

Slade wasn't sure if that's what Diamond needed. But if she did, he wasn't the one willing to give them to her.

Though, he normally didn't mind a challenge, right now he wanted easy.

No lip. No attitude. Fuck, tuck, and go.

Another reason he kept landing face down on Dawg's girls. Couldn't get easier than that. For the most part, anyhow.

They knew better than to cling afterward.

"What's 'er name?" Slade asked Dawg, who was coming from the back room with Moose on his heels. Slade had been so caught up in his thoughts, he hadn't even noticed he'd left.

Damn.

"Don't think it's gonna matter when you wake up tomorrow mornin'."

"It *is* tomorrow mornin' already," the prospect told Dawg.

"No, once he lands in his rack, he ain't wakin' up 'til tomorrow mornin'."

Moose laughed and nodded.

Nope, that couldn't happen. Slade had to work The Iron Horse tomorrow night... tonight... what-fucking-ever. "What time is it?"

"Three."

"Fuck," Slade groaned.

"Yeah, an' I wanna hit my own rack. So get the fuck outta here."

Slade tilted his head toward the still passed-out stripper. "Didn't fuck 'er, right?"

"No. Didn't make it off that couch 'fore you both passed out. Got a sloppy lap dance an' then you were both out fuckin' cold."

"Fuck," Slade muttered again.

"Yeah, owe me a hundred bucks."

Slade's eyebrows shot up his forehead. "For the lap dance?"

"No, owe *her* for the lap dance. Owe *me* for the loss of tips since she missed her last dance on stage."

"Shit."

Dawg nodded. "Yeah, *shit*. This shit's gotta stop, brother. Bad 'nough when you're gettin' wasted, but gettin' my girls wasted ain't good. Got me?"

Slade sucked in a breath. "Yeah. Got you."

"Gotta carry her, Moose. Make sure she gets inside her place an' it's locked up 'fore you leave."

"Got you, boss."

"An' don't be copin' a feel, either. Got me?" Dawg said louder than what was necessary, which made Slade wince.

The heavyset prospect lifted his palms in front of him. "Ain't takin' advantage of some unconscious lady."

Dawg snorted at the prospect's use of "lady." But no matter what Dawg thought of his "girls," he treated them well and made sure they stayed safe. That's why he never had a lack of talent on stage.

"An' that's why I pay you well, prospect. Now get 'em both outta here so I can go crash."

Moose leaned over, picked the stripper up like she weighed nothing, even though she was dead weight, and Slade reluctantly climbed to his feet. His head spun for a second but once he leveled out, he was good to follow Moose out of the club's back door to the employee parking lot.

However, out in the parking lot on the way to the prospect's vehicle, he had to take a quick pit stop and rid his gut of its liquid contents.

And that didn't make him feel one fucking bit better.

———

"The big three-oh!" Jewel practically screamed in her ear.

Diamond winced at her sister's loud enthusiasm. Who the hell was excited when they turned thirty? Not her. Di was not looking forward to her thirtieth birthday. No way, no how. Thirty and still single. Thirty and still not an ol' lady. Thirty and still didn't have anyone in her bed on a regular basis. Thirty and her steady boyfriend took batteries. And a lot of them.

She frowned.

"Okay, so what are we planning?" Bella asked, leaning back into the counter at Sophie's Sweet Treats.

They were having an impromptu meeting of the DAMC women. Somehow, whenever that happened they always ended up at Sophie's bakery.

Well, the reason why was simple.

Fucking awesome, sweet, fattening cupcakes. The best in western Pennsylvania if you asked Diamond. But that was neither here nor there...

The point was the women wanted to do something for her birthday.

"We could do a ladies' night out!" Kelsea chirped.

"Where?" Ivy asked.

Kelsea shrugged. "Find some hot club in the 'Burgh?"

"I'm not going to some club," Bella muttered.

"Why not? It would be fun!" Kelsea exclaimed.

"Well, that would leave me out," Sophie said, holding onto her huge belly. "All I need is my water to break in the middle of the dance floor."

Sophie looked like she was about to pop out Zak's kid at any second. Di wrinkled her nose. It actually looked painful with her body stretched enormously out of its natural shape. It looked like she shoved an overfilled beach ball under her maternity top. She couldn't imagine Sophie's former hot body would ever be the same again.

The woman waddled over to the display case and groaned as she tried to lean over to pull out a tray of cupcakes for them to devour.

"Oh!" Sophie gasped.

"What?" Kiki yelled, eyes wide.

Sophie straightened, making a face. "I think I just peed myself a little. Freaking kid is riding on my bladder like it's a Harley."

"Let me get that," Bella said, putting a hand on Sophie's back and gently moving her out of the way. She pulled out a tray of cupcakes that looked mouth-watering.

"What are those?" Diamond whispered in awe, mesmerized by the hip-widening confections.

Bella did an elaborate hand sweep over the tray. "S'mores cupcakes. Chocolate cake filled with a swirl of fudge and marshmallow filling, topped with toasted marshmallow frosting and graham cracker crumbles on top."

Ivy sighed as she stared at the baked goodies.

Di felt the same way. "Give me one of those right now!"

Bella laughed and handed them out. Everyone got very quiet as they shoved all the sugary goodness into their cupcake holes. Eye rolls, passionate groans, and lip smacking ensued.

Then the bells over the door jingled and they all turned their attention in that direction.

"How'd you know we were pigging out on the newest cupcake flavor?" Bella called out.

Axel pushed through the door, wearing his uniform and a heavy patrol jacket since it was March and winter still hadn't completely vacated Shadow Valley. He smiled and shrugged. His gaze bounced from the tray of cupcakes to Bella.

"I've been thinking about them all morning. Especially since you mumbled something about S'mores cupcakes in your sleep."

"I did not," Bella scoffed.

"I swear you did! Give me one of those." He approached the display case and Bella handed him a cupcake.

All the women held their breath as Axel peeled the baby blue paper baking cup off the bottom of the cupcake and waited for him to tongue the icing in the sensual way he was known to do. But he didn't. He just took a big bite.

All their breath rushed out at once.

"What the fuck, Bella? You ruined it now that he's in your bed every night," Ivy muttered under her breath to her sister.

Bella smirked and shrugged.

After swallowing his bite, he cocked an eyebrow toward the group of women behind the counter. "Am I interrupting an important meeting?"

"Yes, since your cousin's turning thirty in a couple weeks. We're making plans."

"Oh fuck," Axel muttered. "Like what?"

"Going clubbing or male strippers. Or," Kelsea shrugged, "something fun."

Axel frowned. "Male strippers?"

"Yeah, why not?"

Di didn't miss it when Axel's gaze hit Bella's. Something went unsaid between the two.

"We're not doing male strippers," Bella said softly, rolling her lips inward to contain her amusement.

"Says who?" Kelsea asked, disappointed.

Diamond was surprised she didn't stomp her foot for good measure. She was known to do that on occasion.

"I could tell you who would have something to say about it." Axel's gaze landed on Jewel. "Diesel." It moved to Sophie. "Z." It bounced to Ivy. "Jag." Then finally landed on Kiki. "And Hawk. Maybe that's who."

"But not you, right?" Kiki asked, just as amused. "You'd be fine with Bella going to see male strippers?"

Axel's inhale of breath and his chest puffing out was unmistakable. He yanked up his duty belt. "I have no problem with it."

Kelsea's laughter peeled through the shop as she slapped her palm on her thigh. "Right!"

"I wouldn't. Bella's free to do what she wants!" he exclaimed.

"Riiiight," Kelsea said again, still laughing.

Bella moved around the counter and up to Axel, slipping a hand into his open patrol jacket and planting it on his belly. "Maybe it's best if you leave us women to finish our little pow wow. Go fight some crime or something."

He planted a quick kiss on her lips before shoving the remainder of the cupcake into his mouth. He nodded, chewed and swallowed before saying, "Can I take one to go?"

Kiki grabbed another cupcake and held it out to him. He moved to snag it and then leaned into Bella, putting his mouth to her ear.

Diamond wondered what he whispered to his woman and felt a pang of jealousy. It wasn't that she wanted Axel, hell no, she didn't. He was her cousin, for fuck's sake. But she was envious of what those two had.

Hell, she was envious of what all the women in the room, who had hooked up recently, had with their men. All but her. Well, and Kelsea, too.

Bella beamed up at him and after another quick kiss to her forehead, Axel left.

Bella turned to the group who was staring at her and she clapped her hands together sharply. "Now, let's get down to the business of planning Di's thirtieth birthday bash!"

The women hooted and held up their cupcakes, tapping them together like champagne glasses.

"I know part of my plan is that I'm getting laid for my thirtieth," Di declared with a nod.

"Easy enough," Ivy said, licking icing off her finger.

"No, seriously."

"We believe you, sis," Jewel assured her. "All we have to do is plan a pig roast and there'll be plenty of dick to choose from."

"Like who?" Di asked and before anyone could answer, she added, "And don't say Slade."

"Okaaay. I won't." Jewel frowned. "Like hang-arounds. And... we can invite the Dark Knights. I'm sure one of them would drag you by your hair upstairs and bang the shit out of you."

"Yeah, I'm sure our brother would love to watch me being dragged upstairs by a Knight. Your ol' man might have something to say about it, too."

Jewel waved a dismissing hand in the air. "Then don't do it at church. Take whoever it is back to your place."

Di tilted her head as she considered her sister's suggestion.

"Okay, but we still need to plan what we're doing," Kelsea said.

"I think we need to do it somewhere other than church," Kiki said. "We want it to be special. You only turn thirty once and we don't want it to turn into a club party just like any other."

"True," Ivy said, tapping her bottom lip with her finger.

"So we don't want to do it at The Iron Horse, either..." Kiki said, clearly giving it some thought.

"No. Plus, do we really want the men busting in and being all up in our business? Making sure we're not doing something *they* don't approve of?" Jewel said, reminding them all of how bossy and domineering the club members can be.

"Right. I thought you liked driving your man so crazy he gives you those "lessons" of his?"

Jewel smiled, her eyes sparkling. "I do. But still..."

"Right. They'll spoil it. It has to be elsewhere."

"So we go to a club and go dancing. Simple as that," Kelsea said.

"Somebody *really* wants to go out clubbing," Kiki murmured.

"What else is there to do?" Kelsea, the youngest of all the club sisters, asked.

"Not goin' out dancin'," came the deep grumble from the direction of the bakery kitchen.

"Ah, fuck," Kelsea muttered next to Di as Zak came through the door.

"Ain't goin' out runnin' 'round puttin' yourself in danger with the fuckin' Warriors on the warpath," he continued.

"The Warriors aren't going to be at a night club in Pittsburgh," Kelsea huffed.

Z shook his head, making his dark shoulder-length hair swing, and stepped up to his wife, curving a hand along the bottom of her extended belly. "How's he doin'?"

"*She's* doing fine," Sophie corrected him.

"Why didn't you guys find out the sex?" Kiki asked with more than a little exasperation in her voice.

Sophie waved a hand around, then laid it over Z's. "We want it to be a surprise. And I already know it's going to be a girl."

"Ain't gonna be a girl," Z grumbled.

Bella snorted at the argument that kept being repeated for almost the last nine months. And it was driving them *all* crazy.

"What are you going to do if it is?" Kiki asked, her eyes crinkling with amusement at his stubbornness.

Z opened his mouth and shut it. His eyes narrowed, and he frowned. Then he said, "You women wanna party, do it at church."

"Z! No!" Kelsea yelled.

"No, we're not doing it at church," Jewel seconded Kelsea.

"No lip. Ain't gotta choice."

"The fuck we don't!" Kelsea cried.

Z raised his brows and swung his head toward her, laying down the law. "Church or nothin'. Got me?"

"What the fuck," Kelsea muttered. "We're not having our meetings here anymore."

Di sort of agreed with Kelsea. It was difficult to have their meetings at the bakery now when it always seemed that Z was around. Instead of working in any of the other club businesses, he decided he'd help "manage" the bakery, which, to him, pretty much meant he got to boss his wife and Bella around and *sometimes* do paperwork.

But really, Diamond thought the reason he wanted to "work" in the bakery was to keep an eye on and protect his pregnant wife.

Sophie cupped her man's cheek as she grinned up at him. "Then you men have to promise to stay out and we can have male strippers come in."

His blue eyes swung back down to his wife. "What?"

"You heard me," Sophie murmured, her grin widening to a smile.

His eyebrows hit the top of his head. "Strippers?"

Di tried not to laugh at the way he spit that word out of his mouth.

"Yeah, you know, like the ones that are always at all the club parties, except these have dicks instead of tits," Kelsea said, crossing her arms over her chest. "Shouldn't have a problem with that, right? With equality and all that."

Z's eyebrows dropped low and his expression turned dark and stormy. "Equality? Have you lost your fuckin' mind?"

"Nope. Time for this club to come into the twenty-first century. We're demanding equality," Kelsea declared as she stomped her foot. *Ah, there it was.*

Z snorted, dropped his head to stare at his boots and shook it. "Brain musta got scrambled," he muttered to the floor. He raised his gaze to his wife. "You ain't goin' nowhere with my kid in your belly, got me?"

Sophie pinned her lips together as she patted his chest reassuringly. "First off, I'm not going out dancing in this condition."

"In any condition," he corrected her in a mutter.

"And your concern with our safety is duly noted."

"Reason for it."

"Right. I get it, baby," she whispered. She glanced toward the rest of the women. "But it's Di's thirtieth birthday and we *are* going to celebrate it, whether you like it or not."

"That so?"

"Yep, that's so," Sophie repeated with a nod.

Di rolled her lips under in an attempt not to beam at Sophie's control over her husband. As club president and badass biker, he wasn't normally willing to bend for a woman, but Sophie had him wrapped around her little finger. And right now she was wiggling that powerful pinky.

The rest of the women were pretending not to notice Sophie's control over her old man. Di eyeballed Kelsea, hoping the younger woman kept her trap shut and didn't blow it for them.

Kelsea's eyes slid to hers and she bugged them out in a silent message. Di gave her a slight nod.

Zak finally sighed. "Gonna get Hawk to close down The Iron Horse an' get Dawg to book you some male strippers. Ain't gonna let any of the brothers over there to bother you. Drink, dance, eyeball some strange dick, have fun. Still safe. Got me?"

"Got you," Sophie whispered, her eyes sparkling.

"Invite Dawg's girls."

"No," she said firmly with a shake of her head.

His eyebrows furrowed. "The sweet butts."

"No."

"The Knights' ol' ladies," he muttered finally.

"Fine."

"Gonna set the prospects out front to guard the door. Keep an eye out for trouble."

"Fine. As long as they don't come in."

His nostrils flared. "Whatever," he muttered, pressed a kiss to her forehead and moved back in the direction he had come from. No one said a word until the door to the back kitchen swung shut. Then they even waited a few more seconds until they knew he was out of hearing range.

Then they all looked at each other and beamed. Di rushed up to Sophie and gave her a high five. "Good job."

"Now, I just hope I don't pop until after the party. I want to see the results of my negotiations."

"Strange dick?" Ivy asked, quoting Z.

"Hell yes!" Kelsea crowed.

Ivy snorted. "Dawg should have connections to find a hot traveling troupe of male strippers on short notice."

"Up to him, he may find the ugliest ones."

"I'll call him and make sure he doesn't," Jewel assured Kelsea. "And I'll make sure there's a lot of them. One for each of us."

"Oh, brother. You know Z was only the first obstacle. Some of us will have one of our very own," Kiki said.

"Like Hawk?" Jewel asked.

"Mmm. And remember that big, serious, overly protective brother of his?" Kiki asked her with an arched brow.

"How can I forget?" Diesel's ol' lady answered with a frown.

"Right."

"Bah," Jewel answered, waving a dismissing hand. "They'll all get over it."

Di was suddenly glad she didn't have to worry about a possessive man like most of them did. She was free to enjoy her birthday and hot, naked men as much as she wanted.

And she was going to make sure she took full advantage of her birthday celebration. Maybe she'd even be able to talk one of the strippers into a private dance. At her place. With both of them totally naked. And horizontal.

No batteries required.

Yeah, that sounded like a great idea.

She couldn't wait.

CHAPTER TWO

S lade groaned, pressed the heel of his palm into his eye socket and ground it hard. His head was splitting open and he hadn't even opened his eyes yet. He held his breath for a moment and listened carefully.

Breathing.

That wasn't his.

He cracked one eye open and stared at a stained dropped ceiling that was not the one in his room at church.

Fuck.

He opened the other eye and slid his gaze over to the side without turning his head. Because that might be too painful.

He did a mental body scan. He was naked. Something alive was next to him. And he was laying on something somewhat soft.

Possibly a bed.

He sucked in a breath to steel himself and finally forced his head to turn.

Fuck.

That was a lot of long, dark hair covering the woman's face. But hair was the only thing covering her. Otherwise, she was as naked as he was.

For a moment, his heart stopped thinking that somehow he hooked up with Diamond and ended up in her bed.

Because that would be a fucking mistake. A huge one.

Sticking his dick in her would be like sticking your finger in one of those Chinese finger traps. The harder you pulled away the tighter the trap got.

He carefully pushed some of that hair out of the woman's face and studied her.

Fuck. What was her name?

Sarah. Sally. Sierra.

No. It was more stripperish. Sa-something.

Her eyelids lifted, and blue eyes stared at him. His heart stopped again.

Dark hair. Blue eyes...

Just like Diamond. *Fuuuuuck.*

She yawned and pushed herself over, curling into his side.

Oh, fuck.

"Morning, soldier," she greeted with a smile, reaching out to run her red-painted fingernail over his dog tags.

Was it morning?

"Not a soldier," he grumbled, his voice rusty.

"You're wearin' tags."

"Yeah," was all he grunted. He needed to get the fuck out of there. He glanced down at his dick.

"We fucked, right?" he asked her.

Her eyes got wide and Slade realized her blue eyes didn't have the same intensity as Diamond's. Fuck no they didn't. This one's eyes were a bit dull.

"You don't remember?"

"Will you be mad if I say no?"

When her eyes narrowed, he took that as a yes.

"How 'bout if I don't remember your name?"

She pushed away from him and sat up. "You don't know my name?"

He groaned quietly. "Know it. Just drawin' a blank right now.

Starts with an S."

She bit her bottom lip, studied him and when she finally released it, said, "Savannah. Not surprised you don't remember. You kept calling me Di or Diamond or something like that."

Ah, shit. "So we fucked?"

She nodded.

"Wore a wrap, right?"

She nodded again.

Thank fuck!

"Wait. How many times did we fuck?"

She held up three fingers.

Jesus fuckin' Christ.

"Wore a wrap all three times, yeah?"

She nodded again.

Oh, thank Christ!

"This your place?"

"Yeah."

He looked around the small room. She was not a neat person. Clothes, whether they were dirty or clean, were in piles everywhere. The top of her dresser was so full of shit, he couldn't even see an inch of the wood top. A trashcan overflowed nearby. Dust covered the little bit of space that was visible on her nightstand. This woman was not squared away at all.

He was afraid to inspect the sheets they were laying on to see if they were clean or dirty.

He shuddered, pushed to a seat, and dropped his legs over the side of the bed. "Gotta go."

"Don't want to have breakfast? Kids will be up soon; I can make us some pancakes or something."

Kids.

Fuuuuuuck.

He glanced over his shoulder at her. Now that he was upright he realized how much she looked like Diamond. But in a more "ridden hard and put away wet" type of way.

"How many kids you got?"

She smiled as if he was asking because he was interested. He wasn't really. He didn't want to be a daddy to anyone else's offspring.

"Four."

Holy fuck. He needed to get out of there. He didn't want to be daddy to number five, either. He hoped she was telling the truth about him wearing protection each time they fucked. Because the woman was apparently very fertile.

"Got four kids an' you're strippin'?"

She shrugged. "Pays the bills."

He pushed to his feet and searched for his clothes. He was relieved when he found them neatly folded up on top of what he hoped was a pile of clean clothes. His boots were nearby, and he spotted his cut hanging from the knob of her bedroom door. At least that hadn't ended up on the dirty floor.

He pulled on his clothes quickly.

"So... breakfast?"

"Gotta go."

"Gonna be at the club again tonight?"

Ah, fuck. "No, gotta work."

"Thought you said you worked last night."

He froze as he pulled his long sleeved thermal shirt over his head. "Yeah."

"You stopped by after work."

That he did. "Yeah. Gotta close tonight. Gonna hit the rack after that."

"Another time, then."

He tugged his shirt down his torso and grabbed his cut. "Yeah, 'nother time."

Shoving his feet into his boots, he didn't bother to even lace them before yanking the door open.

"It was fun," she called out.

If it was, he couldn't remember. "Yeah," he grunted, not looking back. He needed to get to church and take a damn shower to wash stripper off him. All these months he'd avoided actually fucking any of them. He'd done a couple sweet butts just to relieve the load in his nuts, but that was it. He tried not to stick his dick in anything that hung around the club on a regular basis. He didn't need that hassle.

And since Dawg tended to bring some of his girls to the club parties, he wasn't in the mood to have one of them trying to lay their claim on him.

At least most of the sweet butts knew the deal. They were available to any of the brothers simply for the opportunity to hang around the club. Why any woman in their right mind would want that, he didn't know. But when he was sick of yanking on his own dick, he'd take them up on being available.

Though, sometimes he thought he'd better double wrap it. Even though some of his club brothers were going down left and right, getting trapped with ol' ladies, enough single brothers remained to keep them busy. Worse, some of the sweet butts had this notion that they might become an ol' lady.

Not his. No fucking way. He was not hooking up permanently with a sweet butt. Hell, he wasn't hooking up permanently with anyone.

And that included Diamond Jamison.

———

Slade slipped in through the back door of church and groaned. He looked right into blue eyes framed by long dark hair.

Diamond was heading in his direction like a woman on a mission. He braced as she approached but she ignored him and was about to blow right by him when she suddenly slammed on the brakes. He went solid since she was only inches from him, but facing the opposite direction. He turned his head, so did she, and her narrowed eyes met his wide, *he-was-sure-as-shit* bloodshot ones.

Her nose wrinkled as she leaned in and sniffed him. "Smell like pussy." He froze as she shifted even closer, her nose now barely inches from his neck. "And cheap perfume. Must like them easy."

"Nobody wants a ballbuster, princess," he muttered.

"Don't call me that."

"Which one? Ballbuster or princess?"

"Either. I'm not a ballbuster."

Slade snorted. "Right. What're you doin' here?"

She arched a brow at him. "Getting shit together for my party."

"What party?"

"My birthday party. The Iron Horse will be closed down for the night so us ladies can party."

"When's that?" he asked, surprised at this news.

"Thursday night. We won't need your services."

"Wasn't offerin' 'em."

"All the brothers will have to stay out. No men allowed but the strippers."

He cocked a brow. "What strippers?"

"The male exotic dancers we're getting for my birthday."

"What the fuck," he muttered. So not only was Hawk allowing the women to shut down The Iron Horse for a night, the brothers were allowing male strippers to come in to entertain the club women? She had to be bullshitting him. They'd never allow that.

No fucking way.

"Going to bang one, too," she announced with confidence.

Slade put two fingers to his ear and rubbed it hard. He could've sworn she said she was going to bang a male stripper. "What the fuck you talkin' 'bout?"

"I'm going to fuck one of the dancers."

Every muscle in his body went solid. Even if Hawk and the rest were allowing male strippers to come in... "They won't fuck you."

"Why not?"

"Because they don't do that kinda shit."

She planted her hands on her hips, her attitude seeping out enough that he swore he could almost see it. "Didn't one of them just bang you?"

He opened his mouth, then snapped it shut.

She made a little noise. "Thought so."

"Whatever," he muttered. "Hawk know you're bringin' male strippers into his bar?"

"Yep."

What the fuck? "Know they're all gay, right? Ain't gonna fuck you."

Her eyes snapped. "Why do you care if they do?"

"They?"

"Yeah, it's my birthday, maybe I'll have more than one." She smiled. A big fucking one, too.

Slade's jaw tightened, and he sucked in a breath. "Don't do anything stupid."

"You should talk."

He sucked at his teeth, feeling his temper rise. He was tempted to teach her one of those "lessons" Diesel taught his ol' lady all the time. But Slade still had the remnants of another woman's snatch on his dick, so that wouldn't do.

That reminded him, he needed to clean up. "Gotta shower."

"Yeah, you do."

He shook his head and headed toward the stairs. "Don't be fuckin' strippers, princess," he tossed over his shoulder.

"Maybe you should take your own advice."

Yeah, maybe he should.

CHAPTER THREE

The *thump, thump, thump* coming from The Iron Horse shook the wall behind the bar at church.

"For fuck's sake, swear that music's louder than when Dirty Deeds is playin'." Jag griped, downing a shot of whiskey and wiping the back of his hand over his mouth. He slammed the shot glass onto the bar and as soon as it landed, Hawk filled it up again.

Hawk poured more into his own recently-emptied shot glass then raised the bottle of Jack to eyeball how much was left.

Slade should've left, that's what he should've fucking done. He wasn't needed tonight to bartend or even act as a bouncer since The Iron Horse was closed to the public. He had no reason to stick around.

But he also didn't want to head over to Heaven's Angel's Gentlemen's Club. He wasn't in the mood to run into Sierra... Sarah... *fuck*... Savannah. Whatever.

He'd stayed out of the strip club the last few nights, working late at Hawk's bar and afterward hitting his rack to catch up on some much-needed sleep.

But, fuck him, here he was, sitting in church drinking with his club brothers whose women were over next door about to get down and dirty with some so-called male *exotic dancers*.

Man-hos. That's what they were.

Probably going to be wearing microscopic banana holsters to keep their tiny pricks contained.

Fuck.

He held out his empty shot glass and Hawk splashed some more of the amber liquid into it.

Diesel was on a tear, pacing back and forth behind them, his fingers clenching and unclenching into fists as he muttered to himself.

Slade had to admit, he'd never seen the massive man so bent out of shape before. Well, maybe when that crazy-ass Warrior, Black Jack, snatched Jewel.

"Brother, gotta calm the fuck down. Nobody's gonna be touchin' your ol' lady," Hawk called out.

"Better fuckin' not," D grumbled.

"All those male strippers are gay, anyway," Slade mumbled, hoping that was true.

"Better be," Z said, next to him.

"What do *you* got to worry 'bout? Your ol' lady's already knocked up an' about to pop," Jag said. "An' it was your genius suggestion to let 'em have this over there."

Z swung his gaze to his cousin. "Want 'em runnin' wild 'round the 'Burgh dancin' an' drinkin' an' who knows what the fuck else?"

"No," Hawk grunted, slamming the Jack Daniel's bottle onto the bar top and sliding it down to the other end of the bar where Grizz and Crow sat; Crow nursing his whiskey, Grizzly nursing a beer.

"So glad I don't got no ol' lady over there starin' at some strange," Crow said into his liquor, then laughed. He turned his head in their direction. "You guys look like a buncha sorry asses."

"How long's this thing supposed to last?" Hawk asked Z.

"How the fuck am I supposed to know? Dawg set it the fuck up."

"Music only just started," Crow reminded them with a snicker from his stool down the bar.

"Maybe we should all head down to Dirty Dick's an' hang with the Knights 'til this is all over with," Jag suggested, raking his fingers through his hair.

"Ain't leavin' the women here without protection," D barked.

"Got Jester an' Coop standin' outside the front door keepin' watch," Hawk reminded him.

The two newest prospects were given the shitty job of standing guard outside the front door of the bar in the cold. Slade was glad he never had to prospect for the DAMC, since he'd done it once already for another club. He'd vowed never to do it again since prospects were treated lower than dog shit. Z had made an exception to him prospecting since Slade helped with some trouble the Warriors brought on the club's women at a fundraiser the summer before. "Helped" as in knocked a Warrior the fuck out.

"Don't give a fuck who's standin' out there. Ain't leavin'," D insisted.

Hawk came from behind the bar and shoved a glass of whiskey at his brother. D took it, downed it in one swallow and shoved the empty glass back at his brother, who whacked D on the back and let the agitated man go back to pacing.

"Gonna pace for the next two hours?" Z asked him.

D abruptly came to a halt, turned his dark eyes their direction and barked, "Fuck no." He strode around the bar, opened one of the cabinets, and turned on a hidden monitor.

Fuck! Slade forgot D had installed security cameras and a digital video recording system in The Iron Horse. He did it after the Warriors shot up bar during the club's Christmas party almost three months ago. They had also reinforced the front walls of the bar during the reconstruction, but still... those cameras...

He wondered if the women knew. Probably not. Because Slade worked there almost every night and forgot all about it himself. The cameras were small enough not to be noticed.

"D, don't know if you should watch," Hawk warned.

Diesel ignored him and flipped through the feeds until the one that pointed toward the center of the bar came into view.

This was not a good idea. It was like waving a red flag in front of an annoyed bull.

Nothing good was going to come of watching the woman getting all hot and bothered by oiled-up, buff men wearing G-strings while grinding against their women.

Not one damn good thing.

Diamond's chair sat in the center of the large circle of women. It was a better turn-out than she'd thought. Kiki, Ivy, Jewel, Sophie, Kelsea, Bella, Jayde, and Ace's wife, Janice, showed up. As well as Ace's sisters, Annie and Allie. Even Di's mom, Ruby, was there. And they couldn't forget Mama Bear, Grizz's ol' lady. Some of the Knight's ol' ladies and regular pieces arrived, too, like Magnum's woman, who, surprisingly, was a tall, pretty blonde named Stacy.

But it was Di's birthday and tonight she was the center of attention. Kelsea started bouncing anxiously in her chair when the loud, bass-heavy music started.

Di had a flashback of the movie *Magic Mike* when a long line of hot men, unfortunately still wearing clothes, came running out of the kitchen's swinging doors.

She sank her teeth into her bottom lip and her nails into her palms to contain her excitement as they all climbed up onto the bar and began to dance in a row.

All the breath rushed out of her as she eyeballed their bodies. Even in clothes, they were clearly not rough and tumble bikers. Hell no, they weren't. Their hair was neatly trimmed, their faces not at all scruffy and their clean-cut clothes didn't have oil or grease stains on them. Not at all. There wasn't one leather vest in the room, either.

And they probably didn't smell like well-banged pussy.

Hot damn!

She groaned as one at a time they moved to the center of the polished wood bar and stripped down to skin-tight shorts that didn't leave anything to the imagination. Their skin was tanned and shiny like they had rubbed baby oil all over themselves.

Fuck. She wanted that job.

Even over the loud music, she heard the women behind her whistling, cat-calling and shouting out their encouragement.

Then as one, they ripped off their shorts and all leapt off the bar and began to circle the women, gyrating and thrusting their hips, straddling their laps, touching and rubbing anyone who was willing. Or anyone who held out a dollar bill. Or two.

Then two of the dancers broke off and came right to her. One with dark hair and not a damn tat in sight. And the other a blonde with beautiful green eyes and silver barbells piercing both nipples. She sucked in an excited breath.

Their bodies were perfect, muscles cut, thighs powerful as they danced around her. Di didn't know which one to stare at first.

Happy fucking birthday to her.

The dark-haired one approached her from the front, while the blond from behind. She was about to be the center of a man sand-wich. She couldn't scrape the smile off her face even if she tried.

She looked up at the dark-haired one. "What's your name?"

"Robby."

Di jerked her head toward the blond. "What's his?"

"Bobby."

No fucking way. She was about to be man-handled by Robby and Bobby. Fuck yeah, she was.

A giggle slipped from her. She covered her mouth in shock. She *never* giggled.

She raised the wad of ones she had in her fist. "What'll you do for a buck?"

"You're the birthday girl, right?" Robby asked, his eyes twinkling.

Another giggle threatened to spill out. "Sure am!"

"Then whatever you want."

Hell, yes! "What'll you do for a hundred bucks?"

"You."

Di nodded and beamed up at him. "That's exactly what I wanted to hear."

Then Robby was straddling her, grabbing her head and thrusting his groin into her face with the music.

Another giggle slipped out and she sucked in a breath. She wasn't even drunk, but she was giddy as fuck.

Who would've thought having male strippers would be so much fun.

Di tucked a folded dollar bill into her cleavage and without hesitation, Robby pulled it out with his teeth, his breath hot skimming along her skin. Her nipples puckered to hard peaks under her deep V-necked top.

Oh yeah.

Fuck Slade and his statement that these men were gay. That man didn't know shit. He only wanted to ruin her fun.

Bobby switched off with Robby and the blond began to run his hands all over Di's body, then he shoved his face into her breasts and motor-boated her.

She let out a squeal of laughter, digging her fingers into his hair to hold him there as long as possible.

When he finally came up for air, she turned her head enough so she could see the other women in the circle all enjoying themselves as the dancers stripped down to their G-strings and were bumping and grinding to the music.

Not one of those women weren't smiling and laughing.

Not one.

Diamond had to admit, Kelsea had finally come up with a good idea for once.

"That fucker touchin' my wife's belly?" Z shouted, his eyes wide and his face red.

Slade leaned over the bar a little more to see what the club president was freaking out about, but he couldn't see shit since the monitor was surrounded by Z, Hawk, Diesel and Jag. And that combination of bulk was hard to see through.

Might as well be a brick wall.

However, he could see that their bodies were tense, and Jag had his hands wrapped around the back of his neck, like he was trying to keep his shit together.

"What the fuck," Hawk muttered as he leaned closer to the monitor. "That... No. He did not... fuck that. This shit's gonna end."

D slammed his fist on the counter in front of the monitor. "Fuck that shit!" he bellowed.

Slade slipped from the stool he was sitting on, his gaze meeting Crow's amused one as he rounded the bar to join his brothers.

"Can't be that bad," he said, pushing between Z and Jag. His eyes hit the screen and he froze.

Then he squinted, shook his head to clear it, then looked more carefully at the color monitor.

"Did..." he started, but then his brain exploded from what he was seeing. It looked like one of those gay men was humping Diamond's face. He only wore one of those tiny banana hammocks in red and he was... Yes, he was thrusting his junk right into Diamond's face and she was...

Smiling and laughing, her hands wrapped around his ass, encouraging that shit.

No, she wasn't.

Oh fuck, yes, she was!

And that wasn't even the worst of it. Another of those gay dudes was behind her, shoving his hands down her shirt and grabbing her tits!

He twisted his head toward Jag. "See what they're doin' to your fuckin' sister?"

Jag's eyes were glued to the screen as he yelled, "Fuck my sister! See what they're doin' to my woman?"

Slade's gaze swung back to the monitor and he found Ivy, her long red hair twisted up in a dancer's fist as he tugged her head back and shoved his face into her neck.

Oh fuck.

The worst part was Jag's ol' lady wasn't pushing the guy away. Hell no, she kept waving a dollar bill around, encouraging the man.

The only one that had a lick of sense was Bella as she sat outside the circle just watching, but she was laughing at the chaos going on inside The Iron Horse.

Complete utter chaos.

"Fuckin' stoppin' this shit," D barked, pulling out of the huddle.

"No," Crow shouted, making everyone freeze. "Don't do it. Told 'em you were stayin' out. Was the deal."

D's head swung his direction. "Ain't gotta woman over there, brother. Don't got much say."

"The fuck I don't. That was the deal, remember? They stay here, they don't get bothered by any of us."

"No one said dick 'bout touchin'," D bellowed, his eyes a bit wild.

"Also didn't tell 'em about the cameras. Want 'em to find that out right 'bout now? Think any of you gonna get to enjoy the spoils of this night after," Crow lifted his chin toward the monitor, "those guys get 'em all horned up? You go bustin' in over there, you guys ain't gettin' shit but a cold shoulder tonight. Think 'bout that. Let 'em have their fun an' they'll all be climbin' onto your dicks tonight an' ridin' you hard."

Slade's eyebrows raised. That might be the most words he ever heard Crow say at one time.

He turned back to the monitor. Problem was, the rest of the men crowding the monitor *would* get to enjoy their women all horned up tonight.

Unlike him. He wasn't getting shit except annoyed.

He ground his teeth as he watched Diamond get pulled from her chair and sandwiched between two dancers. One was dry humping her while the other smacked her ass.

Even though there was no sound with the camera feed, it wasn't hard to figure out that the fucking bitch was laughing her ass off. Her head was thrown back and she was now grinding against the dancer who was pinned to her front.

His nostrils flared, and he sucked in a sharp breath.

She said she was going to get laid for her birthday. She clearly stated it would be by one or possibly more of those dancers. And by the way she was acting with two of them, she had found her targets.

"Suggest you turn that shit off before you all fuckin' blow a head gasket," Grizz growled from the end of the bar.

Hawk shot a look in the old man's direction. "Don't wanna see how your ol' lady's actin'?"

Grizz tugged on his long, grey, scraggly beard and his eyes crinkled deeply at the corners. "Fuck no. Don't give a shit. Just know I'm gettin' laid tonight an' it's been a long fuckin' time. She can do whatever the fuck she wants as long as she ends up with my dick between her legs."

Crow snorted, lifting his glass of whiskey. "See? Man's got the right idea. Shut that thing off an' let 'em be."

"Anyone touches that monitor, I'll break your fuckin' fingers," D growled. "Need to know how many lessons my woman's gettin' tonight."

Jag barked out a laugh and moved away from the show, shaking his head. "Can't watch anymore. Better be right, old man. Ivy better be spinnin' on my dick like a pole dancer later."

Grizz waved a dismissing hand toward Jag and grunted.

D glanced down at Slade. "What the fuck you standin' here for? Thought you gave up the chase on that snatch."

"Wasn't chasin' nothin'," Slade grumbled.

"Coulda fooled me," D said, his eyes going back to the monitor. He leaned forward, squinted then stumbled back a step. "Oh, fuck no."

D spun on his heel and Hawk grabbed his arm, shaking his head. "No, brother, Grizz an' Crow are right. Promised them. Let 'em go."

D swung a meaty paw toward the monitor. "Your fuckin' woman's got her face shoved in a man's junk."

Hawk took a visible breath and closed his eyes for a second. "Yep. Saw it. Gonna forget it. Also gonna make 'er pay for it later."

D surprised everyone by grinning, something the man hardly ever did. "Yeah."

Hawk gave him a chin lift and a grunted "yeah" back. Then he grabbed the Jack and poured them both a double shot.

When he was done, Slade grabbed the bottle from him, put it to his lips and let the liquor slide down his throat.

Z snorted. "Looks like someone ain't done with the chase."

Slade finished off the remainder of whiskey, hissed out the burn, and swiped his hand over his mouth. "Just commiseratin' with you all."

Z snorted again. "Right."

Slade shoved himself away from the monitor and moved down the bar to where he couldn't see it anymore. He needed to leave. He needed to get the fuck out of there. He couldn't watch anymore and couldn't stand to hear the music thumping.

He closed his eyes and all he could picture was Diamond naked in a bed, sandwiched between those two guys as they were sucking and fucking her.

He ground his back molars and then slammed his hand on the bar.

When he opened his eyes, he saw everyone was staring at him. Some more amused than others.

He wasn't finding any of this funny.

Jag sat on the stool next to him. "Know she's my sister, but she can be a fuckin' bitch."

"Know it."

"Long as you know it an' are prepared to deal with it."

"Ain't havin' to deal with shit."

"Right," Jag murmured, running a hand over his jaw. "Got it bad, brother."

"Bullshit," Slade spat.

"Recognize it 'cause I had it bad, too. Fuckin' Ivy jerked me 'round for years."

Slade turned his head to study Diamond's brother. He was surprised to hear Jag admit that since Ivy and Jag seemed like they were made for each other. Any time they were near each other they were always touching in one way or another.

Jag downed another shot of whiskey. He placed the glass on the bar with care as if he was doing his best not to smash it. "Watched her fuckin' all kinds of geeks an' nerds. Drove me to the point of doin' stupid shit."

"Like what?"

"Like fuckin' Goldie on one of those couches," he tilted his head toward a worn, old couch along one of the walls in the common room, "during a party. Everybody watchin', includin' her. Was draggin' around one of her nerds that night an' I lost my shit."

"Who's Goldie?"

"Used to be one of Dawg's girls. Let's just say she made 'er rounds... a few times."

Slade grimaced and thought about the stripper whose bed he woke up in a few mornings prior. One that happened to remind him of Diamond when he crossed his eyes and squinted. Or drank a whole lot of liquor. Which he'd been doing too much lately.

"Gonna take on a woman who can flip the bitch switch in an instant, gotta be willin' to deal with the challenge an' the claws."

Slade stared at the empty Jack bottle sitting in front of him.

Jag wasn't done yet. "But you tame 'er, might be worth it."

"Talkin' 'bout your sister," Slade said with a frown.

Jag nodded. "Know it. Just tryin' to give a brother some advice."

"None needed," he muttered.

The man next to him snorted. "Keep tellin' yourself that." Jag shouted down the bar, "Hawk, get us a fresh bottle. This brother needs a fuckin' drink."

That was one thing Slade could agree with.

CHAPTER FOUR

S lade leaned back against one of the counters in the commercial kitchen between the private side and public side of the building and waited. With both his arms and ankles crossed, he was trying to appear a lot fucking calmer than he actually was.

The Jack Daniels had helped smooth out the edge a little, but not enough.

If that fucking woman thought she was going to get laid by a couple of strippers, she had another thing coming.

That was for damn sure.

Most of the women had already split, heading home with their still agitated men. Even some of the dancers had come into the kitchen to get dressed before heading out, most of them eyeballing him and even a couple of them giving him some chin lifts.

Not that he returned them.

Fuck no, he didn't.

"Cool tats, bro," one of them even said.

Cool tats, bro.

Slade grunted and kept his eyes pinned to the swinging double doors that lead out to The Iron Horse.

He didn't know what was taking the woman so long. She'd better not be getting fucked in the middle of the bar. He was tempted to peer through the scratched, plastic windows of the doors, but he forced himself to remain in place.

His chest was tight, his blood pressure sky-high, and his imagination was starting to spin out of control.

"Wants to get laid for her fuckin' birthday," he mumbled.

"What?" one of the dancers asked as he passed Slade, carrying a large duffle bag. Slade couldn't imagine why the man needed one that big since they hardly wore anything when they were thrusting their dicks into the women's faces. And they call that dancing.

"Fuck off," he growled at the guy, whose eyes widened as he rushed out of the kitchen.

Then, just who he was waiting for pushed through the doors.

Not with one dancer, fuck no. With two. The two he saw dry humping and spanking her.

"I'm parked out back. We can go back to my place..." Her voice drifted off and the big smile she was wearing dropped quickly once she spotted him.

Slade glared at the two men flanking her. "Get your shit an' get gone," he growled.

Diamond put her hand out and stopped them both from moving away. "Nope. Don't got a say in this, Slade." She plastered a smile on her face and said, "Robby and Bobby are coming home with me."

Robby and Bobby? Was she shitting him?

He pushed off the counter and dropped his fists to his sides. "Get your shit an' get gone," he said slowly so the Bobby twins didn't misunderstand him.

Diamond's mouth gaped as both dancers bolted from her side, grabbed their bags and pushed back past her still only wearing their G-strings.

Within seconds they were gone.

"What. The. Fuck!" Diamond screeched.

Slade grabbed her upper arm and dragged her through the doors that led into church.

"What are you doing?" she screeched some more, digging in her heels and pulling back.

Slade was glad to see that the common room was empty, and no one was about to witness him losing his fucking mind.

"Want to get fucked for your birthday? That what you want?" he tossed over his shoulder as he pressed forward, still dragging her along behind him.

She stumbled, caught herself and then jerked backwards. But he was not releasing her. No fucking way.

"Yeah. But not by you."

"Bullshit," he growled as he closed in on the stairs.

"You like easy. I'm a ballbuster, remember?"

"Don't always like it easy, princess, sometimes I like a little fight in my fuck." He got to the bottom of the steps and stopped, his breath ragged, more from anger than from exertion.

For some reason she was panting, too.

He tightened his fingers around her bicep and her bright blue eyes turned dark. "What are you going to do?" she breathed.

"What I should've done a long time ago," he muttered to himself more than her. "Allowed you to get under my skin an' work your way 'round like a fucking flesh-eating virus. Gotta get you outta my system."

"What?" she whispered. "I'm not going upstairs with you. Especially since you think I'm a *flesh-eating virus*!" Her whisper ended in a shout and he winced.

"Ain't D, can't carry your ass upstairs. But we're doing this, princess. Givin' you your birthday wish an' I'm gettin' you out from under my skin."

"Well, that's sounds like a pleasant fucking time!"

He met her fiery gaze, his jaw tight. "Gonna keep screechin' at me like a harpy?"

"A what?"

"A fuckin' harpy!" he shouted. He'd had enough of this shit. He swore a vessel in his forehead was about to pop. He leaned in close, so close that when he breathed, he inhaled her: her scent, her warm, sweet, alcohol-tinged breath, her wrath. "Listen. Gonna fuck you good. Gonna make you come. Gonna give you what you want for your fuckin' birthday. Then we're done. Got me?"

She raised a brow at him. "Only once?"

He jerked his head back. "Only once what?"

"Only going to make me come once? Is that all you're good for?"

He pinned his lips together and released her. He stared at his boots, shaking his head, until the urge to strangle her passed. "Won't know 'til you get your fuckin' ass upstairs."

She cocked her head and planted her hands on her hips. "Is that right?"

"Woman," was all he could manage.

Then out of nowhere, she smiled and started hiking herself up the stairs.

He blew out the breath he didn't realize he was holding and watched as her ass swung back and forth with each step.

"Holy fuck," he muttered under his breath, and followed her up, wondering how much of a mistake this was.

As they hit the top landing, she glanced at him and he lifted his chin in the direction she needed to go. He watched in shock as she headed toward his room down the hall.

He took his time following her because he was waiting for her to turn and try to bolt past him. But, fuck him, she didn't. She kept moving even though she had no idea which room was his.

He heard a noise behind him and a low voice exclaiming, "Oh, brother, good luck with that," then a door slammed shut and locked.

He wouldn't be surprised if everyone was battening down the hatches with the hurricane named Diamond moving down the hallway.

"Hold up," he called out and pulled his room key from his pocket. She stopped, turned and moved back toward him. He unlocked his door and pushed it open and as she stepped past him inside, he leaned in and hit the overhead light.

"Jesus," she muttered, wrinkling up her nose. "This is a shit hole."

He looked around his small room. Wasn't the Ritz, but every-thing had a place and was in it neatly. He wasn't one of the brothers who had dirty laundry tossed all over the floor or mold growing in their bathroom. Fuck no. It was organized and clean.

"It's clean. I'm clean an' you better be clean."

Her blue eyes slid to him in surprise. "What the hell does that mean?"

"Means I make sure to wrap it tight. Hopefully, all the dick in you's been wrapped tight, too."

"Damn, Slade, you make a girl feel warm all over," she murmured.

"Ain't no girl," he muttered.

"What?"

"Ain't no girl," he repeated louder. "Just turned thirty. Far from a girl."

She tilted her head to study him. "Well, that's true enough."

He moved to the bed, sat on the edge and began to unlace his boots. When they were loose, he pulled them off, as well as his socks, which he tucked inside, then set his boots out of the way. He pushed to his feet, slid his cut off and carefully laid it over the back of the chair in the corner. When he turned, Diamond was still in the center of his room but watching him intently.

"Gonna get naked?"

"Still deciding," she answered, her lips curling at the corners. "You've been pretty much a dick lately and I'm not sure you deserve to get what I could give you."

He snorted and yanked his long-sleeved thermal over his head. He heard her sharp intake of breath and finished pulling the shirt off before neatly folding it and placing it on the seat of the chair.

He cocked a brow in her direction. "Problem?"

She shook her head, her eyes heated as her gaze raked over his torso. Her eyes continued to follow his hands as he moved to his belt. "Ain't one of those strippers. We're both getting' naked here, princess."

. . .

N o. No, he wasn't one of those strippers. He was so much better. Di sucked in a ragged breath as her gaze explored Slade's chest. Both of his arms were solid tattoo sleeves and his ink continued over his upper chest and up his neck, stopping only under his jaw. His muscles were well-defined, and his dog tags hung between his drool-worthy pecs. He had a line of dark hair that started at his navel and disappeared into his worn jeans that she was dying to follow with her tongue.

She watched him jerk at the belt he had unfastened, slipping it from the loops, pop open the top button of his jeans and slowly slide the zipper down. Like slower than normal.

Her gaze rose at that deliberate slowness and when she met his dark brown eyes, he smiled.

"Likin' what your seein'," he stated, sure of himself, his voice low and grumbly.

Di shivered, her nipples peaking hard under her shirt.

Jesus, she wanted to see this man naked last summer when he first showed up and thought she was going to until he pushed her away unexpectedly.

They had made out a few times on a couple of the club runs but it never went farther than that. But now...

Now, holy shit...

She wiped the saliva from the corner of her mouth as he pushed his jeans over his hips and down his legs. He kicked them off and when he straightened her eyes fell to his cock, which was standing straight out from his body.

She was about to start singing "Happy Birthday" to herself.

She couldn't pull her eyes away when he grabbed his hard-on and stroked it a couple times.

"Still waitin'," he grumbled, snapping her into action.

She sank onto his bed and pulled off her high-heeled boots, throwing them across the small room. His eyes followed them as they smacked into the wall. He frowned as she tugged off her socks and threw them the same direction.

After standing up, she had her top and jeans off within seconds and thrown out of the way. Her breathing shallowed as she stood in her bra and panties before him, waiting for him to make the first move.

Because she couldn't wait for his hands, his tongue, his lips to be on her, his cock inside her.

Yes. *Happy, happy birthday to me.*

They stood staring at each other and she wondered why he wasn't moving. Even his hand had stilled on his cock. She questioned if he was even breathing.

"Slade," she whispered.

Suddenly, she was knocked back onto the bed, all the air rushing from her lungs and he was over her, tearing at her bra and panties, ripping them off and tossing them over his shoulder.

Fuck, yes.

His fingers dove into her long hair and he ripped her head back, shoved his face into her neck and scrapped his teeth down her throat, down her chest until he latched roughly onto one of her nipples. He tugged it with his teeth before sucking it deep.

"Holy shit, yes," she hissed, her eyes rolling back in her head as the pull of his mouth on her nipple made her core clench tight.

She bucked her hips beneath him, feeling his hard length pressing into her thigh, his hot, silky precum leaking onto her skin. She groaned into his mouth as he took it, shoving his tongue deep, reminding her who was the stronger of the two.

She tangled her tongue with his, challenging that notion. Then she bit his bottom lip and he jerked back, his eyes dark, his breath rapid as he stared down at her.

A slow smile crept over his face. "That's it, give me some of that fight with my fuck."

He wanted fight? He'd get it.

She slammed her palms into his chest and he shifted back from the impact. With a growl, he snagged her wrists and pinned them to the mattress and took her mouth once again, making sure she tasted the blood she drew. A groan bubbled up from deep at the back of her throat.

Releasing her mouth, he moved his way back down, biting and nipping her flesh as he went. After letting her wrists go, he snagged one nipple with his mouth and the other with his fingers, twisting it hard.

She whimpered and arched her neck, dragging her nails down his back, scoring his flesh. He made a noise against her breast but didn't stop the intense attention he was giving them.

Wet and throbbing, her pussy clenched tightly as she dug her fingers into his ass and shifted beneath him. "Fuck me," she groaned.

"Not yet, princess," he murmured against her damp flesh, working his way lower, dislodging her hands from his ass. They slid up his body as he settled between her thighs. He shoved her legs up and out, planting her feet on his shoulders, opening her wide to him. And then he dropped his head and his mouth found her...

A low wail escaped her as he teased and sucked her clit hard. He gave her no mercy at all and she wasn't going to ask for any. The rougher he became, the better it was.

Tonight was her night and she wanted it all from this man. Whatever he was willing to give her, she'd greedily accept.

She dug her fingers into his short hair to keep him in place as his tongue worked her wickedly. She gasped as his fingers slid deep, curving to stroke her sensitive spot. She bucked her hips once more as he tortured her with exquisite pleasure. It snuck up on her unexpectedly, probably because it had been so long... but the orgasm raced through her body, curling her toes, clenching her fingers into his skin, her teeth sinking into her bottom lip until her mouth opened wide and she let out a loud cry.

She struggled to catch her breath as he continued his pace, not letting up even for a second. She dug her heels into his back and cried out his name as one climax turned into two. And as she slowly floated back into her body, she tilted her head to see him still buried between her thighs, at the apex of her legs. But his mouth was no longer on her. No, his eyes were tipped up to her, his lips shiny as he gave her a grin.

"Fuck, princess. Never woulda expected that from you."

She wanted to ask him why, why wouldn't he expect that reaction? Did he think her cold and unfeeling? But at this moment, she didn't care about anything but him climbing up her body, and feeling his cock hard and heavy as he did so.

He pressed his lips to hers and she tasted herself.

"Slade..." she murmured.

He pulled away, shaking his head. "No. Don't fuckin' ruin it." He reached for the drawer of the nightstand next to the bed, jerked it open and dug around. He pulled out a long strip of condoms and ripped one off, tore it open and rolled it down his length.

"If you're like that with just my mouth on your pussy, can't wait to see how you are with my dick inside you."

He settled back between her legs, his cock pressing at her entrance but not pushing forward.

She closed her eyes and begged, "Fuck me."

But he didn't, instead he fisted his fingers into her hair and pulled it tight, making her gasp.

"Lemme see those blue eyes of yours, princess."

She lifted her lids to meet his dark gaze and when she did, he thrust forward, taking her deep with one stroke.

All the breath rushed from her lungs as he filled her up, stretched her, making her feel something she hadn't felt in a long time. A warmth spiraled through her from her center out. She didn't want to explore that feeling because she knew the answer might scare her.

That aside, if all she had was tonight with this man, she was going to make sure it lasted all night long.

"This time I'm on top, next time you are, got me?"

She couldn't argue with that.

Then he grimaced as he continued to thrust, his hips tilting just right, his cock hitting her in all the right places.

She couldn't stop the noises that escaped her. She knew she was loud and could probably be heard throughout the second level of church. But she couldn't contain them, couldn't hold back as he continued to grind against her, driving into her, making her buck wildly against him.

She wanted more, so much more.

Fuck, he was good with his hips. And she couldn't forget his mouth, which, at the moment, pressed into her neck as he sucked and nibbled on her skin.

She met him stroke for stroke, thrust for thrust, and he took her hard and fast, as if he was afraid the night would be over too quickly.

She trailed her fingers over his tattooed neck, his broad shoulders, down his colorful arms that flexed and bunched as he took her again and again.

"Yes, that's it..." she breathed. "Give it to me harder."

"Fuck," he groaned into her neck, then moved down to sink his teeth into her breast, biting down enough to make her cry out.

She loved it. The rougher he got, the more she liked it. She'd never been with a man who wanted to give it to her like this. She had no doubt that Slade was the man who could do it.

He was not worried about hurting her and she was glad for that. She wouldn't break and could take anything and everything he wanted to do to her.

In fact, she welcomed it.

He sucked her skin so hard, she knew it would leave a mark and encouraged him to continue by digging her nails deeper into his back.

Suddenly, he lurched up, yanked her head back by her hair and he pressed his mouth to her ear.

"Fuckin' need you to come, princess. Gotta do it now."

She bared her teeth and demanded, "Make me come."

"Gonna," he grunted.

"Now!" she shouted, losing her mind as he continued to pound her hard, driving his cock deep.

She slapped his ass hard and he jerked, his rhythm skipping a beat.

"Fuck!" he barked in her ear.

"Fucking make me come," she yelled.

He pulled his head up to stare down at her. "Fuck yeah. My princess likes it rough."

"Do it. Fuck me."

His mouth found her ear again. "Doin' it. Your wet, hot pussy's squeezin' me tight. Ain't givin' that to any other man. Only me. That's my fuckin' pussy now. All fuckin' mine."

His words, his rough claim on her, drove her over the edge. Her vision blurred, and her mouth opened as the climax ripped through her, making her twitch beneath him.

"Fuck yeah, babe. Gonna come inside you," he growled. He drove deep one more time, stilled, his body tensed above her as he released a grunt then came. He didn't move for the longest time, remaining deeply connected to her as the last of his pulses inside her faded away.

She melted bonelessly into the mattress, his solid weight on top of her, and she wrapped her arms around him tighter to keep him there as long as possible. Shoving her face into his damp neck, she breathed him in.

She closed her eyes and let out a long, satisfied sigh. She hadn't had sex that good in a long while. Hell, she may have never had sex that good before.

Slade shifted off her and finally broke their connection as he slid to her side. "Crushin' you, princess."

"Don't care," she said, missing the weight of him immediately.

"Right," he grunted. "Gotta get rid of this," he said, pulling off the condom and climbing to his feet.

Her gaze followed him as he moved toward the tiny bathroom that was attached to his room. She studied the DAMC colors he had tattooed onto his back as he crossed the doorway. Before he shut the door, he turned to pin her with his dark stare. "You move from that goddamn bed, I'll tie you the fuck down." Then he slammed it shut.

Diamond laid back, stretching her limbs out across the queen-sized bed that took up most of his room and stared at the ceiling.

Then she smiled.

CHAPTER FIVE

Slade blinked his eyes open to see why a heavy weight crushed him.

Long dark hair draped over his torso as Diamond's cheek pressed to his bare chest.

Moving a strand of silky hair out of the way, he saw her eyes were still closed, her lips slightly parted, as she continued to sleep.

He had no fucking clue what time it was. He only knew they'd been up most of the night fucking.

He rubbed his fingers over the bite marks and bruises she had left behind on his skin and grinned. If he'd known how rough she liked it, he would've dragged her up to his room a long time ago.

But then, the woman lying across his body was different when screaming out that she was coming versus when she was just screaming in general. His grin flattened out. The first he liked, the second he didn't.

Maybe giving her dick on the regular would change her bitchy attitude. But he doubted it.

He pushed his head deeper into his pillow and blew out a breath as he stared up at the ceiling.

This might have been a colossal mistake.

Was the sex good? Fuck yeah, it had been awesome. The woman's sexual appetite matched his. They had fucked four times. And there would have been a fifth if his dick hadn't gone on strike. By that time, his nuts had been drained dry and cried for mercy.

He needed to piss, but there was no way he could slide out from underneath her without waking her up. And he didn't want this peaceful time to be disturbed. Watching her sleep, he realized how beautiful she truly was. Too bad she could turn into a raving bitch so fast.

He traced his fingers over the smooth skin of her shoulder and down her arm, where he then brushed the tips of his fingers over her delicate, long ones. Her nails weren't super long but long enough to leave gouges in his back last night. He only hoped she didn't fuck up the club's colors that covered his back. Those tattoos weren't that old, and he didn't feel like sitting for a few more hours while Crow fixed them.

When he landed in Shadow Valley, he wasn't looking to stay. He was actually just passing through, searching for something that had gone missing until he ended up at The Iron Horse one night. He'd already left one club because he didn't like the direction things were headed and he hadn't been looking to patch into another club so soon.

But Z convinced him to stick around, at least for a little while, and then he jumped in to help the women at the *Dogs & Hogs* event last summer when the Warriors tried to steal the money the DAMC was raising for disabled vets.

Being a vet himself, that hit home. He had always been good with his fists. It just came naturally since he never shied away from a good fight. And that day gave him a good opportunity to show his skills by knocking out a Warrior when the asshole attacked the DAMC women.

Don't hit a woman. Don't disrespect a vet. Simple rules to live by.

He used to box when he was in the Marines, but it had been awhile since he'd been in the ring. He missed it since it was a good way to relieve frustration and stress.

And sometimes he'd even win some decent money by winning a match.

He might have to find a gym nearby where he could get back to it. The club's gym, which was tucked into a tiny back room at Shadow Valley Body Shop, was a joke. No punching bag, no decent equipment, nothing but some old free weights and a couple bench presses. And fuck trying to work out when someone was already in there. There was barely enough room to move around for one brother.

He might have to say something to Z about starting another club business. He wouldn't mind stepping out from behind the bar at The Iron Horse to manage a gym, which would be both open to the public and available for all of DAMC to use. They definitely needed a set-up better than what they had now. And it would be another source of legal income for the club coffers.

The DAMC was different than his former club as they *tried* to stay on the right side of the law, even though the Warriors kept dragging them down. They treated their women a little better than his previous club. They were deeply loyal to each other, even though they had to oust their former president, that asshole Pierce. And they took care of their community.

Since he patched into the club, he felt like he'd become part of the "family." The only one who still seemed to look at him sideways was Diesel. But then that man was overprotective of everyone. However, Slade held the ultimate respect for D's crew at In the Shadows Security since they were all former military special ops. Fellow vets.

He combed his fingers through Diamond's long tresses, smoothing her hair over his skin. She groaned as her lids lifted, then stared at him with her sleepy beautiful blue eyes.

"Mornin', princess."

"Hey," she breathed, and he was relieved to see that she was still relaxed and satisfied and had no fight in her since he was not in the mood to deal with a raging bitch this morning. If it *was* morning.

"What time is it?" she asked.

Trying not to dislodge her, he leaned over and grabbed his cell, hitting the power button to check the time.

"Nine."

Her head lifted. "In the morning?"

"Sure as shit hope so. If it's nine at night, been passed out way too long an' I'd be late for my shift at the bar."

"Have to work tonight?" she asked, her question tinged with slight disappointment.

"Yeah, princess, gotta work almost every night. Comes with the territory. Wanna live here, eat here, be a part of the club, gotta do my part."

Her eyes tipped down and she traced her finger over his dog tags, then grabbed one and flipped it over.

"Stone," she said softly, reading his tag. "Slade D. What's the D stand for?"

"David."

She skipped his social security number, then read out his blood type. "O pos. USMC, L. What's that?"

"My gas mask size."

"No Pref." Her eyes tipped up to him. "No religious preference?"

"Yeah," he grunted, getting sucked into those deep blue eyes of hers.

"Seen combat?"

"Yeah. And, princess, this line of conversation's stoppin' right here."

She frowned. "Why?"

"Ain't gonna answer that, either."

"Okay, then what's with calling me princess?"

"Act like one."

"No, I don't. Biker chicks are nothing like princesses."

He snorted. "Biker chick."

"Yeah. Born and raised in this club."

"Know it, princess. Don't need to remind me." He brushed his thumb over her bottom lip. "Never wanted out?"

She shifted until she laid on him, staring down into his eyes. "No.

This is my family. I don't know anything else, don't want to know anything else. We all take care of each other. No matter what."

"Got you. Loyalty's big with you."

"Big with all of us. We might get annoyed with each other and sometimes fight, but, honestly, no matter what stupid thing we do, we're always forgiven. And it's not all blood in this club, either, as you well know. You don't have to be from Doc or Bear's line to be considered family. Once you're in, you're in."

"What about Pierce?"

Her eyelids lowered as she thought about their former president who'd been ousted from the head of the table a few months back. "Pierce overstepped a few times."

"Yeah, he did," he answered, thinking about the danger the man put Ivy in by letting her go into Knights territory by herself to gather intel. At the time, the outlaw MC wasn't an Angels' ally like they were now. It could've turned ugly. Luckily, Jag found her and dragged her ass home.

"Disrespected some of us."

He cocked a brow. "Us?"

"Us women. We always had to watch getting caught alone with him."

Slade's body got tight. "He touch you?"

"Man thinks he's God's gift to women."

That wasn't an answer. "Asked you a fuckin' question. He touch you?"

She avoided his gaze and his question.

He grabbed her chin and made her look at him. "Answer."

"Yeah," she whispered.

With a twist, he had her flipped onto her back, trapped underneath him. "How'd he touch you?"

"Slade..."

She closed her eyes and he felt his blood rush through him and his chest tighten. He wanted to smash that fucker's face in.

"It wasn't... He didn't..."

Now his blood was no longer rushing but raging. "Didn't what?"

"I was young and didn't know to keep away from him then."

"How young?"

"I don't know. Fifteen?"

His head jerked back. Fifteen? "Who'd you tell?" Because he certainly can't believe that asshole remained club president after touching a fifteen-year-old.

"No one."

"Not D?"

Her eyes widened. "Diesel's only three years older than me, Slade. He wasn't even patched in yet. He certainly wasn't the enforcer back then."

Jesus. It was hard to think of that man as a teenager. "Your father?"

"He was already in prison."

Slade's nostril flared. "You told no one."

"No."

"Shoulda told Ace, at least."

She turned her head away. "It was embarrassing. I was a teenager. He got me alone when I should've known better."

He grabbed her chin and made her face him. "Like you said, was a teen. No man should touch a young girl."

"He tried it with almost all of us."

"All of you?" Slade ground his teeth together. "Fucker needs his colors stripped. Gonna talk to D."

"No! Don't you fucking dare. I don't need my stupidity out there."

"Babe..."

"No, Slade. Keep that shit to yourself."

She shouldn't have told him. Now every time he saw that fucking asshole he'll want to thump the fucker into the ground. The man hardly came around the club anymore after the coup for the presidency, but he still showed up every once in a while and refused to just hand over his colors and disappear.

Something kept him hanging around even where he wasn't wanted. Slade had no idea why. The reason had to be more than the former president still running the club's gun shop and range. Had to be.

"Stay away from him from now on," he grumbled. "Got me?"

"Don't need to tell me that," she said sharply, her eyes narrowing.

"Tellin' you that," he said, not caring if she was getting pissed. He now knew the corrective measure for turning off her bitch switch. And he wouldn't hesitate to use it to mellow her back out. In fact, he'd enjoy another go at her.

He frowned when he thought about last night and how she almost ended up in bed with someone that wasn't him. Fuck, actually two someones.

"Didn't get Bobby an' Bobby's numbers, right?"

She snorted. "You mean Robby and Bobby?"

"Know who the fuck I mean," he grumbled, not finding it nearly as amusing as her at the thought of her taking those two strippers home. Climbing in bed with some strange.

"Guess you were wrong about them being gay."

Hell, they probably were gay or bi and was just going to do her for some hard-earned cash. In fact, they had a wad of green in their hands when they had come into the kitchen last night. Those women's wallets were probably a lot lighter after that so-called birthday celebration.

He thrust his hips against her, making sure she felt his morning wood. "They ain't gonna give you dick like I can."

Her eyes widened and then she laughed. Fucking burst out laughing!

He frowned. "Didn't hear you complainin'. In fact, my ears are still ringin' from that screamin' you did all night. *More. Harder. Faster. Rougher. Fuck me, Slade!*"

"If you were doing it right, I wouldn't have had to give you all those instructions," she said, her eyes twinkling.

Now she was being a complete smart-ass. He snorted. "Uh-huh. Next time try to keep your mouth shut. See if you can do it."

"Next time?"

He opened his mouth to answer her, but a pounding on the door interrupted him.

What the fuck.

"What?" Slade barked over his shoulder, his head twisted toward the door.

"Brother, just checkin' to make sure she didn't stab you in your sleep."

Slade shook his head, not knowing whether to find Crash's concern amusing or not.

"Get gone, Crash!" Di yelled.

"You're late for work," grumpily came through the door.

"So are you," she snapped back.

"Yeah, 'cause nobody got any fuckin' sleep with you caterwaulin' all fuckin' night."

Slade called out, "Brother, she's gonna be even later. Just sayin'."

After a slight hesitation from the other side of the door, he heard, "Better you than me... *just sayin'.*"

"Brother, my suggestion's to head to the shop or get some earplugs. Shit's about to get loud again."

"Fuck," came mumbled through the door.

Once Slade heard Crash's heavy footsteps move away, he turned his head back to study the woman beneath him. "Gonna give you more of that dick you liked so much last night."

"Hmm. Are you asking or telling?"

He blinked at her question. "Want it?"

She grinned. "I like it better when you're taking what you want and not asking."

Oh, yeah. He grinned back. "Like the Diamond who ain't a bitch. Can we keep 'er around?"

"I'm not a bitch."

"Princess, when you flip your switch you can shrink a brother's balls into raisins. No one wants to deal with that mouth."

She pointed to her lips, still puffy from all the use they got throughout the night. "This mouth?"

He grinned. "Yeah, that one. Need to put it to good use instead."

"Like what?"

He rolled off her and settled onto his back, arms folded behind his head. "Sure you can figure it out, babe."

He smiled when she slipped down his body, nipping at his skin as she went until finally settling between his legs. He reached down and wrapped his hand around his now hard dick.

She slapped it away. "I don't need help. I got this."

He pulled his hand away, looked at the ceiling and grumbled, "She got this," with a chuckle.

His eyes quickly tipped down to watch what she was doing once her hot, wet mouth encircled the head. All the breath left him as she sucked him deep.

"Fuck," he groaned, his heels digging into the bed.

"Mmm," she hummed against his throbbing shaft.

He reached down and grabbed her hair, pulling it away from her face and into his fists. Watching her cheeks hollow out with every bob of her head made him almost lose his shit right then and there.

He couldn't watch it. No fucking way. Watching *and* feeling that sweet, hot suction on his dick was too much. Where did she learn to suck cock like that?

Fuck! That was the last thing he wanted to think about at this moment.

Didn't matter. Did not fucking matter who she wrapped that talented little mouth around before him. Didn't fucking matter, he told himself once more to get it through his thick skull.

All that mattered right now was that it wasn't one of the Bobby twins getting this stellar head.

She tightened the two fingers she had encircling the root of his dick and squeezed it hard. The nails on her other hand raked along his balls, making them tighten.

"Fuck yeah, babe, that's it," he groaned. "Oh *fuuuuck.*"

His hips rose off the mattress when the tip of her tongue circled the edge of his crown and she flicked it around the top.

Jesus fuck.

He dug his fingers deeper into her hair and fisted them tight, keeping her in place as his hips rose and fell, fucking her hot mouth.

His eyes closed, and a low groan rose from his chest and out of his parted lips as he panted.

"Fuckin' Christ, babe." His chest felt as if it was caving in as her teeth scraped softly along the top of his dick.

And when she took almost his whole length...

He felt like crying like a baby. *Jesus*, she could suck a knob off a door. But his knob was about to blow.

"Gonna come," he panted his warning. He tugged on her hair, but she resisted, not letting him go. "Babe, gonna come," he warned her again.

Like seriously, this was her last chance to bail.

But she sucked him harder and he grunted, his hips shooting off the bed as he blew his load down her throat.

And the fucking woman... Took. It. All.

As soon as his brains landed back in his head, he tipped it to peer down at her. Her shiny lips stretched into what looked like a satisfied grin.

He bet his satisfied grin had her beat, though.

She reached up and wiped the corner of her skilled mouth with her finger. Not that there was anything to wipe away. No, there fucking wasn't. She was just being cocky since she swallowed every last drop.

"Keep your fuckin' mouth busy like that, no chance to sear my ears with your bitchin'."

She made some noise like she was offended as she smacked his thigh, then climbed right up his body to give him all her weight. She dropped her head and kissed him.

He pinned his lips tight and turned his head away. "Fuck, babe, you just swallowed my load. Don't wanna taste it."

"Oh, so it's okay for you to kiss me after eating me out?"

"Fuck yeah. That's hot."

"But I can't kiss you after sucking you off?"

"Fuck no. Gotta have rules."

"No rules."

With a twist of his body he was back on top, staring down into her blue eyes. They were so piercing that they got him in the gut. A feeling he did not want to explore. Not now. Maybe not in the near future, either.

"Gotta have rules," he murmured as he studied how her dark hair spread out over his pillow.

Fuck, she looked good in his bed. His heart began to pound wildly and a bead of sweat popped out on his forehead.

Uh-uh. No. He was not going to be tied down to Diamond. Nope.

He pushed off her and sat up on the edge of the bed, running a hand over his short bristly hair, then he wrapped it around the back of his neck and squeezed.

"We're not going to fuck again?" she asked softly, disappointment tinging her question. She traced a finger gently down the line of his spine.

He closed his eyes and slowly let the air in his lungs escape from between his lips.

"Gonna be late for work, princess."

"Okay? You told Crash I would be. He's not going to care."

Jesus. How did he get her out of his bed, out of his room, without being a complete dick?

He couldn't.

Fuck.

Without looking at her, he said, "It was fun, but it's morning an' I got shit to do."

The bed shifted as she jerked to a seated position. "What?"

"Got shit to do," he repeated.

"Like what?"

"Like washing the pussy off me an' gettin' somethin' to eat. That's what."

She said nothing. He only heard her breathing. Then the bed shifted again as she climbed out of it. He avoided looking in her direction.

"Got your birthday wish," he mumbled.

He expected her to freak the fuck out on him. Expected a boot or something to clobber the back of his head. But he heard nothing but her getting dressed. He had a feeling the silence should scare him more than her bitching.

From experience, he knew a woman's silence could be deadly.

The door opened and he braced himself for the slam.

The soft click of it closing made him close his eyes and scrub his hands over his face.

He could barely make out the sound of her boot heels heading down the hallway. They weren't rushed at all. They were slow and methodical until he couldn't hear them anymore.

He turned his head and stared at his empty bed. Placing his hand in the center of it, he could still feel the warmth she left behind. He groaned.

Fuck him.

———

Diamond slowly moved down the stairs, her eyes on each step so she wouldn't tumble down them, break her neck and end up in a heap at the bottom. She had her lips pressed together tightly so they wouldn't tremble. If she kept concentrating on putting one foot in front of the other, then maybe she could keep the sting that burned her eyes from escaping down her cheeks.

She should have gone home with Robby and Bobby. That way the morning after wouldn't hurt so damn much. Even her stomach felt like it had been carved out with a spoon.

As she hit the bottom of the steps, she looked around to make sure she wasn't going to be taking a walk of shame in front of any prospects, or skanks, be it sweet butts or any of Dawg's girls.

Because right now she felt no better than a patch whore. At least with Robby and Bobby, she'd never have to see them again afterward. Unlike Slade.

She searched the common area and her eyes widened as she

spotted Crow leaning against the counter in the corner drinking a cup of coffee.

His dark, almost black, eyes were on her, but she couldn't read them. She took a right, heading toward the back door to escape and he cleared his throat.

She ignored it and he made a louder, more deliberate noise, making her halt mid-stride.

She closed her eyes as his low, honeyed voice washed over her. "Get over here."

Without opening her eyes, she whispered, "Can't."

"Did you say 'Can't?' Since when's that word in your vocabulary?"

"Crow," she groaned.

"Fuckin' get over here, baby doll." When her feet refused to move, he added a firm, "Now."

Opening her eyes, she twisted her head in his direction to see that he had put his coffee cup down and was now crossing his arms over his chest. He wasn't going to take no for an answer.

She sucked in a deep breath to bolster herself then crossed the large room toward him. When she got close, he opened his arms and she walked right into them, pressing her cheek against his warm, broad chest.

His lips brushed over her hair at the top of her head. "Shouldn't be lookin' as though someone died after gettin' laid, baby doll."

She nodded against him.

"Do I need to beat someone's fuckin' ass?"

"No," she murmured into his chest.

"Who fucked you over?" his question was low and asked close to her ear.

She sighed. "No one."

"Bullshit. Was your fuckin' birthday last night. Had a good time. Drove the brothers fuckin' nuts, though. Even..." He drifted off, then finished with a growl. "Slade."

Her fingers curled into his back as he pulled her tighter against him.

"That you an' him makin' all that fuckin' noise last night?"

Diamond didn't embarrass easily, but him asking that question made the heat crawl up her neck into her cheeks. She buried her face farther into his shirt to hide it.

"Jesus," he whispered when she didn't answer. He rubbed a hand up and down her back in a soothing manner. "Thought you wanted his dick?"

"I do," she said then quickly corrected it with, "I *did*."

"Got it. Now what?"

Good question. Now what? "Says I'm a bitch."

"After he fucked you?"

"No, before." Di felt his body shake with silent laughter against her. "Am I really a bitch?"

His shaking stilled abruptly. Then he snagged her chin and lifted her face to his. He held her gaze when he admitted, "Yeah, baby doll, you can be a fuckin' ragin' bitch. But you're smart an' can be fuckin' sweet as one of Soph's cupcakes when you wanna be."

"I don't try to be that way, Crow," she said softly.

"Know it, baby doll. We all just accept that's the way you are. We all just figure you ain't gettin' enough dick."

She laughed and smacked his arm. "That's not right."

"True, though. Catch-twenty-two, baby doll. Not gettin' dick turns you into a bitch, you bein' a bitch ain't gettin' you dick. Somethin's gotta give to break that endless cycle." He sighed, his chest rising and falling under her cheek. "Look how sweet you are all cuddled up in my arms right now. Got dick, made you sweet." He pressed his face into her hair. "Even if you are a bit heartbroken right now."

"I'm not heartbroken."

"Yeah, you are. Watch you 'round 'im. Your pretty blue eyes always landin' on 'im, watchin' 'im, hungry for 'im. Hard to miss." Crow paused then his chest continued to rumble under her ear as she pressed it against him. "Tell you somethin', think the man's a rollin' stone. Don't think he's gonna settle here. Searchin' for somethin'."

"What?"

"Dunno, baby doll. Until he finds it, gonna keep movin'."

"Crow, I saw the colors you tatted onto his back. Can't get more permanent than that."

"Yeah, surprised me he got it done. Think he did it to appease D's suspicion of 'im."

"The guy's a former Marine," Di murmured.

"Don't mean shit, baby doll. Maybe it's best he tossed you from 'is bed."

"He didn't toss me—"

Crow pulled her away enough to give her a look.

"Whatever," she grumbled, then pressed herself against him again. "You feel good."

He chuckled softly. "Ain't givin' you dick to keep you sweet."

She smiled into his shirt. "Would it be so bad?"

"No. But it ain't gonna—" He suddenly stopped talking and his whole body went solid against her. She turned her face enough to see what made him react that way.

Slade was coming down the steps, his hair still damp. His dark eyes hit hers, held for a second, then lifted to Crow's.

"Brother," he grumbled as he crossed the room in their direction.

Crow gave him a chin lift but held Di closer. "Brother," he returned the greeting. "Coffee's fresh."

Slade nodded and headed over to the pot, his eyes not leaving them. He only turned away long enough to grab a mug and fill it, then he turned back, took a swallow and said, "Wanna let 'er go?"

"Nope."

Di tried to pry herself out of Crow's arms, but he tightened them.

"Need to let 'er go, brother," Slade said, this time not asking as he took another sip of his coffee and placed his mug carefully down on the bar.

Crow cocked a brow in his direction. "Why? She yours?"

Slade's dark eyes got even darker and after a few beats said, "Ain't yours."

"Toss a bitch from your bed, shouldn't care where they land."

Slade's nostrils flared, and his jaw got tight. "Wanted to be fucked for her birthday. She got fucked."

"That all it was? Generous birthday gift?"

"You talkin' for her now?" Slade asked, his eyes narrowed. They flicked down to Di as she stood perfectly still, then they flicked back up to Crow.

"Nope."

Slade gave a sharp nod. "Then let 'er go," he growled.

Di couldn't miss the slow smile that crossed Crow's face. He didn't lose that smile when he leaned down, kissed her forehead and then murmured quietly in her ear, "Go home, baby doll. Clean up, go to work. That man ain't had enough of you yet." He lifted his head and gently pushed her away. "Just do what I said," Crow said louder, so Slade could hear him.

Diamond nodded and without looking back, straightened her spine, lifted her head high and walked out the fucking door.

CHAPTER SIX

The loud music vibrated deep in his chest as Slade lifted his gaze. He had snagged a stool at the bar that ran the length of one side of the long stage. Two poles, one on each end, had a female wearing nothing but a G-string swinging from them. Those fucking women had it going on with their leg and arm strength. They could probably crack a walnut with their thighs.

Luckily it was Sierra... Sandy... Savannah's night off, so he didn't have to worry about her hanging on him and trying to make another breakfast date.

The stripper nearest to him cocked a leg around the pole and hung upside down as she twirled in circles, her *what-looked-like-new* fake tits hardly even jiggling.

Unlike Diamond's when she rode his cock two nights ago. There was nothing fake about those. Soft and heavy with suckable pink nipples that were just the right size for his mouth.

Fuck.

As he dropped his gaze to his beer, a hand landed on his shoulder and he felt someone lean into him, big tits pressing into his arm.

A husky female voice whispered in his ear. "Lap dance, baby?"

He shook his head. "Ain't interested."

"Sure?"

"Yeah," he grunted and glanced over his shoulder at Dawn, one of Dawg's newest girls.

She was cute. But blonde with blue eyes. Not a brunette. She seemed sweet. But not his type.

No.

He thought he liked easy.

Until he realized easy was boring.

He was relieved when Dawn moved on to her next potential customer down the bar.

"Dawn's fresh, brother," Dawg said as he stood behind the bar, eyeballing him. "Might wanna grab her while she is."

"Had her?"

The brother shook his head. "Nope. Never fuck my own girls."

That was probably a good policy.

Slade lifted his pint glass. "Like I told 'er, not interested. Just tryin' to enjoy a beer."

Dawg grunted and leaned back against the stage, oblivious to the high heel that swung inches from his head as the stripper did her on-stage stunts. The crazier they danced, the more tricks they could do on the pole, the more dollar bills were tossed their way.

"Heard it was you an' Diamond keepin' everyone up the other night."

It was Slade's turn to grunt, avoiding Dawg's narrowed green eyes.

"Dangerous shit, brother, stickin' your dick where it might get stuck."

Slade didn't need that little reminder. He was well aware of it.

"Also a reason why none of us has chased that."

Slade's spine stiffened, and he ground his molars as he met Dawg's gaze, holding it hard and fast. "Don't like a challenge?"

Dawg's smile grew, and he stroked his fingers lazily down his beard. "Oh no, brother, love a challenge. Don't like a headache, is all."

"Think she's a headache?"

"Know she's a headache."

That answer made him wonder. "Any brothers do her?"

Dawg's head tilted as he regarded Slade. "Might wanna ask 'er that."

"Askin' you."

"Gotta problem if they had?"

Slade's nostrils flared. Would he? Fuck yeah, he would. And that shit right there made his gut churn.

Dawg suddenly pushed away from the stage and came closer, whacking Slade's arm hard enough to jolt him. "Too much available easy to hafta deal with somethin' difficult. Got me?"

Yeah, Slade got where he was going. He watched the man walk away shaking his head and chuckling.

Problem was, Slade suddenly had a hankering for not-so-easy. Someone that had a little bite to her. Sharp teeth, sharp nails and a sharp mind.

His phone lit up and vibrated on the bar with a text message from Hawk.

Z's kid's coming.

Fuck, Sophie was in labor. Slade didn't bother to reply right away since the text was sent out in mass, probably to everyone on the man's phone.

He wasn't sure if he was expected to show up at the hospital or not. He wasn't sure what to do at all.

He ended up texting Hawk back. *Need me at bar?*

Got it covered.

Suddenly, Dawg was standing in front of him again, holding his own cellphone. "Got the text?"

"Yeah," Slade grunted. "You headin' over?"

"Yeah, this is fuckin' big. Next gen of DAMC's comin' into the world. Gotta be there to support our prez."

Slade nodded. He really didn't want to hang out at the hospital for what could be hours and hours. And he hadn't been a part of the MC for that long where he felt the need to see the next generation to be born. Unlike long-time members like Dawg. But still... He did want to be there for Z.

"Headin' over now if you wanna catch a ride. Got Moose coverin' for me."

Slade sighed as he slid off his stool.

This was going to be a long fucking night.

———

Slade leaned against the wall, one leg cocked, his boot firmly planted against the wall, arms crossed over his chest as he surveyed the waiting room in the maternity ward. The place was packed solid with a bunch of excited but exhausted people. Every seat was full, every available wall space taken, and some of the women even sat on their old man's laps.

"What are they goin' to name 'im?" Crash asked no one in particular.

"They're goin' to name *her* Camryn," Diamond answered him.

"Oh, fuck. Better not be a girl," Rig grumbled next to Crash, dropping his head into his hands and shaking it.

"If it's not a girl, they'll name him Cameron," Diamond added.

Slade stared at her from across the crowded room. She'd been avoiding him all night and it was starting to piss him off. Especially since she was sitting next to Crow, who kept running his fingers down her arm and over her thigh that was closest to him.

He knew the brother was doing it on purpose to try to rile him up and so far, Slade had kept his shit together. But he was exhausted due to the long hours of waiting and his patience was running thin.

Especially since Diamond did nothing to stop the man.

Bella sat on Crow's other side, her head on his shoulder as she tried to nap. Slade wondered what her old man would have to say about that. Though, Axel hadn't shown up at the hospital, yet.

Crow's fingers were doing the walking all over Bella, too, since he had his arm wrapped around her shoulders. Seems as though the women trusted him like a real brother. However, Slade had to wonder if Crow had the same brotherly feelings or he was just taking advantage of the women's trust.

Either way, he didn't like the man touching Diamond. Not at all.

He scowled and pushed off the wall. A hand snagged him and kept him from marching over there. He stared down at the big paw wrapped around his arm, then followed it up to its owner.

Hawk shook his head. "Ain't the time."

Slade's eyes flicked from Hawk to Crow and back.

Hawk continued, his voice low, "Just tryin' to get you goin', tryin' to make you see what's right in front of your face. The man ain't dumb. Also ain't foolish."

Slade sucked in a deep breath in an attempt to heed Hawk's words and as he opened his mouth to respond, two things happened. Z came swaggering into the waiting room from one direction, wearing what looked like a hospital gown, or something similar, over his clothes and Axel entered from the other direction wearing his uniform. Slade watched curiously as the brothers' gazes met and something went unsaid between them. Then Z addressed the room since everyone suddenly was at attention, waiting on his news.

"I..." His voice broke and he dropped his head for a second, blinking hard. The room got so quiet a pin being dropped could've been heard. He cleared his throat and then looked up, his bloodshot eyes sweeping through the room. "Got a son."

Nobody made a sound for a heartbeat, then two, before a deafening roar went up.

"A fuckin' son!"

"Fuck yeah!"

"Fourth generation DAMC!"

"DOWN AN' DIRTY..." someone shouted.

"'TIL DEAD!" rose up from everyone.

Slade was sure the whole hospital, if not awake previously, was now well aware that a new life in the DAMC had entered the world.

Ace moved forward, grabbed Z and hugged him tight, whacking him hard on the back. Both men swiped at their faces and, understandably, no one said a word about it.

Even Slade felt a tightness at the back of his throat with the emotion moving through the room.

One by one, the brothers approached Z, congratulating him. Eventually, even Axel moved up, clasped hands with his brother and bumped shoulders. It took them a few moments to move apart.

When Axel finally stepped back, he wrapped a hand around the back of Bella's neck and pulled her to him and into his arms. She was crying, and Slade didn't know if they were happy tears, but he sure hoped so. He knew the woman had a strong reaction when it came to things like babies and pregnancies, though he wasn't sure why. He only knew she couldn't have any kids of her own. Axel buried his face into her hair and they simply held each other while everyone celebrated.

"Well, is he Cameron?" Hawk yelled out, his arm wrapped around his ol' lady, Kiki, who had tears running unchecked down her own face. She didn't bother to hide them as most of the females in the room didn't.

"Nope. Sophie had a change of heart when she was squeezin' the shit outta my fingers an' cursin' me out."

"Well, spit it out, boy!" Ace yelled, holding onto his wife Janice.

"My woman insisted on a Z name after she held him for the first time. So, his name's Zeke."

Diesel, standing next to Zak, nodded his head, grumbling, "Good strong name for a future brother."

That it was.

"How's Sophie?" Diamond called out, drawing Slade's attention once again.

"Doin' great. Still a bit pissed at me for gettin' her knocked up an' makin' her suffer through that shit. But she'll get over it."

A few chuckles moved through the room.

"She'll forget it and before you know it, you'll be having your fourth kid," Janice said.

"You only had two," someone reminded her.

"Yeah, well, have you seen the two I had? Should've stopped after the first one ripped me open."

"Fuck," D muttered at his mother's confession.

"Had Ace get snipped after pushin' out a second ten-pound

watermelon," Janice continued, her eyebrows raised at Diesel, "Had enough after that one there. Never was the same again."

"Jesus fuckin' Christ," D muttered some more.

Jewel patted his stomach as she wrapped an arm around her ol' man's waist. "We may never have any after hearing that," she murmured, her eyes wide and face pale.

"Fine with me," D mumbled.

"Aaaanyway," Kiki said loudly. "When can we see him?"

"Ace an' Janice can come back now. The rest's gonna hafta wait."

A grumble of disappointment went through the room.

Hawk moved to the center. "Kid'll be home soon enough. Why don't we all clear out an' leave 'em be for now. As soon as they're home, we'll throw a pig roast to celebrate."

Heads nodded, "yeahs" went up and everyone began to clear the room after patting Z on the back one last time.

"Now we need to bet on who's gonna be next," Rig stated next to Slade.

"Ivy," Hawk announced.

"Kiki," Jag suggested.

Both men looked at each other and frowned.

"You're next," Hawk grumbled.

"Fuck no. Kiki's older than Ivy."

"So what?"

"Gotta knock her up while she's in her prime," Jag said.

"What the fuck," Hawk mumbled.

"Do I have a say in this?" Kiki asked, hands on her hips as she frowned at the two of them.

"Do I?" Ivy asked.

"Just know it ain't gonna be me," Dex muttered on his way past.

"Me neither," Rig said, following him out.

"Not it," Crash said, smirking, making his way to the exit.

"Not me," Nash laughed and left.

Crow snorted, and Dawg laughed as they cleared the room.

All remaining eyes landed on Grizzly and Mama Bear. The old

man swatted a gnarled hand their direction as he steered his wife out the door, grumbling.

"Brother, you comin'?" Hawk asked Slade as he put a hand on Kiki's hip and turned her toward the doorway.

"In a minute."

"Need a ride?"

He did since he caught a ride over with Dawg, but he had another idea. "No, got it covered."

Hawk's eyes slid to Diamond, who was standing in a corner talking to her sister, and he nodded.

After they left, Slade remained where he was on the opposite side of the waiting room, watching. Her back was to him, her body animated as she talked. Jewel's gaze rose from her sister to over her shoulder and met his.

Slade gave her a chin lift and Jewel, keeping a poker face, dropped her gaze back to Diamond. Then she said something and moved back to Diesel. Diamond turned and met his gaze, frowned, then went to leave.

Slade followed her down the hallway toward the elevators, his gaze landing on her ass as she moved. After hitting the down button, she crossed her arms over her chest as she waited for the car, completely ignoring him.

Slade moved faster when he heard the ding of the elevator and when the doors whooshed open, he shoved her inside and quickly hit the button to close the doors before she could object.

They didn't say a word to each other as the car descended to the main floor. Another ding sounded as it stopped, and the doors opened.

Diamond began walking at a quick pace through the hospital's lobby, but Slade kept up, following her closely.

"You don't have to follow me," she snapped over her shoulder.

He didn't answer.

"Find a ride back to church with someone going that direction."

He ignored her suggestion.

"You're not getting in my car," she stated, still staying ahead of him as she hit the parking lot and weaved through the cars.

When they got to her Nissan, she beeped open the locks. He snagged the key fob from her fingers before she could protest, then shrugged off his cut and turned it inside out before sliding it back over his shoulders.

"I'm drivin', princess."

"Uh, no." Her eyebrows drew low. "You're not getting in my car, remember? Did you miss that part?"

He grabbed her elbow, steered her to the passenger side of her bright red 370Z, ripped open the door and muttered, "Get in."

She stiffened. "You must have this mistaken idea that I answer to you. Not sure when you started to think that, but let me clear it up for you... I don't."

"Get. In," he repeated through clenched teeth.

"Must be deaf," she shouted as if he truly was hard of hearing.

"Must be blind, too, 'cause I don't see you gettin' in your fuckin' car."

"Slade—"

He took a deep breath, then blew it out slowly. "Princess, please... get in the fuckin' car."

Adding the "please" must have done it, because she blinked at him once, twice, then got into the passenger side without another word. He shut the door and hurried around the front of her small sports car.

He grunted as he folded himself up to get into the driver's side and adjusted the seat so he wasn't eating the steering wheel. Pushing the start button, the car came to life and he shoved the shifter into reverse.

After backing out of the spot, he pushed in the clutch, shoved it into first gear and turned his head to look at her. Her face was closed, unreadable.

"Gotta give me directions."

"To where?"

"Your place."

"Why?"

"Because we're gonna get noisy an' don't feel like hearin' shit from everyone again."

"Oh."

Yeah, *oh*.

"Think I want to do that with you, again?" she asked with the Diamond attitude she was known to embrace.

"Don't you?"

She turned her head to stare out of the windshield and, with a small smile pulling at her lips, said, "When you pull out of the parking lot, make a left."

A hell of a big smile curled Slade's lips up as he let the clutch fly, making the car jerk forward. He exited the parking lot and made a left.

CHAPTER SEVEN

"Like that man touchin' you?" Slade growled as he thrust in and out of Di at a slow pace.

Slow enough to drive her crazy. But she really couldn't complain, he'd already made her come twice, just with his mouth on her alone.

However, since he didn't mention the name of "that man," she could only guess he meant Crow.

She tilted her head back, arching her neck as his teeth sank into the flesh around her nipple. He bit down hard, and she cried out. He was on top, totally in control, so her movements were limited due to his weight and size, but she managed to slam her hips up to meet his.

"Slade..." she moaned.

"Asked you a question, woman."

One she wasn't going to answer. Not while she was in her right mind. Though, she was quickly slipping from her right mind the more he drove her toward the edge. He might be taking it slow, but there was nothing gentle about the way he was fucking her. Each thrust jolted her body hard. Enough so, to keep shoving her up the bed. Every time her head became dangerously close to the head-board, he'd pull out, yank her back down and start fucking her all over again.

Yes. He. Would.

She grabbed his head and pulled him into a deep kiss, then bit his lip hard enough to draw blood.

He grunted but didn't pull away, instead biting her back. She jerked, their kiss broke, and she smiled up at him. With her thumb she wiped the blood away from his bottom lip, then tucked it into her mouth to lick it clean.

"You're fuckin' crazy," he grumbled, his eyes heated as he watched her suck her thumb.

His cock twitched deep inside her. That had turned him on. He liked it as rough as she did.

"Must be to bring you back to my place," she answered. "You must be crazy, too."

"Fuckin' am after watchin' that man put his hands on you right in front of me. Not once but two fuckin' times."

"I don't belong to you," she reminded him.

"Just done fuckin' you, shouldn't be in another man's arms."

She realized he was talking about the other morning when she'd just left his bed at church. Seeing her in Crow's arms must have bugged the shit out of him. "Says who?"

"Gotta have rules."

"No rules," she stated, then gasped as he ground himself deep.

"Got my dick inside you, makin' rules."

"Rules were meant to be broken," she murmured.

He stilled, planted his palms firmly into the mattress and curled himself away from her to stare into her eyes.

She was definitely getting under his skin. "What do you want from me, Slade?"

"What we're doin'."

Sex. That's all he wanted from her. "Just this?"

"For now."

That answer surprised her. "Then what?"

He didn't answer, his eyes sliding to the side. He blew out a breath then lowered himself again but didn't resume moving inside her.

"Right now more fuckin', less talkin'."

That was one rule she could live with. She slapped his ass so hard it stung her own hand. "Then fuck me and shut up."

His eyes slid back to her and they crinkled at the corners. "You got it, princess."

Finally, he shut up and fucked her.

Not twenty minutes later, as Diamond felt like every bone had deserted her body, she watched Slade slip from her bed and hit the master bathroom. The light went on, the door closed and so did her eyes as she listened to him clean up and get rid of the condom.

She sighed.

Crow had been right. Slade wasn't done with her.

Crow was surprisingly intuitive when it came to the DAMC women. And he also knew what to do to force the men to face what they desired. Or *who* they desired. Crow tended to throw it in their face then laugh at the results.

Funny how the man always came out unscathed himself. Never had an ol' lady, never pursued one, either. He just enjoyed watching his brothers fall to their knees around him. And still he remained unencumbered, standing tall.

Di had a feeling his days were numbered, though. One day he'd be the one fighting his feelings, maybe fighting off a woman from clamping a ball and chain around one of his ankles.

When that day came, she just bet the rest of the brothers would make him, well... eat crow.

She laughed softly at the thought. Then the bathroom door opened, and Slade swaggered naked across the room, clearly comfortable in his own skin.

Her gaze slid over his body, taking in his short military-style haircut, his dark eyes and his many tattoos, and she couldn't find one damn thing wrong with him. Not one.

Crow might be right. Getting dick smoothed out her edges. Maybe not just any dick though...

The bed shifted as Slade climbed back in, pulled her into his arms and drew the sheet over them both. She fit perfectly into the curve of his body, and she sighed with contentment.

"Was wrong," he grumbled.

Di turned her head slightly, even though he had her back pulled tightly against his front so she couldn't see him.

He pressed his mouth to her ear. "Ain't a bitch."

Her eyes widened, but she said nothing. Instead, pressed her lips together, hoping he'd continue.

"Just a strong woman not takin' shit from anyone. Got a fuckin' flame inside you that burns bright. See it now."

She blinked quickly as her eyes began to burn. She refused to break down and show him weakness after he just said she was strong.

"Not gonna share you. Tellin' you now, that man touches you again, gonna break every one of his goddamn fingers."

She couldn't stay silent any longer. "He doesn't mean anything by it. That's just the way he is."

"Princess, he ain't a relative an' ain't attached. No reason to touch you when you're in my bed."

Maybe she should point out that he was in *her* bed and this was only the second time they've slept together, but she thought better of it. "Again, he's harmless and I've known him a long time."

She felt him shake his head behind her. "Said I got rules. That's one of 'em. Got me?"

Di pursed her lips as she considered his rules. Or, really, the only one he mentioned... so far. He was laying down the law when he really had no right to. Having sex twice with the man didn't allow him to suddenly dictate her life. "Is there an expiration on these so-called rules?"

"In effect long as you're gettin' my dick."

"So just until you're done with me."

He didn't say anything.

"Or I'm done with you," she continued softly.

His body went solid behind her and his arm tightened around her waist.

"Just want to make sure I'm clear about that," she added. She turned in his arms until she faced him, both of them laying on their sides.

His eyes appeared dark as he studied her face. "Ain't sharin' you, princess," he grumbled.

"Nobody says you have to." She arched a brow before asking, "Should I tell you the same thing?"

He traced a finger down her cheek and when it got near her mouth she snapped at it playfully. He was brave enough to brush his thumb over her bottom lip and she snagged it with her teeth and tugged on it gently.

"Like to use those teeth of yours," he murmured. She released his thumb when he asked, "You do any of the brothers?"

She frowned at the sudden switch in topics. "What do you mean?"

"Know what I mean, princess."

Her brows furrowed. "Does it matter?" She raised a *wait-a-minute* finger. "Hold up. *Should* it matter?" She felt her blood pressure rise to borderline bitch mode.

"Got a right to know."

She stared at him incredulously then shook her head. "No. I don't think so."

"Yeah, babe."

She pushed herself to seat and stared down at him. "No. You don't."

"That answer's pretty tellin'."

"Is it?"

"Yeah, babe, it is. Instead of simply denyin' it, you're fightin' it. Makes me think you have."

She struggled to keep from lashing out at him and his double standards. "Did you fuck Lola?"

A look crossed Slade's face. He couldn't deny it. The sweet butt herself made it well known that she'd had sex with Slade. And not just once, either. She also knew that Diamond had an interest in Slade, so the woman bragged about it loudly whenever she could. It took everything Di had not to throat-punch the skank.

Sweet butts aka patch whores were one of the reasons Di hated attending the club parties. All a brother had to do was look their direction and they spread their legs and crooked their finger at them.

No matter what Slade thought, Di had never slept with any of the club brothers. No way. She was either related to them or they felt like brothers to her even if they weren't actually related by blood. Even as hot and tempting as Crow could be, there would be no way she'd sleep with him, even if he wanted to. He was like a sibling and just the thought skeeved her out.

But Slade being new, and more importantly, since she didn't grow up with him, made him different.

Like her sister Jewel, Di was born to be an ol' lady. It was in her blood and in her soul. Hell, her mother was a DAMC ol' lady, her father a life-long Angel, and her granddaddy a founding member.

To her, nothing would be more freeing than to be on the back of a sled with the wind in her hair and the open road in front of her and her man.

Her man.

However, until Slade came along, she held no hope of finding an old man of her very own. She had almost given up. Then Slade walked into The Iron Horse one night and everything changed.

But the thought of him fucking Lola, or one of Dawg's girls or any of the patch whores, made her stomach churn. Yes, that was life in the club and it was nothing she wasn't used to, but then the rest of the brothers weren't Slade. She didn't want any of them in her bed.

Now that Slade *was* in her bed, she had to stop thinking about who all came before her in his. Even after she sat on the back of his sled on some of the club runs last summer, he'd found relief elsewhere.

And that shit hurt.

He had pushed her away because he thought she was too difficult to deal with.

Di admitted she had her moments. She was as hard-headed as any of the club brothers. But still...

"Here's the deal," she finally said when he never answered her question about Lola. "Crow was right." She felt his body go solid again at the mention of the ink slinger's name, but she pushed on. "I can admit that when I'm getting laid, my bitchiness tends to retreat. So you'd probably become the club hero if you're giving it to me on the regular."

He opened his mouth, but she raised her hand up to stop him.

"You want to be in my bed, then you're in *my* bed. Not Lola's, not some other patch whore's. Not one of the stripper's." She leaned in closer to him to make sure he knew just how serious she was. "I'm not sharing, either. *Got me?*"

Something she didn't recognize moved across his face, but it quickly disappeared.

But she wasn't done yet. "I catch you at Heaven's Angels, you're no longer welcome in my bed. I catch you touching or sucking face or... whatever... with any of those skanks, I'm done. You wanted rules? You got them."

"Woman..." he grunted, and she couldn't tell if he was amused at her little speech or pissed. Maybe more like stunned.

"Might not be the only rules, either. I'll have to think more on that."

He snorted and shook his head. "Not lookin' for an ol' lady."

"Okay."

His eyes widened for a split second then narrowed as if he didn't believe she'd accept that.

She would.

One reason why was loyalty was important to Di. And she wasn't ready to explore being Slade's ol' lady anyway until she knew for certain that he could keep his dick out of other women.

Over the years, she'd seen some ol' ladies come and go because their men couldn't keep their dicks in their pants. She didn't want that heartbreak. She wanted something solid, like Sophie, Kiki, Jewel and Ivy. Hell, she wanted "forever" like Janice and Mama Bear.

Her mother was emotionally destroyed when her father, Rocky, was sentenced to life in prison for murder.

Whatever man Di decided to settle down with, she wanted it to stick. Crow mentioned Slade might be searching for something, that he may be a rolling stone. She didn't need to invest her emotions and tie up her heart with someone who may, one day, decide to move on.

Because if he did, she would not go with him. She would not leave the club or her family. Her roots were deeply planted in Shadow Valley, in this club, and no one, not even a man she might end up loving, could uproot her. No fucking way.

She wanted to see the fourth generation DAMC grow up and carry on the same traditions she was brought up with. She wanted to help raise every child that was born amongst the sisterhood. They were a tight knit group of women that she would be hard-pressed to find anywhere else.

And she would never, ever give that up.

So, yeah, she wasn't ready to be Slade's ol' lady since he had no roots in this club, nothing to keep him from moving on.

Not only that, she realized she knew *nothing* about his past or his family. And she wondered if anyone else did. She couldn't imagine Diesel would allow anyone with such a mysterious background to patch in, but she couldn't be certain. She never asked him, but maybe she should.

"Princess, ain't lookin' for an ol' lady," he repeated again.

She looked him straight in the eye and said again, "Okay."

"Just like that," he muttered.

"Yeah, Slade, just like that. I'm not looking to tie anyone down who doesn't want to be." She held his gaze when she asked, "Are you just passing through?"

His brows shot up. "Whataya mean?"

"Are you just here for a little while? And once you get restless you'll move on?"

His eyes slid to the side and he sucked in a breath before his gaze returned to her. "No need to patch in an' get the club colors on my back if I'm plannin' on leavin'."

And that was the kicker. What he said was true. Who in their right mind would go through days of having Crow tattoo the club's rockers and insignia into their skin if it was only temporary?

No one.

She brushed her fingers over his dog tags. "Won't talk about your service, but what about your family?"

He rolled onto his back and tucked his arms under his head as he stared at the ceiling. "Not much to talk about."

She curled against his side and traced the outline of some of his many tattoos. "Brothers? Sisters?"

"Nope."

"Got to have a mom and a dad," she prompted.

"Single mom. My uncle, her only sibling, had been in an MC. The one I patched into."

"The one you left."

"Yeah."

"They were doing shit you didn't like."

"Right. Left before I got caught up an' landed behind bars. Wasn't in the mood to do time in a concrete box after doin' my time in the Marines."

She nodded and studied his profile. "What were they doing?"

"Shit."

"What kind of shit?"

He turned his head to look at her. "Shit. Just shit, princess. Not worth talkin' 'bout."

"What about your dad?"

"Don't know 'im. Never met 'im."

"Your mom never talked about him?"

Slade made a noise and rolled over until he was over top of her, staring down into her face. "Babe, this an inquisition?"

"No. Just trying to get to know you better," she murmured, starting at his lips just inches from hers. She ran her tongue over her bottom lip.

"Not much to know."

She doubted that was true. She just might have to have a little discussion with Diesel.

"My turn... It bug you your pop's doin' time?"

She didn't even hesitate. "Of course. He's doing life. I don't remember a time he wasn't in prison."

"How old were you when he went in?"

"I was a baby. Maybe a year old. Jewel was born right after he went in."

"Fuck," he muttered.

"Yeah. My mom might as well have been a single mom like yours."

"Visit 'im?"

"I really don't know him well. Sometimes he writes letters. Sometimes he calls. On a rare occasion I visit. Says he still loves my mom and I believe him. Ripped my mom to pieces to see him get sentenced to life. Three young kids and no man to help."

"Ace stepped in."

"Yeah, Ace and Janice stepped in. Grizz and Mama Bear, too, since my grandfather was killed by a Warrior. Grizzly has always been like a grandfather to us all since Bear was murdered. And Doc was thrown in prison just about the same time as my father."

"Gotta be hard."

"That's why we all stick together."

He nodded, then he said something that didn't need said. "Warriors have been fuckin' with you all for a long time."

"Yeah," she breathed.

"Gotta suck. Gotta hate 'em all, yeah?"

"No reason not to hate them. They've killed, raped, kidnapped some of us. Stole from us. Whatever they can do to fuck with us, they do it."

"Long-standin' war."

"For years DAMC tried to take the high road. That didn't do us any good."

Slade stared down at the women beneath him. "Right," he murmured. "Think you're safe out here? Out in the country?"

All these months he'd been a part of DAMC and he'd never been out to Ace's farm once. Until this morning. From the hospital, Diamond had unexpectedly directed him out of town. When they had pulled down a long lane and past a farmhouse, she mentioned that was where Ace and Janice lived along with Ace's ancient, crotchety mother, Lonnie.

She continued to direct him past the house and once they traveled farther down the lane he started to see large cabins. She explained that Ace's sisters, Annie and Allie, each lived in one of their own and helped Janice take care of Lonnie. Kelsea still lived at home with her mom, Annie.

She also mentioned that some of them were rented out long-term since Ace got a good amount of rent for them since they were all two-bedroom places. However, her rent was dirt cheap which was why she could afford the newer, expensive sports car she drove. Her cabin was the farthest from the farmhouse and sort of isolated.

And Slade did not like that at all. She shouldn't be living out there by herself with all the shit that had been going down lately with the Warriors. She could be kidnapped, raped—hell, even killed —and no one would hear her scream for help.

"It's safe out here."

He frowned. "Too far away from anybody."

"I have a phone."

"Gotta weapon?"

"Like a gun?" she asked, surprised.

"Yeah, a fuckin' gun to protect yourself with."

Her eyes softened as she stared up at him. "Are you worried about me?"

Fuck. Was he?

"Should move to town," he said.

She snorted softly. "I'm not moving to town. I've got it good here. Got my own place, family nearby, and loads of privacy."

Even though that was all true, Slade didn't like that she was out there by herself. Especially since most of the family around were only women. Ace always seemed to be at the pawn shop that he ran. From what he heard, it was to avoid that cranky old woman that Diamond mentioned.

"Anyway, I don't need a gun." She yanked on the dog tags that hung from his neck and pointed at the USMC logo tattooed onto his bicep. "Have a Marine in my bed, remember?"

Did she think he would land in her rack every night?

"Princess, I work 'til early mornin' at The Iron Horse. Sometimes it takes all I got just to drag myself up the stairs to my room. Ain't gonna drive all the way out to the middle of bumfuck every night to warm your sheets when you'll already be asleep an' gotta get up early for work."

"Not that early."

"Early enough. An' anyway, just said I don't want an ol' lady. Me bein' in your bed every night's just like havin' one. Ain't happenin'."

She shrugged. "Okay."

His eyes narrowed on her. Every time she became agreeable, he wondered what was going through her head, how she was scheming. Diamond was not the easiest woman to deal with. Not even close. So her being so agreeable made him suspicious.

He dropped his head and murmured against her lips, "Will come out the nights I ain't workin' too late."

When she opened her mouth to answer, he dipped his tongue inside and explored every inch of it. The groan he got from kissing her thoroughly was felt all the way down into his dick.

Even though he'd been exhausted from being up all night waiting for Z's kid to be born, then up all morning fucking Diamond, he suddenly found his second wind.

Oorah.

CHAPTER EIGHT

Diamond couldn't believe she was at one of the pig roasts when she normally couldn't stand to be at them. Though, this one was different. Sort of. She was here only to celebrate the birth of Zeke. And she couldn't wait to hold the new bundle of joy.

However, the new parents were inside church and surrounded by a crowd. She'd approach Sophie later when things died down.

She sat close to the bonfire since there was still a chill in the night air. A bottle of Iron City beer hung from her fingers as she tracked Lola walking across the courtyard toward the stage and Nash's band. Dirty Deeds had been jamming out all night doing classic rock and roll.

The music was being piped into The Iron Horse so the customers over there could enjoy it live. The band usually drew a good crowd for the roadhouse even when the patrons couldn't physically see the band, because they were just that good.

A big crowd meant a busy bar and loads of money in Hawk's pocket, as well as, the club's coffers. It also meant that extra hands were needed on deck over there to serve drinks, kick out underage patrons, and bounce drunk assholes.

Because of that, Di hadn't seen hide nor hair of Slade. He was tending bar and bouncing belligerent drunks when necessary, while

Hawk partied on the private side and kept a close eye on his future wife.

Yes, *future wife*.

It hadn't been officially announced, but Kiki had showed up tonight with a freaking blinding boulder on her left ring finger. She didn't have to say a word since it was immediately spotted from a mile away. She said she didn't want to make a big deal out of it since the attention should be on Z's baby.

So, besides the excitement of Zeke's arrival, there was Hawk's engagement to celebrate. If it wasn't celebrated tonight, it would just be one more excuse for *another* pig roast. Because apparently no one in this club knew how to do anything else to celebrate but run a rod through a pig's ass, drink and fuck. And even sometimes the fucking wasn't done in private. Di never ate at the picnic tables under the pavilion for a reason. A pretty good one at that.

At least Kelsea had come up with the male stripper idea for Di's birthday. Thank fuck.

While Dirty Deeds was worth listening to, the parties at church were as boring as shit. She'd heard Nash's band play one million and one times and was pretty much at her limit with hearing covers done of AC/DC, Black Sabbath, ZZ Top, and the like. Not that she had anything against those bands, she didn't. But after a while, it got old.

She bit back a yawn, then tipped her bottle to her lips and let the cold beer slide down her throat.

She eyeballed Lola talking closely to one of the newer prospects, Jester, and she wondered why the newest recruit wasn't working The Iron Horse instead of Slade.

She might have to have a word with Hawk about that.

She also needed to talk to Diesel about digging into Slade's background if he hadn't done so already. If D gave her any shit, she would go to Axel and express her concerns. Bella's man might help her out and do a little background check.

She'd hoped Slade would spill more about himself after a couple more nights in her bed, but he hadn't. He hardly talked about himself at all, which made her even more curious.

Her sister came from behind her and settled into the empty chair to her right. Jewel's hands were empty, and she shoved them into the pockets of her leather jacket.

"Why don't you have a drink?" Di asked suspiciously.

Jewel stared into the blazing fire and shrugged. "Couldn't hold the baby and a drink at the same time."

"Don't see a baby in your arms now."

"Yeah."

Di studied her sister's profile in the glow of the fire. "You know, if I ever see any of us without at least a beer now, I'm going to suspect that sister is knocked up."

Jewel shot her a wide-eyed look. "Believe me, it isn't me. If it's anyone, it's Kiki."

Di laughed. "True."

Jayde suddenly came bounding around the chairs they were sitting in and bounced on her toes in front of Di and Jewel, making her long dark pony tail bounce along with her. "Holy shit! Did you get to hold Zeke yet?"

"No," Di answered.

"Yes," Jewel said at the same time.

"Oh my God, he's so adorable. I want one!"

Di looked up at the youngest DAMC sister and rolled her eyes at her.

"I need to get a man and have *lots* of babies," Jayde continued, not catching what Di did.

"Are you even supposed to be here? I thought Mitch told you to stay away from the club."

Jayde waved a dismissing hand. "He doesn't know I'm here."

"Of course not," Di mumbled. "Because if he did, he'd probably drag your ass home."

"He needs to see his grandson," Jayde said with a frown.

Di didn't know anyone who didn't agree with that statement. "No shit. But until he gets that stick out of his ass, he won't."

"I'm going to bring Mom to the bakery so she can see Zeke."

Di sighed. She wanted April, her aunt, to see Zeke, but she also didn't want Jayde and April going behind Mitch's back and tearing their family apart more than it already was. Baby or not.

Things had improved between Axel and Zak since Axel and Bella now lived together, but even their relationship was still tenuous and strained. Right now they were tolerating each other because of Bella and because of Z's baby.

But it wouldn't take much for that thin olive branch to snap.

"Have you seen Linc?" Jayde asked out of the blue.

Di frowned at her cousin. "Maybe you should stay away from Linc tonight since you're in 'I need to have lots of babies' mode. You coming home knocked up by a biker will make your father lose his mind."

Jayde leaned close to her and Jewel and whispered loudly, "I know how to have sex and not get pregnant."

Di snorted, shot her sister a look then turned her attention back to Jayde. "How about you just leave Linc alone so the poor guy doesn't end up with two bullets in his ass. One from your father and one from Axel."

She scowled down at Di and then stomped away, mumbling, "Whatever."

Di sighed and shook her head. She had a feeling Jayde was going to do something stupid and send shit sideways with the rest of the family.

Bella came up and squatted between the two chairs, holding a full red plastic cup. "Who pissed in her Cheerios?"

"Di did," Jewel answered with a snicker.

Bella swung her head toward Di. "What did you do?"

"Warned her off Linc. I don't think you want your man going to jail after plugging a round into Linc."

Bella's raised her brows. "For what?"

"Simply accepting something that's being waved in front of his face."

Bella turned back to look in the direction Jayde went. "Shit. Hopefully Linc has a better head on his shoulders than that."

"It's not the head on his shoulders he has to worry about."

Bella laughed.

Di leaned over and peered into her cup. "What are you drinking?"

"Jack and Coke. You?"

Di lifted her I.C. Light bottle and Bella winced. "Not that light stuff."

Di shrugged. "Hey, it's low on calories and carbs."

Jewel laughed. "You know, so she can stay lean and mean to kick some ass."

"Speaking of that... Did you ever finish your certification?" Bella asked.

Diamond glanced around quickly to see if anyone was nearby and could overhear them. It wasn't like what she was doing was bad, but she had a feeling it would be frowned upon by the guys and they might give her shit about it. And when they were on someone's case they could all be annoying.

For that reason, she never talked about it in front of any of them. What they didn't know they couldn't complain about.

"Yeah, I finished it and started subbing at the gym."

"Subbing? Substitute instructing?" Bella asked.

Di nodded.

"That's so cool!" Bella exclaimed. "Are you going to start teaching full-time?"

Jewel leaned forward and said, "No, she isn't. For some reason, she has this fear that the guys will find out and be assholes about it."

Bella snorted. "When aren't they assholes? But, seriously, that's crazy. It's just a workout."

No, kickboxing was more than just a way to keep in shape. She started doing it when she wanted to protect herself. After Pierce cornered her all those years ago, she knew she had to take steps to keep herself from being vulnerable, becoming a victim, so she got her mother to enroll her in a self-defense course. Di never told her why she wanted to take it, and Di definitely didn't want anyone to know what Pierce did because she still felt stupid for putting herself into that situation. So she ended up learning some basic moves and while at the gym, she watched a kickboxing class and then begged her mom to sign her up for that next.

Ruby was just happy her teenaged daughter found some sort of interest that kept Diamond out of trouble.

Jewel and Bella were pretty much the only ones in the DAMC who knew that she still kickboxed and was serious about it. Occasionally even competing. Her brother Jag knew she had done it when they were teenagers but most likely thought she eventually stopped, that it was just a phase Di went through.

But she didn't stop. And to get a discount and help pay for classes and training, she ended up working the front desk at the gym. Eventually, the owner convinced her to get certified as an instructor because she was so passionate about it. A natural from what he said. And he needed someone to sub for him when he couldn't teach for whatever reason.

Unfortunately, the job had paid shit and it was a half an hour away, so Di agreed to take over managing the office at Shadow Valley Body Works when Jewel went to work for Diesel. But she still drove up to the gym to train whenever she could.

All those years she worked at the gym, not only did the guys not know she was kickboxing, but the gym owner pushed her to get better and stronger. A few times, Di considered turning it into a career somehow. And Jewel had actually encouraged her to do just that.

"You should talk to Z about having the club finance your own gym," Bella said to her. "That would be so cool. You could teach us all to kickbox and do self-defense. Learn to kick some ass!"

"I don't know..."

"Why not? I know if I had known some self-defense or..." Bella drifted off.

Fuck. Di did not want Bella remembering the abuse her husband had put her through. Tonight was supposed to be a celebration.

So she quickly said, "Do you think they'd go for it? Sophie's bakery and Kiki's law firm are the only club businesses run by women. And you know why? Because Sophie already owned her business when she met Z and Kiki had enough of her own money to start her own firm and didn't need any help funding it. Do you think the Executive Committee would agree to fork over a wad of dough to help me start a business?" She shook her head. "They'd probably laugh."

Jewel made a noise. "They could only say no, but it'd be better than working in the shop's office."

"*You* worked in the shop's office," Di reminded her sister.

Jewel lifted a shoulder. "Yeah, but now I'm not."

"Because D demanded you run his business instead. It's just another way for him to keep an eye on you."

"I think we could convince them," Bella cut off Jewel's response before things got heated. "Think about it, these guys like to work out. All they have is that shitty little room in the back of the body shop with half-assed equipment. If the club owns our own gym, they could have whatever equipment they'd want, and they'd have a lot more room to grunt and sweat. As it is, that room's so small, it's tight if more than one person is in there lifting. And forget any of us women trying to use it. Honestly, I'd think they'd go for it."

"And," Jewel added, "there's no competition. There isn't a decent gym in Shadow Valley. It'd give the club more money in the coffers and another place for prospects to work, which could help expand the club. It's a win-win for these stubborn men. It's all on how you present it."

That was true. Though, Di had considered it many times, she had always pushed the thought away. It was one thing to take over managing an established business like Shadow Valley Body Works. Quite another to start one from the ground up. But even if Z and the others agreed with it, she'd need a lot of help and everyone was busy enough already.

"I'll think about it." Di eyeballed Jewel. "You might have to do some negotiating since asking for funds to start a new business needs to go to a vote and your beast of a man doesn't think us women can or even need to protect ourselves since we have him. To him, we're helpless—"

"Woman..." came a deep, scary voice behind them.

Oh, fuck.

All three of them looked at each other, then up over their shoulders at Diesel. His eyes were pinned to his ol' lady. "Whataya yappin' about?"

Di watched her sister's face go blank.

"Nothing," Jewel answered.

He stared down at her for a moment, then said, "Better not be lyin' to me."

"Why would I lie to you?" Jewel asked with a smirk.

He grunted.

Diamond leaned toward her sister and whispered, "Because you want one of his *lessons.*" Then she jumped out of her chair, grabbed Diesel's *thick-as-a-tree-limb* arm and pulled. "Need to talk to you about something."

"What?" he grunted with a frown.

Di's eyes fell on Jewel and Bella, then she gave them a slight chin lift. She tugged on his arm again even though he didn't budge. "Come with me."

He studied her for a moment, then finally his big booted feet began to move in the direction she tugged.

"Got a question for you. Or maybe even a favor..."

D's brows snapped together as he reluctantly followed her. "What about?"

"Well, it's more like a who..."

———

S lade stepped out into the cool night, the smell of smoke of both the legal and illegal kind, as well as the bonfire variety, still lingering in the air. The band had just packed up their equipment and left, and the fire burned low in the pit. He'd missed the party, but the bar had been so busy he couldn't find even a minute to get away. Even when Jester and Coop came in to relieve him.

Hawk had dropped in a few times to survey the bar patrons,

make sure everything wasn't going to shit and to remove money from the cash register every so often.

Last year, Slade had showed up at The Iron Horse about the same time Kiki entered Hawk's life, so he only had to go by what the other brothers said about Hawk spending most of his waking hours at the bar until his woman came along. Now, the man tried to stay away as much as possible.

He trusted Slade and Linc to handle the day-to-day management, and the prospects, Jester and Coop, to help. Plus, he had some outsiders work the bar part-time and in the kitchen as line cooks, dishwashers and just general *get-shit-done* employees.

Slade could easily see why Kiki was more important to him than the bar was. But it was the revenue from the bar that helped buy that enormous diamond that the club's attorney showed up wearing tonight.

Slade couldn't even imagine what it cost but agreed Kiki was probably worth it. She was Hawk's world. His everything.

It was hard to miss that Hawk's eyes tracked his woman constantly when she was in his vicinity. And it wasn't just Hawk who did it. D did it with Jewel, Jag with Ivy and Z definitely watched his woman and now his newborn closely. He didn't blame them one bit.

All those brothers had landed themselves some fine ol' ladies. Loyal and *bangin'* hot, as well as smart.

Slade's eyes swept the courtyard, disappointed that Diamond didn't stick around until his shift was over. He scrubbed a hand over his hair, then headed over to one of the remaining kegs by the fence, grabbed a plastic cup and poured himself a draft. He headed back over to what was left of the bonfire and settled his exhausted bones into a chair. He released a long sigh, put his head back and closed his eyes.

He had no idea how long he was out, but when he woke, the fire had died to glowing coals, the courtyard was dark, and a head of dark brown hair bobbed in his lap as his dick was sucked.

What a helluva way to wake up.

His fingers slid into her hair, fisted and he tilted her head up. "Princess..." he groaned.

He blinked in shock. It wasn't Diamond's lips around his cock. Oh, fuck no, it wasn't.

Fuck!

Slade shot to his feet, his chair falling behind him into the dead grass.

Lola looked up at him from her knees, a smile on her lips. "Didn't mean to scare you."

"What the fuck, Lola?"

Her smile flipped into a frown. "What? You've never complained before."

His mouth dropped open as he stared down at her. Then he lifted his gaze quickly and searched the courtyard. Relief flooded him as it seemed empty except for the two of them.

"What the fuck?" he asked again.

"I thought you'd enjoy waking up that way. The fire had died down and you were going to get cold. I figured I'd get you warmed up." Lola slowly climbed to her feet, running a hand over her mouth.

Slade carefully tucked what was left of his hard-on into his jeans and struggled to zip them shut. "Can't just whip my dick out an' suck it."

She laughed. "What fucking man complains about a head job?"

"One who doesn't want it from you."

Her eyebrows knitted. "Why? Like I said, you've never complained when I've done it before."

Even though she was right, things had changed... "Didn't ask you to do it now."

"C'mon, Slade. I didn't mean to make you upset. I was just looking for a little company."

He shook his head and blew out a breath, pinning his narrowed eyes on her. "Why are you still here?"

She shrugged. "I was hanging with Jester until he went to work the bar."

"Jester can't fuck you." Prospects could not get a piece of any sweet butt. If Jester was touching Lola, they'd both be kicked out on their asses.

"Didn't say he was. He was just being friendly."

Friendly. *Riiiight.* Slade shook his head again. "Lola, you need to get gone."

"You don't want some company?"

He wanted company but not Lola's. Not now. He didn't need that headache since he was landing in Diamond's bed on the regular. "Fuck no."

"Damn, Slade. That's harsh. You had no problem fucking me in the past."

"That was before."

"Before what?"

"Before we set rules," came a low female voice from behind him.

Lola's gaze lifted as she looked over his shoulder at whoever was behind him.

Slade knew exactly who was behind him. *Fuck.*

"What kind of rules?" Lola asked, her eyes narrowed.

"Like not having skanks suck his dick."

"Well, that doesn't apply to me then, since I'm not a skank..."

Diamond snorted.

"Ain't talking to you, bitch," Lola snapped. Her eyes slid back to Slade. "So I'm asking *you*, want some *good* company for the rest of the night?"

A hair-raising noise came from the woman behind him and Slade was afraid to turn around. He had a feeling that Diamond's bitch switch had been triggered.

"No, he doesn't want your used-up skanky snatch."

"Does she talk for you, Slade? Is she your ol' lady now?"

There wasn't much Slade was afraid of, but if there was, it was two pissed off women fighting over a man. That would be at the top of the list.

"I might not be his ol' lady, but I'm smart enough to know he shouldn't stick his dick where he could catch something! Who knows where the fuck that mouth of yours has been. Could be like a petri dish."

"Diamond..." he murmured and before he could turn around to get her away from Lola, he was knocked to the side as Lola rushed past him with a shriek and tackled Diamond to the ground.

"Fuck!" he shouted and before he could grab Lola off her, Diamond did a move that stopped him in his tracks. Her fist was lightning fast as she stunned Lola with a quick punch to the face.

"Damn," he breathed.

With moves like a pro, Diamond had the sweet butt flipped over onto her back and she straddled Lola's waist and restrained her, using her weight. There was no hair pulling, no scratching, no bitch fighting at all.

Unfortunately, he didn't have the time to appreciate Diamond's skill since Lola had her arms flailing as she tried to grab Diamond's hair and scratch her face. And if that happened...

But it didn't... Diamond skillfully trapped the sweet butt's wrists and pinned them to the ground. Lola's body bucked underneath her wildly as the woman screeched. Somehow Diamond hung on and kept herself from being attacked.

Slade rushed over, grabbing Diamond under her arms and hauled her off Lola. Her chest was heaving, her eyes wild, her hands still clenched into fists. "You're out of this club, bitch!" Diamond snarled, lifting one of those very skilled fists and shaking it at the sweet butt.

Lola pushed herself to a seated position, wiping at her mouth. "Fuck you, Cubic Zirconia."

Oh, fuck. Bitches were crazy.

Slade pointed at Lola. "Stay down. Don't you get up 'til I have her outta here. Got me?"

Lola turned her head and spat blood onto the ground. "Fuck you, Slade. You want that biker cunt? She'll have your balls in a vise and you'll get sick of her bitching."

Diamond jerked forward in Slade's arms, practically growling. He tightened his hold by wrapping his arms around her chest and walked backward, dragging her with him.

"Diamond, quit it," he said in her ear.

"That bitch is out of here!"

"Yeah, it'll get handled," he assured her, hoping that he didn't trip while walking her backward. If he loosened his grip on her even the slightest, he was worried she'd tear back after Lola, who was pushing to her feet and brushing herself off.

"I was waiting for you and you're fucking down here getting your dick sucked!"

"Not now," Slade said quietly. "Gonna come with me calmly? We're goin' inside. Don't need you tusslin' with her, got me?"

"I can take her," Di snapped.

Slade fought back the chuckle that wanted to escape. *She could take her.* After the little bit Slade saw, he had no doubt Diamond could do it.

He turned them around and released her, except for the firm grasp he kept on her wrist. "Inside," he told her.

With a huff, Diamond moved toward the side door that went into church and when they finally got through it, he steered her toward the stairway.

"Your place or here?" he asked.

She didn't answer for a minute, instead she just stood there, still breathing a little faster than normal.

"How about you stay here, and I go home," she finally said then moved toward the back door to the parking lot.

Slade reached out, snagged her wrist again and hauled her back to him. "That ain't gonna happen," he muttered, staring down into her eyes still flashing with anger.

"Think I want you with skank spit on your dick?"

Slade caught his bottom lip in his teeth and closed his eyes for a second, just long enough to let the irritation run through him so he didn't say anything he'd regret later.

He released her wrist. "Fine. Fuckin' go, then." With a shake of his head he moved toward the stairs. He didn't look behind him, but he knew she remained in the same spot and he could feel those blue eyes of hers burning holes into his back. He expected her to call out, to stop him before he reached the bottom of the steps, but she didn't.

He sighed in relief when he heard her yell out, "Where are you going?"

Without turning around, he said, "Upstairs to wash 'skank spit' off of me, then comin' over to your place to fuck you good. Be ready. Better be in sweet Diamond mode, too."

Then he stomped up the stairs not waiting for her response.

———

S lade brushed a lock of hair out of Diamond's face as it rested on his chest. Their breathing was finally back to normal after the rough and tumble sex they had. He was surprised they hadn't broken her bed, because that's how badass it was.

He was beginning to appreciate the fact that Diamond's cabin was isolated. Otherwise, Ace, or the any of the others living on the farm, might bust in thinking he was killing her.

The fucking woman had a mouth on her, but he was not one to curb her enthusiasm. Hell no, he wasn't. Speaking of enthusiasm...

"Where'd you learn to fight like that?"

Her blue eyes tipped up to his and suddenly something ran through him that he didn't recognize. Something he wasn't ready to figure out, either.

"You should know what the club motto is," she answered.

"Yeah. And?"

"I know how to get down and dirty."

"That you do. Don't fight like a girl, though."

"No."

"Why?"

Her bare shoulder lifted and fell back into place. After a long hesitation, she finally said, "I've done some kickboxing."

He shifted until he could see down into her face a little better. "No shit?"

She nodded, a small smile curling the corner of her lips. "No shit."

"Damn. Gotta tell you, princess, that shit was hot."

"Yeah, well, I saw that patch whore on her knees while you were tucking your dick back into your jeans and it..."

"Pissed you off," he finished for her. That unrecognizable feeling swept through him again.

"Yeah, it pissed me off. Unfortunately, I forgot to remind myself that no man's worth fighting over."

He stifled a chuckle, then became more serious. "Just to be clear, didn't break the rules," he murmured.

"I know. That's the only reason why you're in my bed right now."

"Fell asleep. Woke up to..." No point in making her relive it and get her temper flaring again. "Thought it was you," he finished softly.

She sighed, her warm breath blowing across his still damp chest.

When she remained quiet, he added, "Wished it was you, princess."

And that was true. What they had going on right now was a good thing. And he didn't want to blow it. Whatever it was, worked for them. For the past couple of weeks, they'd gotten together whenever they could, usually in her cabin, and the sex was fucking amazing. Mind-blowing.

No matter how rough he got with her, she ate that shit up. And she gave as good as she got.

So yeah, he could definitely see her kickboxing. But her form was... really, really good. It made him wonder where she learned to kick box, why she never mentioned it until now and whether she was still doing it. But mostly, he wanted to know why.

"Got in a lotta scraps when you were a kid?"

She mumbled something against his skin.

He lifted his head. "What?"

"No," she mumbled. "I started doing it after Pierce cornered me." She hesitated, then blew out a breath. "I needed to find a way to protect myself."

He stilled. Fury begin to bubble up from his chest. Not at Diamond. Hell no. But at that piece of shit former DAMC president. That man needed to stay clear of Slade if he knew what was good for him.

He tried to push away his rage at the thought of a fifteen-year-old feeling so vulnerable around an adult like that, she felt the need to take steps to protect herself. Most teenagers would have run to tell someone, not Diamond. Instead, she took it upon herself to solve a problem in the best way she could think of.

He sucked air into his flared nostrils, trying to lower his blood pressure. "Nothin' surprises me 'bout you, princess. nothin'. You abso-fuckin-lutley impress me with your courage." She really did.

When he looked back down at her she was smiling, which made him blink in surprise. It had to be his compliment making her eyes twinkle like they did when she was happy. He loved seeing her like that. Content and happy. Especially when she was sprawled over his chest after a bout of a sweaty session of knocking boots.

Since she just gave him a little insight about herself that he didn't know, he decided to do the same.

"Boxed in the Marines," he admitted.

"Were you good?"

"Yeah, enough to make some good scratch at it."

"Didn't want to continue with it?"

"Not good enough to go pro."

She traced a fingernail around his nipple and a shiver ran down his spine. "How long were you in the Marines?"

The question was innocent enough, but Slade knew once he started answering questions about his time in the military, she'd want to know more, and he just wasn't ready to talk about it. Or at least some of it.

"Eight years."

"Eight?"

"Yeah, six active, two reserves. Did my time, got out."

When she opened her mouth to ask the next question, he pressed his finger to her lips. "Done talkin' 'bout it. Wanna know more 'bout you."

"What about me?"

He asked the first question that popped into his head. Especially since Lola had called her Cubic Zirconia earlier. Which wasn't funny at the time but was now that he thought back on it. "How'd you get the name Diamond?"

"You know my mom's name is Ruby, right?"

He nodded.

"Mom made a deal with my dad. She got to name any girls. He got to name any boys. Jag was born first and since Dad loved the Rolling Stones, he named him Mick Jagger Jamison."

"Mick?"

Di snorted. "Yeah. He hates it. Only Ivy gets away with calling him that and only in private, if you get my meaning. She says it's a way to make Mick only hers, when the rest of us get Jag. So anyway, Mom went with a theme for Jewel and me, obviously."

"Like your name?"

She shrugged against him. "Doesn't bother me. Jewel doesn't mind her name, either. So, I guess we're luckier than Jag."

"Princess Di," he murmured, stroking the back of his knuckle down her cheek.

"Mmm. Classy lady. I'm nothing like her."

Slade chuckled. "Don't want classy. Like that you can get down an' dirty. Got some spunk, woman. Turns me the fuck on."

"I thought I was too bitchy for you. I assumed that's why you pushed me away last summer."

"Keep you full of dick an' that bitchiness disappears."

"So, you're sacrificing yourself for the good of the club?"

His lips twitched. "Yeah, babe, I'm sacrificin'."

She whacked his arm.

He continued, "But you still have enough fight in you to make the sex interesting."

"Interesting, huh?"

Slade flipped her over and covered her body with his. "More than interesting."

She smiled up at him and his chest tightened. When the woman smiled she was *lose-your-breath* stunning. A woman that might make other men jealous because she didn't belong to them.

But she didn't belong to Slade, either. Not now, maybe not ever.

Though, he was happy for Z going down that road of claiming an ol' lady, putting a ring on her finger and then creating a family, Slade wasn't so sure that was for him.

He had shit he needed to do, to get off his plate, before even thinking of settling down.

Settling down.

Fuck. Did that phrase even enter his head?

He sucked in a breath.

"What's wrong?" she asked him, her eyes worried.

"Nothin'." He slipped to her side and pulled her against him, her back to his front, strumming his thumb absently over her nipple. He tucked his chin into the crook of her neck and inhaled her scent.

And again, that fucking feeling that he couldn't identify rushed through him. His heart began to pound against his chest and he closed his eyes trying to beat back the panic.

Months ago when he landed in Shadow Valley, he didn't plan on staying. He was only there to poke around for a little while and then move on. And now, here he was a fully-patched member of the Angels and had a DAMC woman in his bed. Or her bed. Whatever.

He wasn't here to put down roots. That wasn't his intent.

But the nights he ended up with Diamond in his arms, he felt those roots growing, spreading, sinking deeper into the ground.

He couldn't let that happen. He needed to fight it.

He'd be smart to roll out of her bed, her place, and go back to his room to forget she ever existed. Then he needed to do what he came to do in the Valley and get gone.

But as much as he knew that needed to happen, he couldn't pull away from her. Not now. Not today.

Maybe tomorrow. Or possibly the next day.

Because today he was staying put. Her bed was warm, Diamond was hot, and at this very moment, there was nowhere he'd rather be than the exact spot he was in.

And, fuck him, that scared the hell out of him.

"Slade," she said softly.

"Yeah, princess?"

"I can feel your heart pounding."

"Yeah," he breathed and pressed his face deeper into her neck.

"Are you sure you're okay?"

Fuck no, he wasn't sure.

He wasn't sure at all.

CHAPTER NINE

Diamond sat at her desk in the office at Shadow Valley Body Shop and stifled a yawn. These late nights with Slade were kicking her ass. But they were definitely worth the dark circles under her eyes and her constant exhaustion.

In the beginning, he was showing up a night here and there. Lately, it'd been almost every night. The only time he hadn't made the effort to drive out to the farm was the couple of nights he closed the bar and didn't get done until three or four in the morning. But normally he showed up around midnight and they'd bang one out. Or two. Then they'd talk for a little bit. Never about himself, though. Never that. He'd tell her the crazy stuff that happened at the bar that night or he'd ask about her day. They talked about nothing of importance.

Then they'd fall asleep. And since she had to wake up a lot earlier than him, when she'd leave for work, he'd still be crashed in her bed. Every morning that happened, she'd stand in the doorway as he slept and watch him for a few minutes.

And she felt *it* creeping in. Every morning that feeling got stronger as she studied him, even though she knew she shouldn't let it, that falling for him might come back to bite her in the ass. But no matter what she told herself, it kept creeping. Not like an avalanche but more like lava flowing from a volcano.

What Crow said about Slade being a rolling stone was lodged at the back of her mind, but her heart ignored it. And that was a dangerous thing.

Problem was, when Slade mentioned about how he didn't like her leaving the door open at night for him since she was usually asleep when he first crawled into bed with her, she offered him a key...

Surprisingly, he accepted it. It shocked the shit out of her, but she chalked it up to him being worried about her safety with the Warriors on the prowl and her cabin being secluded.

Even so, she wondered if taking that key meant anything to him or it was just a means to end.

No matter what, she realized that Jewel was right, as was Slade, when she was getting laid, the ragged edges of her temper smoothed out. Who would have thought all it took was a bit of dick? Maybe it was more due to the man attached to that appendage.

As she got to her feet to pour herself her fourth cup of coffee of the day in her struggle to keep her eyes open, Crash came crashing through the door from the shop into the office.

His nose wiggled, and he spotted the fresh brewed coffee in the corner. "Thought I smelled caffeine." He grabbed a mug that hung nearby and filled it, then grunted after taking a sip. "Shit's good, babe. Keepin' you here just on your ability to make fuckin' bangin' coffee."

He was keeping *her* here. Right. Like he had a choice. One thing about being a part of the DAMC was that everyone had to work. Preferably in one of the club-owned businesses. For years, she didn't since she worked at the gym.

Di was going to have to seriously give it some thought as to opening her own gym and instructing kickboxing full-time. Maybe she'd have to drop some hints to some of the guys, like Z and Hawk. Maybe even her brother and Ace. Forget Diesel. She could see him being the most unreceptive of her going out on her own, especially with an idea like hers. With as long as she worked at the gym, she pretty much knew the ins and outs of running one.

Even so, until that day came, she should be "lucky" that Crash was "keeping her." *Uh-huh.*

Di held out her mug to him. "Pour me some."

He eyeballed her mug and lifted a brow. "Right."

She frowned. "Seriously, Crash, I made the shit, you can't pour it for me since your ass is standing right there, blocking the coffeemaker?"

"Nope. Get it yourself."

She pushed past him and did just that. When she turned, he was staring at her.

Did she have something on her face? "What?"

"What's the matter with you?" he asked, wearing a suspicious look.

"What do you mean?"

"Just told you to get your own coffee an' you didn't flip out on me. Somethin's up."

She took a sip of her coffee and settled back into her chair. Kicking her feet up on the desk, she leaned back and cradled both hands around the warm mug. "Why do you think something's up?"

He cocked a brow at her but stayed silent. He propped a hip against the counter where the coffee stuff was kept.

"Crash."

"What?" he asked softly, distracted as he studied her like he'd never seen her before.

"Do you think I'm a bitch?"

His head jerked. "What?"

"Do you think I'm a bitch?" she repeated impatiently and more slowly, enunciating each word clearly.

Crash's golden-brown eyes widened, his face got pale, and he straightened. "I... uh..."

Their attention turned toward the shop door as Rig barreled through it, wiping his greasy hands off on a rag. "Just roll-backed in a rusty piece of shit for that total reconstruct you're goin' to do."

Crash's eyes slid to Rig, then back to Di. "Rig can answer that."

Rig stopped short. "Answer what?"

"Whether Di's a bitch."

Rig took a step back, his eyes wide. "What? Why do I have to answer that?"

"For fuck's sake. One or both of you just answer the question honestly. Am I a bitch?"

Rig pursed his lips as he twisted the rag in his hands. Crash stared at Rig.

"Seriously?" she asked, then sighed. "Am I that bad?"

"You run the office real good, Di," Crash said quickly. "Almost as good as Jewel."

"Almost as good?" she asked, her voice rising.

"An' like I said, you make fuckin' awesome coffee."

Well, there was that. *What the fuck!*

"But you've been a lot nicer lately, gotta say," Rig said. "You gettin' laid or somethin'?"

Jesus.

"Yeah, Rig, I'm *gettin' laid*."

Rig stroked a hand down his unruly beard. "By who?"

Crash laughed, then said, "Slade still tappin' your ass, Di?" He shook his head. "Man's got steel balls on 'im if he is."

"What? Why?" she asked him.

Crash snorted. "No reason."

"Bet he's got bruises, cuts an' shit from her if he is," Rig said.

Di rolled her lips under and did her best not to laugh at how ridiculous this conversation was.

"Why you never let me tap that, Di?" Rig asked her, looking at her now like *he'd* never seen her before.

These guys.

"First of all, Rig, you'd have to shave that fucking mess off your face." She circled her hand in front of him indicating his unruly facial hair. "No woman likes that shit. Especially between her legs."

He frowned and ran his fingers over his mustache. "Thought they did."

"Yeah, when it's taken care of and you don't look like some wild-ass mountain man who hasn't seen civilization in like twenty years."

"Nah, bitches like it."

Di laughed and shook her head. "No, bitches don't like it."

Suddenly, he leaned over and kissed her right on the damn mouth. Enough of a peck to freak her out. She whacked at him. "Ew! See? It's so gross. I can smell what you had for breakfast in that forest."

"Can probably taste it, too." He smiled and left the office.

Her gaze swung to Crash. "That was gross."

He snorted and shook his head. "See? The *before-gettin-dick* Diamond would've ripped his balls off for that. I like the *after-getting-dick* Diamond. Think Slade will take bribes?"

"Shut up," she muttered. "Don't you have work to do?"

"Yeah," he laughed. "Can I get a kiss, too?" He leaned over and wagged his tongue at her.

"No!" she screamed and smacked at him. "Go away."

He took his coffee and headed to the door, laughing. "You know what else you do good? Ordering Bangin' Burgers. Get it delivered." Then he headed out and slammed the door behind him.

Di stared at the closed door for a moment, then sighed.

If it wasn't bad enough she just had to deal with Rig and Crash, her brother was the next one through the shop door.

Jag was peeling off his work coveralls. "Why's Rig out there talkin' about doin' you? Why do I have to hear that shit?"

Di raised her eyebrows at him as he made his way to the coffeemaker, grabbed a travel mug and emptied the rest of the pot into it. "I don't know. Did you ask him? How the hell do I know what's going through that peanut he calls a brain?" She frowned when he didn't start a new pot. "Just going to drink it all and not make more?"

He took a sip then his steel blue eyes slid to the empty pot. "That's your job."

"Oh. I see," she said softly, her eyes narrowing. "Making coffee's a woman's work?"

Jag's spun his head back toward her. "Yep."

"Ivy make you coffee every morning?"

"Yep."

"Does she spit in it because you're useless?"

Jag smirked. "Not useless, give her good—"

Diamond slammed her hands over her ears and shouted, "No! Nooooo. Ew. No."

Jag laughed. "Now you know how I feel when Rig's talkin' 'bout tappin' your ass."

"Ew."

"Right," he grunted, dragging fingers through his dark hair. "Anyway, got a call from D. Me an' you need to head over to the warehouse."

"Now? Why?" Di had never been over to In the Shadows Security. Not even to visit Jewel. In fact, D didn't want anyone hanging around over there.

"Dunno," he said and shrugged. "Was hopin' you'd know."

"If he needed to speak with both of us, why didn't he just come here?"

Jag tilted his head and stared at her. "Dunno, sis. Why don't you ask 'im?"

"You're the one who had him on the phone..." She lifted a hand. "Oh, wait. I'm thinking this is how the conversation went... Phone rings, you answer with a grunt. He grunts back. You grunt, then he grunts, grunts, grunts. Then you both hang-up. That the gist of it?"

Jag's lips curled up at the corners. "Yep."

She sighed, put her computer into sleep mode, then pushed to her feet. "Crash and Rig know we're going?"

"Yep."

"You going to say anything other than yep?"

"Nope."

"Crash wants Bangin' Burgers. We can pick it up on the way back."

"Yep."

She snorted and headed out the front door. "I think you were adopted."

He laughed as he followed her out.

———

D iamond pushed through the office door and her gaze fell on Diesel sitting behind his desk. She did a double-take. *Diesel* had a desk? "Why the hell are you summoning us here, Your Ass-Holiness?"

Diesel frowned at her. "Shut the fuck up an' sit down."

Her eyes slid to a man who leaned against one of the walls. She'd never met him before and figured he must be one of D's "Shadows."

The man's expression was closed, unreadable. His eyes cold, his arms crossed over his chest, emphasizing how cut his muscles were. She could see a few tats peeking out from his T-shirt which fit snuggly over his broad chest and hugged his bulging biceps. His hair was military short and reminded her of Slade's.

Well, hello there.

Di swiped her thumb at the corner of her mouth. If she hadn't left Slade this morning in her bed, she might have had to turn on the charm to see if she could melt this one's frosty exterior.

"Sit. Down," D barked with his normal happy-self attitude.

She made a face at him. Three chairs sat in front of his desk and two of them were already occupied by Jewel and Jag. She gave her sister a questioning look and Jewel just shrugged in answer.

So, her sister had no idea what this was about, either. That was weird since she was D's ol' lady.

Then her attention shot back to Diesel when he announced, "Got news."

"'Bout what?" Jag asked, slouching in his chair and not looking at all worried about why all three of Ruby and Rocky's offspring were asked to come to D's warehouse.

Diamond moved around Jag to the empty chair in the middle and began to sit.

"Slade."

She landed hard on her ass in the chair and stared at D, her heart beating a little faster and her blood rushing into her ears.

She had recently asked Diesel to check into Slade's past, but she didn't think he would actually do it. However, she knew D wasn't a fan of Slade's, so maybe that's why he did.

Jag shook his head. "Why am I here?"

"Affects you, too. Affects all of you."

Diamond's stomach churned. What could be in Slade's past that would affect all three of them? Her eyes widened, and she felt the blood drain from her face. "Oh, shit! Please don't tell me he's our secret brother."

Jewel let out a groan and Jag's head swung toward her, looking a little green himself.

Diesel just stared at her, his face unreadable. "Guess you're still fuckin' 'im?"

Di squeezed her eyes shut at the horror of possibly having sex with her own blood relative. Her own half-sibling! "Oh fuck! Holy fuck!"

"Ain't your brother," D grumbled with a frown.

Her whole body collapsed like a rag doll. "Oh, thank fuck!" She dropped her head into her hands and sighed with relief. Because that would've been bad. Worse than bad. An epic fuck up. A shudder went through her as she shook that thought off.

"Hunter," D said with a chin lift to the man against the wall who hadn't even made a sound yet.

Hunter's low, gravelly voice swept over them. "His father was a biker."

"Okay?" Jag asked, confused.

"Name of Buzz."

Di stared at the man, waiting for him to continue. Apparently, getting information out of him was like trying to pour cold honey.

"A Warrior."

Di blinked. And blinked again as what Hunter just revealed sank into her brain. Then that sick feeling overcame her all over again.

"Holy fuck," Jag said, sitting back in his chair. "Does Slade know?"

"Dunno. Dunno what he knows. That's the thing."

"He ain't a plant is he?" Jag asked, swinging his gaze from Hunter to D.

"Dunno that, either," Diesel answered.

Hunter continued, "If he knows his father was a Warrior he may very well have patched in to infiltrate your club."

"There's more," D muttered.

"More?" Di croaked, eyes wide. Slade coming from Warrior blood wasn't bad enough? And she slept with him. Multiple times! And she actually had *feelings* for him. Like deep feelings! If he was a mole for the Warriors...

"Buzz is dead," Hunter stated and straightened to a stand and scrubbing a hand over his severely short hair. "Killed by an Angel."

Diamond opened her mouth but nothing came out. Not air, not words. Nothing. She had somehow lost all her breath and couldn't get it back.

"What?" Jag asked, glancing at both of his sisters.

"Yeah," D grunted. Everyone's gaze landed on the big man behind the desk. D's gaze met hers. "Diamond, gotta keep your shit together, got me?"

Her brain started to spin.

"What?" she whispered. He needed to just spit it out. *Holy fuck.* "Just say it, D."

"Rocky took 'im out."

Spots swam in Diamond's vision and the whole room started to rotate quickly. She dug her fingers into the arms of the chair because she felt like a top that was about to spin out of control and smash into the nearest wall.

She could barely get, "You're fucking lying," out in a whisper. Jewel was suddenly squatting at her feet, her hands gripping Di's thighs.

"Hunter's got no reason to lie, sis," Jewel said. "D's got no reason, either. You know that."

Di's gaze flicked from her sister back to Hunter, who was now standing at the corner of Diesel's desk, his intense sea green eyes pinned on her.

Shaking his head, the man stated, "His real name was Gavin Bussard."

See? She knew he was lying. Slade wasn't from Warrior blood. No fucking way. "Slade's last name is Stone."

"That's his momma's last name."

Fuck.

Diamond thought back to the articles she read on her father's murder trial. She remembered there were two names listed of his so-called victims, but she couldn't remember what they were. She'd have to go back and check with her mother, who had kept the articles.

Holy fuck. This couldn't be happening.

Her father murdered Slade's father.

And she had no idea if Slade knew or not.

Because if he did...

Fuck. He could be setting her up. He could be setting the whole club up.

She raised her gaze to D, who was studying her just as closely as Hunter. "He mentioned his father was a biker, that's it." He'd said that's the only thing he knew about his father. If he knew anything else, he was keeping it from her.

"Yeah," D grunted.

"What do we do?"

"Nothin'. Don't tell 'im we know."

"But... my father killed his, D. *Our* father shot *his*!" Di felt the tightness in her chest growing by the second.

"Diamond, see your mind spinnin'. Need to stay calm."

Stay calm. Well, that was easier said than done.

"It's possible he doesn't even know the man's dead," Jag offered.

"It's possible he does," Hunter answered. "It's possible he knows Rocky did it," his cold eyes pinned Di to the chair again, "an' that he knows you're his daughter."

If Slade didn't know, he'd never forgive Di. If he did, she'd never forgive him.

Hunter continued, "It's very well possible that he plans to exact revenge for his father on you, Diamond, since you're Rocky's daughter. Anything's possible."

"Ain't fuckin' him."

Her head twisted toward D. "What?"

"Ain't fuckin' him no more, got me?"

"D..." she breathed as her heart skipped a beat.

"No lip, woman. Stay the fuck away from 'im 'til we know what he knows or don't know. Got me?"

Her chest felt like it was caving in. "I—" *I just gave him a key to my place.*

"No shit, woman. I'm serious. Break it off," D said firmly.

"D..." Jewel whispered to her man, but her eyes not leaving Di's face.

"No lip from you, either," he told his ol' lady. "Your sister, you, Jag, all of us could be in fuckin' danger. Z might've invited a viper amongst us." Diesel pushed to his feet and pointed a finger right at Di. "Break it off. Don't care how you do it. Find an excuse. Just don't let 'im know what we know. Got me?"

Fuck! She couldn't think straight. How was she going to abruptly break it off with a man who was climbing into her bed almost every night? What good reason was she going to use to get him to stop coming over? How could she get her damn key back without making him suspicious?

Why the fuck was this happening to her when she finally had a man in her bed who she actually liked? Actually, might even...

Love.

Fuck.

She tried to swallow the knot in her throat, but it refused to budge.

Was Slade using her? Was he a bomb ready to implode, ready to destroy their club, their family, from the inside out?

She dropped her head into her hands and sucked in a shaky breath.

"Di," Jewel whispered, her voice sounding so full of pity that it made this whole thing worse. So much worse.

She'd been a fucking fool.

She'd always wanted to be an ol' lady, to belong to a man who'd be loyal to her, to love her completely and she thought that Slade might be the one.

He was someone who she didn't grow up with, who she didn't look at like a "brother." He was new, fresh blood in the club. Not only that, the man was smart, good-looking and had a cool temper, unlike her.

He was someone who'd been a former Marine, one she thought had honor. A man who also understood the club lifestyle, even if she didn't like every aspect of it herself. Like the patch whores and the constant excuses for pig roasts and partying. But everything else she did. The sisterhood, the brotherhood, the family loyalty, the community. They all supported each other. Loved each other. But now this...

They might have an enemy in their midst.

Not only did they allow him into the club, Di allowed him into her heart.

And pretending like she knew nothing about how their fathers were connected was going to be the hardest thing she'd ever done in her life.

Fuck me.

CHAPTER TEN

Slade laid in the dark, listening to Diamond's steady breathing and wondered if she was pretending to sleep.

She had been a bit distant when he slipped into bed with her earlier. But he'd been exhausted, and he couldn't wait to let the stress of a busy night at The Iron Horse slip away when he slipped inside of her.

It took him longer than normal to make her come and, even then, she only did it once. Normally, she was a multi-orgasm type of woman, which he loved about her.

They clicked in bed, and when she was in her smooth-as-silk, sexy-as-hell Diamond mode, she was the best fuck he'd ever had.

And he also loved talking into the night with her, even when he was bone-tired. But tonight, as soon as he rolled off her, she'd turned to her side, faced away from him and went to sleep.

That was not like her, so he wondered what was up her ass, or what she thought he'd done wrong. Because a woman never told a man what they did. They liked to leave a man guessing. "You should know what you did wrong."

Yeah, right. After thousands of years, women should finally realize that men were a bit dense when it came to a woman's feelings and her expectations.

If women gave it to men straight, there might not be so many misunderstandings that could screw with a relationship.

Slade stared up in the dark at the cabin's ceiling and his chest tightened at the thought that him and Diamond may actually be in some sort of relationship.

She was definitely more than just a lay. But how much more, he wasn't sure.

Nor was he sure he wanted to take it much further than that, anyway.

He only landed in Shadow Valley in his search for answers. And now he was burrowed deeper into this club than he originally planned.

He actually regretted getting the club's rockers and insignia tattooed onto his back. But he thought getting it done would lessen Diesel's suspicions of him. Unfortunately, Slade didn't think it did any good. The man still gave him the side eye and probably always would.

He wouldn't even doubt that D would try to turn Diamond against him. He wasn't sure if the club enforcer knew they were sleeping together but with him being Jewel's ol' man and with Jewel being Diamond's sister, he couldn't imagine the man didn't know.

He rolled to his side and stared down at Diamond who was now flat on her back.

"Princess," he whispered and brushed a thumb over her cheek. She shifted but didn't respond. "Babe," he said a little louder and wrapped his hand gently around her throat, feeling her pulse beating under his fingers.

She blinked open her eyes and turned her head toward him. "Yeah. What's wrong?"

"You tell me."

She didn't say anything for the longest time and that caused his heart to thump heavily in his chest. She was not acting herself. Not the bitch Diamond and not the sweet one, either. She was just... withdrawn.

"What's goin' on?" he asked her. He would get to the bottom of this, one way or another.

"I was sleeping." Then she yawned, and he wondered if that was fake, too.

He shook his head. "No, what's goin' on in your head, makin' you distant?"

"Nothing. I'm just tired."

His gut twisted. She was lying to him. "Princess..."

"Slade, I'm tired. I just want to sleep."

Slade sat up and looked down at her. "No. Fuckin' somethin's up an' you need to be straight with me."

She pushed herself to a seat and held the sheet up to her chest covering herself, something she never bothered to do before. She had a great body, awesome tits, and she'd never hid that from him before. They'd only been sleeping together for the past few weeks, but even from the beginning she had never been shy about her body. Not once. She'd strut around her cabin wearing nothing but her long, dark hair many a night.

So something was off.

"You regrettin' givin' me a key?"

When she didn't answer, he wondered if that could be it. That maybe she thought giving him a key to her place was a mistake, a step toward some sort of commitment that neither of them were ready to take.

"That it, Diamond? You want your key back?"

She blew out a shaky breath and he certainly didn't miss it.

"Thought we were havin' a good time, but maybe I was wrong."

"We *were* having a good time," she repeated softly.

He wished the room wasn't dark, wished he could see her face, see her eyes. "Were?" he asked and forced his Adam's apple back down into his throat.

He'd ended up in a lot of different beds over the years and not one had he ever had a hard time rolling out of. Not one.

Until now.

Until Diamond.

The reason he pushed her away last summer wasn't because she could be a bitch. That wasn't it at all. That was just a good excuse.

He did it because he knew he could drown within her blue eyes. That he could get sucked in that pit where he couldn't escape. That she could capture a piece of his heart. That she could be the reason he stopped moving, stopped searching, and ended his nomad lifestyle.

"Want me outta your bed, Diamond? That what you want? 'Cause ain't stayin' where I ain't wanted."

"Yes, Slade, that's what I want."

All the oxygen left his lungs. Until she said those words, he had some hope. But now...

He didn't realize how much it would kill him to hear her say that. He didn't realize just how deeply she was burrowed under his skin.

What he thought was them having a good time together wasn't just that. It had become more.

He didn't want anyone else in her bed or her life. He didn't want to ever share the woman that sat next to him on her bed. The one that opened herself up to him.

Blood rushed into his head as his temper soared. "What fuckin' happened?"

"Nothing."

Again, lying.

"Fuckin' lyin' to me an' I have no idea why." He dropped his legs over the side of the bed and stared at her shadowed figure over his shoulder. "I do somethin'?" He couldn't quite tell in the dark, but he thought her eyes were closed.

He counted five breaths before she answered.

"No... I did."

He twisted to face her. His breathing quickened, and his heart began to race. "Whatdya do?"

"I... uh..."

"Princess," he whispered, trying to keep the anxiety from his voice. What did she do that she'd want him to leave her bed?

"Slade, maybe it's best you just go."

"Fuck that shit. Tell me what you did." He rubbed his bare chest because a sharp ache was building there.

"Fuck," she muttered.

Fuck!

"Diamond, askin' you one more time..."

"I fucked Rig, okay?" she screamed then slammed herself back onto the bed and covered her face with her hands, her body shaking enough he could see it even in the dark.

"What the fuck?" he whispered, his heart now pounding in his throat, a vein throbbing at his temple.

"I've wanted him for a long time and he always resisted... until... It... just happened," came muffled reply from behind her hands.

"Just happened? When?"

"Earlier."

His mind raced, and he jumped to his feet. "I was there after him?"

She didn't respond.

"Diamond! Fucked me after him?" he shouted at her.

She pulled her hands away from her face and shouted, "Yes! I'm sorry. I didn't mean..."

"Didn't mean to? Just happened? Been wantin' him? What the fuck, Diamond? Thought we had somethin'—" he broke off before he revealed something he shouldn't. "He know we've been fuckin'?"

Because if he did, him and Rig were going to have a conversation. It was going to be a short conversation and there wasn't going to be a lot of talking. Brothers didn't fuck other brother's women. They just didn't.

"No."

His lip curled, and he ground out, "You fuckin' goddamn whore."

"We weren't serious!"

He shook his head and found his pile of clothes where he dropped them earlier. "What the fuck, Diamond? What the fuck." He yanked on his boxers and his jeans in one pull. Snagging his long-sleeve thermal, he tugged that over his head. Then he found his boots and socks in the dark and pulled them on. His cut was hanging on the door knob, but at the moment, he didn't have the stomach to wear it.

One of his brothers just fucked him.

The woman still in her bed behind him fucked him.

He needed to fucking puke.

He stormed from her room, jerked her key from his pocket and tossed it onto her table as he headed toward the door. After rushing through it, he slammed it shut behind him.

But that didn't make him feel any better.

He never should've rolled into Shadow Valley. He never should've rolled into Diamond's bed.

He should've just kept rolling.

———

"Y ou fuckin' bitch!"

"Hang the fuck on, Rig," Jag growled, putting out a hand, her brother's eyes narrowing.

"I'd never fuck a brother's woman. Ever."

"Know it," Diesel mumbled.

"Why'd you use me?" Rig turned wide eyes on Diamond, who swallowed hard.

"I panicked. I needed an excuse to get him out of my...," she closed her eyes for a second, "house."

"So, you couldn't come up with some random guy? Make up a fuckin' name?"

"Sorry. After our conversation yesterday in the office, your name just popped into my head. Had to pick someone not attached."

"Great," Rig shouted, throwing his hands up. "Now I gotta worry he's gonna hunt my ass down."

"Ain't gonna do shit," Diesel muttered.

Rig turned wide eyes to D. "Yeah, right. Fucking former Marine. Can probably slip into my room an', an' break my neck without me even wakin' up."

"Everyone just needs to keep cool," Zak announced to the small group that was standing around in one of the garage bays at the body shop. It was the best place to meet to do damage control, a place to talk where they wouldn't risk Slade overhearing them.

"He's a former Marine, not a damn ninja," Jag said.

"Don't think D's crew can do that? They're all former military," Rig exclaimed, yanking on his beard in agitation.

"That's different."

Rig continued, "We don't know if he has any special skills..."

"He was a boxer in the Marines. Was good at it from what he said," Diamond said softly.

All eyes turned to her.

"Great," Rig muttered and shook his head. "I'm a lover not a fighter."

Jag snorted, but quickly stifled it.

"Does anyone even know where he's at?" Z asked.

Jag shook his head. "Hawk checked his room. Was empty." Her brother's eyes landed on her. "What time did he leave your place?"

"I'm not sure. Maybe one or so."

"I'da known you were gonna do it last night, woulda got one of my crew to tail 'im."

Diamond bugged her eyes out at Diesel. "You told me to break it off."

"Yeah."

"Yeah! So I did that. Think it was easy for me? Think I liked lying to him?" D just looked at her and she threw up her hands in disgust. "Not everyone's a cold, unfeeling bastard like you, D."

Diamond didn't miss it when his body went solid. But he didn't disagree with her. Out loud, at least. Nor would he.

She knew the truth about Diesel. What he showed her sister, Jewel, versus what he showed the rest of the world. But still... right now she felt the need to hit him where it hurt. Because she was hurting badly, and she wanted him to feel a little bit of that pain. He was the one who wanted her to break it off with Slade. Not her.

It was possible that she and Slade could have come to an understanding about their fathers. Their fathers weren't them. She didn't kill Slade's father and he wasn't the reason Rocky was in Greene for life. Maybe they could've moved past that somehow. But now there was no chance of that at all.

None.

"So I know the fuckin' details if I'm confronted... when did we do this?" Rig asked her with a frown.

"Yesterday."

His eyebrows popped up. "An' he ended up in your bed last night? D'you tell 'im *after* he fucked you?"

Again, all eyes landed on her. Even her brother's. Heat rose into her cheeks and she pressed her palms against them. "Details aren't important," she murmured.

Rig shook his head, angrier than ever. "Makes it worse, Di. No man wants sloppy seconds."

"We didn't do it for real, Rig!" she yelled.

Rig yelled right back at her, "*He* don't know that!"

"I'm so done with this. It's over. It's done. You got what you fucking wanted, D. Hope you're happy." With that she rushed from the shop and into her office, slamming the door behind her. She leaned against the door and drove the heels of her palms into her eye sockets to relieve the burn.

Her body hiccuped as a sob fought to escape. But she wouldn't let it. She couldn't. If she started, she wasn't going to be able to stop. Not for a long time. And she wasn't going to let those guys see or even hear her break down.

She didn't want anyone to know how deeply she had fallen for a man who could be the enemy. She wanted them to think that she was a cold bitch and that she could shake off anything and move on.

She needed to be hard. Like a diamond. Because that was who she was.

Normally, she loved being DAMC. Today she despised it.

CHAPTER ELEVEN

"Wake the fuck up."

A groan bubbled up from Slade's chest, which felt like someone was sitting on him. Crushing him. His hand flopped to his chest. Nothing was there.

"Thought you were done with this shit."

His head was too heavy to lift. It rolled to the side instead. He opened one eye. Just slightly.

"Moose's takin' you back to church."

"N—" Slade cleared his sandpaper-coated throat. "No. Ain't goin'... back."

A few moments of silence, glorious silence, greeted him. Finally.

Suddenly, Dawg's face was inches from his. "What the fuck you talkin' 'bout?"

Slade winced. Damn. Why was he yelling? Didn't he know people were trying to sleep?

He inhaled so he could push out the words, "Ain't goin' back."

"Ever?"

He closed his one eyelid when the room begin to spin.

"Slade, brother. Don't know what you're sayin'. Just trashed."

"No," he croaked.

"Yeah you are. Moose'll—"

"No."

"Can't stay here."

"Just let me sleep it off here," Slade grumbled, burrowing deeper into the couch. Or so he thought was a couch, though, he couldn't be sure. The bottom half of his body was pretty numb.

Dawg let out a long, loud, very impatient sigh. "Puke on my couch an' you're buyin' a new one."

So it *was* a couch. Slade swatted a hand half-assed in what he thought was Dawg's direction.

"Ain't doin' this again. Cut off here. No more."

Slade attempted to swat his hand again, but it just flopped back onto his chest.

"What-fuckin'-ever," Dawg muttered and finally there was true silence. Then the lights went out.

———

With a deep groan, Slade sat up confused. He blinked and then shook his head to clear it.

What the fuck?

He must have fallen asleep on the couch at Heaven's Angels. *Fallen asleep.* Right. The way his head felt and with how dry his mouth was, he passed out, he didn't fall asleep.

Either way, he was surprised Dawg didn't have Moose haul his ass out of the club. He pushed to his feet and tested his balance. He was good.

Good enough to hop on his sled and ride out of Shadow Valley, that was for sure.

He moved behind the bar and dug a bottle of water out of the cooler. Cracking the lid, he guzzled the whole thing, tossed the empty bottle in a nearby trash bin and then snagged another, downing most of that one, too. He wiped the back of his hand over his mouth and then headed toward the men's room since he had to piss like a racehorse. As he moved along the dark and empty stage, he was overcome with sudden disappointment and disgust. In himself. For ending up here again last night. For getting so trashed he passed out. Again.

He tried to tell himself that Diamond fucking Rig shouldn't bother him. That she was right, they weren't serious. They were just hooking up and having fun, so she could do whatever she wanted. Or whoever she wanted. But his brain wouldn't let him believe that lie. What bothered him more was her doing it, then not stopping him before he did her. Hell no, she didn't.

He also didn't understand the Rig thing. Not once had he witnessed Rig and her flirting or, hell, even talking to each other all that much. At the parties, at church, at the shop. He had no indication that there had been any sort of attraction between them. Though, they did work together, so she saw him a lot more than the rest of the brothers.

Maybe something had developed between the two of them during the last few months she'd been working at the shop.

Or maybe she was lying and using Rig as an excuse to kick him out of her bed and her life. Maybe there was something else going on that she was trying to hide.

Lying or not, Diamond didn't want him, and he didn't want to sleep next to a snake or a whore.

Maybe he just needed a break from the club, to roll out and get his head back on straight, finish what he set out to do and then think about his next move.

He finished his water, crushed the bottle in his fist and hit the bathroom. Not even five minutes later, he was pushing out into the morning light and squinting from the pain that shot through his head.

Whenever he came to the strip club, he always parked around back in the employee parking lot. The only vehicles out there this early in the morning were his sled, Dawg's sled and the brother's truck. He turned his head and glanced up at the large apartment over the club. The windows were dark, and he was sure Dawg was crashed out cold.

Digging into his pocket, he pulled his bike key out and went over to his baby, the one and only thing that was a constant in his life. His Harley. He ran a hand over the custom painted gas tank and the seat that his ass had been planted in for thousands of miles. No matter what happened to him, his bike was always there for him at the end of the day.

He loved his sled, that he fucking did. And he took care of her, too. She was a beauty.

He closed his eyes and sucked in the early morning air.

As was Diamond. She sure looked good on the back of his sled last summer during the couple of runs he invited her on. She was hard-assed and stubborn enough that she didn't bother to wear a brain bucket like some of the other DAMC women. She'd simply slip on a pair of sunglasses and tie a bandana over her long dark hair to keep it from becoming one big knot.

Damn. Yes, she had looked like the ultimate biker chick wearing a snug DAMC tank top that showed off her generous cleavage, skin-tight jeans to hug those curvy hips and thighs of hers and *sexy-as-fuck* boots. And she'd have a black leather belt with the club's belt buckle cinched around her narrow waist.

She had felt good clinging to his back as they road in the pack along the winding roads of southwestern Pennsylvania. A Harley was one of the biggest vibrators known to women and he swore that on a couple of the rides, at least one orgasm had hit her. Though, he couldn't hear her with the wind in his ears, he could feel her reaction against his back and her arms squeezing him tighter. And if that didn't make his dick hard...

But after the runs, he'd walk away from her, leave her alone. He wasn't ready to get caught and sticking his dick in her when she wasn't a sweet butt or one of Dawg's girls could be dangerous. But the night of her thirtieth birthday party was his downfall. He couldn't deny how much he wanted her, whether she was a bitch or not. And he didn't mind a challenge, he didn't. His whole life had been one, so what was one more? And, anyway, he didn't like boring. She certainly wasn't that.

As he mounted his sled, he realized getting involved with her had been a big mistake. Huge. Because now he couldn't stop thinking about her... Whether it was regret at taking that step weeks ago, anger at her for fucking him over, or disappointment at being on his own once more.

He never had anyone of his own. And night after night when he climbed into her bed, he started to believe that maybe he finally would. That someone in his life would finally stick.

But now that wouldn't be possible. And he doubted he'd open himself up to that kind of hurt again.

Yeah, it fucking hurt.

He kicked the starter and his sled roared to life. The deep rumble of his straight pipes filled the early morning air and the familiar vibration of the engine sank into his bones, bringing about the feeling of home.

Because that's where home was. On the back of his bike.

He now was sure of that one hundred percent.

He pulled his wallet out of his back pocket and dug through it until he found what he was looking for. A small, worn photograph taken over thirty years ago. He studied the man in the photo who sat on a motorcycle. Unfortunately, it was taken from a distance and he couldn't make out the face clearly. He brushed his thumb over the old picture then flipped it over to read the name that had been written in blue ink on the back. Though it was almost worn away, he could still make it out...

Buzz.

The photo was the only piece of his father that he had.

He carefully tucked it back away, heeled the kickstand up and rolled out of the lot onto a side street. He had no idea where he was headed. None at all.

He wasn't going back to church. He wasn't heading to Diamond's. He just needed to get gone. Even if for only a little while.

He headed his bike north and twisted the throttle.

———

S lade crab-walked his sled backward into the line of bikes in front of the bar. The lit sign on the roof was barely readable. One of the spotlights had burned out and the painted lettering on the wood sign was old and worn. He doubted the owners of the bar would be upgrading the sign anytime soon. It was a biker bar, not popular drinking hole. Most biker hangouts didn't want to draw just any type of customer. No, there wouldn't be a "No Colors" sign next to the entrance. Bikers wearing their colors would be welcomed as long as they didn't cause trouble.

He shut his sled down and as soon as he dismounted he removed his cut, folded it up neatly and stuffed it into one of his leather saddlebags. Then he reached to the sky with both hands and stretched out the tight muscles in his back and circled his hips once to loosen them up.

Harrisburg wasn't a long ride from Shadow Valley, but he hadn't come here directly. After leaving Heaven's Angels, he had headed north, first to the town he had been raised in. Then he headed toward Manning Grove to visit with one of the guys he had grown up with. After a couple nights of restless sleep, he headed southeast to where he was now.

Wheels of Steel Bar and Grille.

He was hungry, thirsty and tired. He hoped this so-called "grille" had some decent grub. But, honestly, he considered anything other than MRE's good food. As he stepped through the front door, a cloud of thick smoke hit him, and he breathed it in.

He hadn't had a cigarette in ages, not since being in the middle east to be exact. He found the tobacco over there much smoother and would hand roll his own. After buying a pack of American-made cigarettes that cost an arm and a leg in the US, he quickly quit. But as his nostrils flared to inhale that familiar smoke, he suddenly had a hankering for one, even though he knew he'd regret it later.

He scanned the dimly lit bar and saw that a few different clubs were in attendance. Some were rowdier than others as they stayed in their own groups, played pool, threw darts or got shit-faced.

He glanced toward the bar that ran along the back of the room and his eyes were drawn to a half dozen bikers who sat in a row on the stools. Since their backs were to him, he could clearly make out their colors.

Shadow Warriors.

A couple of them looked over their shoulders at him and he gave them a chin lift. They both returned it.

He braced himself as he headed toward the bar to grab the lone empty stool and a strong drink...

Because beer certainly wasn't going to cut it tonight.

CHAPTER TWELVE

"Heard from him?" Hawk asked.

Diamond grabbed the bottle of Gentleman Jack from behind the bar, cracked the lid and filled half her glass with it, then topped it off with a little bit of pop. She stirred it with her finger and then sucked it clean before wiping it on a bar towel.

"Nope," she answered, then took a great big swallow of her Jack and Diet Coke. After the warmth of the smooth whiskey hit her gut, she continued, "Doubt I will, either."

Not after lying to him about Rig. And she didn't blame Slade one fucking bit.

"Good thing I got backup for The Iron Horse."

"Yeah, good thing," Di muttered, not giving a flying fuck that Hawk was now one man down. Maybe Diesel could fill in since this was all his fault.

Him and his damn paranoia.

"Ain't heard nothin' from him, either," Z mumbled as he settled onto a stool at the private bar in church. "Texted him a few times. No response."

"How's the kid?" Hawk asked him.

"Hoggin' my woman's tits, that's how he is. Gotta learn to share."

Hawk snorted and shook his head.

"Just wait, chicken hawk. Gotta rock on your ol' lady's finger, soon she's gonna be poppin' out kids."

"We'll see," Hawk chuckled.

"Yeah, we will. Gotta say, if I was suckin' down all that warm milk, I'd be sleepin' all night. Not my kid, fuck no. That little hellion's up all hours of the night."

Hawk cleared his throat. "All right, well... Who saw 'im last?"

"Him who?" Z asked.

"Slade."

"Right," Z said with a sharp nod. He looked her direction. "Diamond?"

She shook her head. "Not since the night I kicked him out."

Z raked fingers through his shoulder-length hair and blew out a breath.

"Hasn't been up in his room," Hawk announced. "Not in the bar." He turned his head and shouted down the bar. "Grizz?"

"What?" the old man shouted back.

"Seen Slade?"

Grizzly frowned. "Wanna see my blade? What the fuck for, boy?"

Hawk snorted again and waved a dismissing hand toward the man. "Never mind," he mumbled.

Everyone's attention jumped to the back door as Jewel swept through it with Diesel lumbering at a slower pace behind Di's whirlwind of a sister.

Jewel came behind the bar and gave her a hug, asking softly, "You good?"

"What do you think?"

Jewel's lips flattened out in response.

"Beer, woman," Diesel grunted.

Jewel bugged her eyes out at Di and both of them rolled their lips under at Diesel's order. As she reached for a glass, Di slapped her hand away.

"Ouch!"

"Don't you do it. You're not his slave." Diesel's head spun toward her and Diamond met his gaze directly. "Yeah, you heard me. She's not your slave. Get it yourself."

His head jerked back, and he opened his mouth, then shut it and came behind the bar, nudging them both out of the way so he could pour his own draft.

"Why she don't have a man, Jewelee," he muttered.

Di raised her brows at him. "Had one. *You* told me to get rid of him."

"Other dick out there."

She didn't want other dick. But it would be a waste of her time telling that to the monster of a man who stood over her.

She moved away and down the bar closer to Crow, who held his arms out and Diamond leaned into him, snuggling between his thighs as he curled his arm around her and held her tight against him. She leaned her head on his shoulder.

"Told you he was a rollin' stone," he murmured in her ear.

"Yeah, well, I kind of kicked the stone to get it moving."

"Know it. D got his reasons."

"Yeah, then he rubs it in my face that I don't have a man."

"Like he said, plenty of dick out there."

"It's not that easy."

"Got it. Ain't lookin' for a one nighter; lookin' for the rest of your nights."

Di sighed, and Crow gave her a squeeze.

"Gonna find it, baby doll. Don't worry. Just like your name. Solid with sharp edges, but bright as fuck. Someone will appreciate what you offer."

She was so done talking about it. Luckily, their attention was pulled to what Dawg was saying.

"... the other night. Tried to kick 'is drunk ass out again, but he wasn't havin' it. Offered to get Moose to bring 'im back, refused that, too. Last I saw 'im, was crashed on one of the couches in the main stage area."

Diamond's ears perked, and her heart thumped a little faster. The main stage area? Of Heaven's Angels?

"That new? Or been a regular thing for 'im?" Hawk asked Dawg.

Dawg's eyes slid to Diamond. She arched a brow at him, encouraging him to answer. "Yeah."

Hawk frowned. "Yeah what?"

"Been a regular thing 'til a few weeks ago. Then it stopped. Was surprised to see 'im again the other night."

"Think he went on a bender an' landed with any of the girls?"

"Dunno."

"He done any of 'em before?"

His eyes slid to Diamond again, but he quickly looked away before he answered Hawk. "Yeah."

"Anyone in particular?"

"Savannah."

Diesel slammed his hand on the bar, making Diamond jerk in Crow's arms. "Call 'er right now. See if he's holed up there."

Diamond eyeballed Dawg as he moved away from the bar and headed to a far corner of the large common room, pulling his cell out of his pocket. As he put the phone to his ear, his eyes landed on her again before he turned away, so she couldn't watch his face as he talked to this "Savannah."

She must have been the one he slept with the morning they ran into each other at church. The morning he smelled like skanky snatch. She frowned.

Savannah. Such a typical stripper name.

"Diamond, get over it," D growled.

She shot him a glare.

"Gettin' Hunter on it. Havin' 'im do 'is thing."

That was all well and good, unless... "If he was trashed and drove his bike, he could've ended up in a ditch somewhere, D."

"Wearin' our colors? Woulda heard 'bout it by now."

"What if he hasn't been found yet? He could be injured or dying somewhere."

"Could be," was all Diesel grunted.

She curled her fists but fought the urge to punch him in the gut. It probably would only amuse him but break her hand in the process.

"Maybe we should get Axel to put out an APB or a missing person's or whatever they call it on him."

Diesel's lip curled. "Keep that pig outta it. Got me?"

Jewel slid an arm around his waist and planted a hand on his stomach under his cut. "She's just worried."

"Worryin' 'bout the enemy," he growled, meeting his ol' lady's eyes.

"We don't know that," Jewel said softly.

"Right. Can't question 'im either when he goes ghost like that."

"Maybe he left because he was upset," she suggested.

"'Bout what?" he grunted.

Jewel made an impatient face at her man. "Did you ever consider he might *like* Diamond? Maybe *more* than like her. Finding out the woman you've been... *seeing* cheated on you is enough to make anyone upset."

D's eyes landed on Diamond and he studied her as if he'd never seen her before. Almost as if he didn't recognize her.

It was disturbing. Suddenly a look crossed his face, but it was quickly hidden, and he dropped his gaze back to Jewel.

"Yeah, baby, got it," he finally grumbled. "Might be more than snatch to 'im."

Diamond sucked in a breath. Jewel rolled her eyes and pushed away from him, shaking her head.

"Just a bit sharp at the edges, don't take much to smooth 'er out," Crow volunteered.

"Right," D grunted. "Smooth when gettin' dick, sharp when she ain't."

Diamond pulled out of Crow's arms and he let her go.

"I need a cupcake," Diamond announced.

"I'll join you," Jewel said.

She needed to get out of there before her bitch switch was flipped on and unable to be shut off. Maybe she should drive around a bit to check the area. Even if Slade was a wolf in sheep's clothing, she didn't want anything bad to happen to him. And she certainly didn't want him suffering in some ditch somewhere. Shadow Warrior or not.

———

S lade groaned. His head was killing him. He'd done it again. Ended up totally fucking trashed and he wondered whose lap or bed he'd ended up in last night. Whoever it was, it wasn't the one he wanted it to be.

He was lying on his side and realized it wasn't only his head that hurt, but his whole body ached like a motherfucker and his arms felt numb, as though they were asleep.

He yelled out in pain when something hard and heavy connected with his ribs.

"Coulda killed you. But didn't."

What the fuck?

He tried to open his eyes. The left eyelid partially lifted, the right one seemed broken. For some reason he couldn't get it to work no matter how hard he tried.

With his narrowed vision he couldn't see much of anything. Though, directly in his line of sight looked like his DAMC cut lying next to his head. *On the floor.*

Who the fuck did that? His colors should never touch the floor. Doing so was disrespecting the club and the brotherhood. A brother could get their ass beat for that, if not tossed out of an MC.

He thought he had safely hidden it in this saddlebag.

When he attempted to roll over, he discovered with annoyance his arms and legs wouldn't move. Not only were they asleep from being in an uncomfortable position, he was tied up with something, but he couldn't tell what.

Fuckin' Christ.

Fucking Warriors must have either knocked him out cold or drugged him. By the way his head hurt it could've been either.

"Wanna know why you were askin' 'bout Buzz, asshole."

While he was down and out they must have beat the shit out of him. Because if he'd been conscious, there would've been no way he would've let them get in the number of hits it would've taken to make his body feel this badly. It not only fucking hurt to breathe, any movement was excruciating, he couldn't see shit, and he hadn't tried talking yet.

But he was about to.

In his limited line of sight, he saw a boot stomp on his cut and grind it into the filthy concrete.

"Why the fuck was you askin' 'bout Buzz?" came the impatient shout from somewhere above him.

"Pop," Slade forced out on a cough.

"What'd he say?"

"Think 'pop'," said a second male voice.

It took everything Slade had to say, "Lookin' for my... father."

"Buzz ain't your pop."

"Know 'im?" he asked, unable to see whoever was in the room, which put him at a huge disadvantage. Not that being trussed up wasn't one already.

Slade didn't get an answer. Instead he heard some low murmurs a distance away from him.

Then he heard heavy footsteps, a pause, then someone drop kicked him in the ribs.

Fucking goddamn, that hurt. Then a blurry face was near his. "Why you with the Angels when your pop's a Warrior? You're lyin'."

Slade sucked in a breath to answer, but he couldn't.

His father was a Shadow Warrior.

Fuck.

He had no idea. He only knew the man was a biker.

Over the years, Slade had hit so many biker bars, asking anyone who would listen if they knew a biker named Buzz and he'd never got a solid lead.

Now, he finally got his answer...

One he didn't want to hear.

His father was a fucking *Warrior*. And Slade became an Angel, the Warriors' hated rivals.

Life couldn't be so fucking ironic, could it?

Even so, he still wanted answers from his father. He wanted to know why he deserted his mother when she discovered she was pregnant.

Slade wanted to know why Buzz didn't come back when the mother of his son died.

He wanted to know why his father didn't come get him when he ended up in a foster home.

When he ended up with no family.

When no one else wanted him.

When he was fucking raised by strangers who weren't blood.

Why did his father hate him enough to desert him?

"Gotta... talk to... 'im," Slade struggled to get out.

Laughter surrounded him. Slade tried to figure out how many Warriors stood over him. His best guess was the six he had talked to at the bar.

He also guessed that he wasn't getting out of this alive. Unless he could convince them to take him to his father.

"Can talk to 'im on the other side when we kill ya."

"Can't understand why you'd be an Angel when one of 'em killed your pop."

"Asshole got no sense of loyalty."

An Angel killed his father?

"You know, maybe we can get a message to the Angels. Tell 'em to come get their boy. Maybe take out a few of 'em when they come ridin' in to rescue 'im."

"Ambush 'em like they did our brothers in South Side."

"Surprised they patched this fucker in since he's got Warrior blood in 'im."

"Stupid fucks."

"Need a reason to get some of 'em here. Need a good reason why we didn't take his ass out an' kept 'im breathin' instead."

"Think they still got Black Jack?"

"After all these months? Fuck no. Bet Jack's dead an' buried."

"What do they have that we want?"

"Want all of 'em dead."

"Want Shadow Valley."

"They ain't giving up territory for this fucker."

Slade knew that was true. DAMC wasn't giving up their area for his ass. He was new to the club, not born into it, and once they knew he had Warrior blood running through his veins, he wouldn't be surprised if they stripped him of his colors.

He couldn't imagine any of them, especially Diesel, would want to negotiate for him.

He was screwed. The Warriors held his life in their sadistic hands. And it wasn't looking good for him.

"Could tell 'em we want guns an' ammo in exchange. Got that gun shop. We could stock up."

"Yeah, an' then use their own shit against 'em." A couple of them laughed at that.

They had already shot up The Iron Horse during the club's Christmas party. If they had more weapons and ammo, they could do so much worse. Slade had a feeling that D's crew was slowly taking out some of the nomads one by one. But he couldn't be sure, since Diesel never talked about it. He kept that information locked down tight. And he could understand that since D wanted to keep the club off Shadow Valley PD's radar. For the most part.

But the DAMC owed the Warriors a lot of payback. For more than just shooting up The Iron Horse. For setting Zak up and sending him to prison for ten years, for assaulting Kiki and Jazz, for kidnapping Jewel, for fire-bombing the bakery, for destroying Jag's sled. And so much more. From what Slade understood, their rivalry started decades ago.

But it was hard to keep the club legit and not exact revenge on the Warriors. It was a fine line they walked trying to keep everyone out of prison but seeking retribution on the rival MC and, not only that, trying to keep everyone safe at the same time.

It was probably why Diesel didn't trust him. Slade was an outsider and there was a lot of weight on D's shoulders to keep everyone protected. Really, it was too much for one man to handle and Slade now understood why he had his crew, his "Shadows."

"Gimme 'is cell. Gonna text one of 'em an' make a demand."

If they texted D, the man would probably tell them to just fuck off and do whatever they wanted to Slade.

"Maybe we should tell 'em we wanna sit-down for a truce. Still demand some guns an' ammo as payback for Black Jack."

"Think they'll believe we wanna truce?"

"Know they're tryin' to keep their club legit. Buncha fuckin' pussies. Might be willin' if we tell 'em we'll wipe the slate clean. Have a feelin' Diesel's crew's huntin' us down. Haven't heard from a couple members lately. Makes me wonder what the fuck happened to 'em."

"Think they've been takin' us out?"

"Gotta feelin' someone is takin' us out or tryin' to."

"Fuck."

"Right. So let's use this piece of shit to lure a few of 'em here. Got six of us. We'll tell 'em we got two an' to send two. Know they'll send more. Means we'll get to take out more. Gotta get the prez, VP, an' enforcer here, for sure. Wipe out the top first. Then we'll gather our brothers an' sweep into their territory an' take 'the rest of 'em out. Take Shadow Valley, take their businesses. Hell, take their women. *Fuck 'em all.*"

CHAPTER THIRTEEN

Diamond chewed on her bottom lip. Church was packed with all of the club members, prospects and DAMC women. Everyone was there except the older women who were instructed to remain at the farm with Ace, Rooster and Moose.

The demand that Your Ass-Holiness sent by mass text said to be at church by four PM. No exceptions, no excuses.

It seemed to be an emergency church meeting, but normally the women were not allowed at the meetings, so this had to be more than that. Something big.

Di's heart thumped in her chest. This had to do with Slade. No doubt.

Diesel, Hawk and Zak stood at the front of the room by the bar and a low murmur circulated through the common area.

Sophie had baby Zeke on top of the bar in some sort of rocking carrier to keep him quiet and content. Even from where Di stood with Jewel, Bella and Kelsea, she could see Sophie's face was pale and she looked worried. The woman only had eyes for Zeke and Zak.

And Di could understand why. Those two were her life.

Di needed to know what was going on. She couldn't take the wait any longer. She was about to freak out like a lunatic and demand that

Diesel tell them why they were all summoned to the clubhouse when she asked Jewel, "Do you know what the hell is going on?"

Jewel turned worried blue eyes to her but shook her head. "No. He hasn't said a fucking word to me. Sometimes that shit drives me crazy. Whatever this is about is new, though. Something must have happened recently."

"Think it has to do with Slade?"

Jewel curved an arm around Di's waist and gave her a squeeze. "Don't know for sure, sis. But I can't imagine it doesn't."

Di met Ivy's eyes across the room where the redhead was pulled against Jag's chest. Di gave her a look and lifted her chin at her brother. Ivy shook her head slightly and shrugged.

Hell, Ivy didn't know anything either, which meant Jag didn't know squat.

Diesel, Zak or Hawk needed to start talking soon or Di was going to lose her freaking mind.

She blew out a relieved breath when Hawk finally shouted, "'Kay, listen up an' listen good. Got more Warrior shit goin' down. Need everyone not involved to stay here at church 'til this current shit's dealt with. Got me?"

A murmur swept through the room.

"Got all the businesses on lockdown right now 'til it all gets sorted—" Hawk stopped abruptly when Diesel grabbed his arm.

D pinned his gaze on Bella and said, "What you hear ain't for your ol' man's ears, got me?"

All eyes landed on the brunette as she straightened, and it was hard to miss her spine stiffen and her lips flatten.

"Gotta hear an answer, Bella. Nothin' can leave this room. Can't keep this shit to yourself, can't keep your loyalties straight, gotta go."

As if one, all the women in the room sucked in a collective breath. D had always been close to his cousin and very protective of her, so none of them ever expected Diesel to say something like that to her. Never. But they all understood the club business had to remain just that, in the club. Especially if it concerned   anything   illegal   or   something   that   could   be conceived as not on the up and up. Even though Bella's ol' man was Zak's brother, Axel was still a cop. And that could mean trouble.

And with Diesel drawing the line in the sand with Bella, it became clear that there was something going on that they didn't want the police to find out about. This made the pit in Di's stomach deepen and she dug her fingernails into her palms to keep from dropping to her knees into a bundle of nerves.

It was also clear that none of the brothers up at the front of the room would continue until they heard Bella's answer.

Diamond felt sorry for Bella having to choose sides. These were instances where it was impossible to remain loyal to both her man and her family. And that had to tear her apart.

"Won't leave this room," Bella finally said with a frown.

Watching the woman struggle with her conscience drove it home that Diamond was struggling with it, too. Knowing Slade had Warrior blood in him made it hard for her to stand by him, but it was also hard to push away her feelings, to just turn away from him like he meant nothing to her.

Because he did mean something to her, that was for damn sure.

But the club meant more. The DAMC would always be her foundation, her rock, one that she could rely on no matter what happened. And she couldn't toss that aside. She wouldn't.

As she glanced around the full room, the fact that she loved this club, loved this family as much as any of the patched brothers, was cemented deep inside her.

"'Kay, then," Hawk yelled out. "Here's the deal... D got a text from Slade's phone. Someone who only identified himself as a Warrior stated they got Slade."

A roar rose throughout the room. Hawk lifted a hand and Diesel pounded his fist on the bar to get everyone to quiet down.

"Said in exchange for Slade they want a sit-down..."

"For what?" came an outraged voice from the other side of the room.

"A truce."

Grumbles and curses rose around Diamond. She didn't believe they wanted a truce, either.

It had to be a set-up.

"Since findin' out that Slade's father was a Warrior, we really don't know where his loyalty lies. Could be usin' him to lure us in. Could be they really want a truce. Can't imagine that's true, though."

"Sneaky fuckin' bastards," Crash yelled out.

A whole lot of answering "yeahs" were shouted.

Hawk raised his hand again. "Not only want a sit-down, want some guns an' ammo as payback for Black Jack's... *disappearance*."

Black Jack was the Warrior who kidnapped Jewel. He was also one of the Warriors who assaulted Kiki and raped Jazz. Everyone had been told he escaped when Diesel, Hawk and Zak, as well as D's crew, went after him.

Apparently, that wasn't true. Diamond hoped they took that fucker out. And made him suffer while they were at it.

Di's eyes slid to Bella. Her face was pale, and she was leaning against Crow who had an arm around her.

Maybe it would have been better if Bella had left, the more details she heard the more she had to keep from Axel. And Diamond didn't want anything pulling those two apart. Axel was good for Bella and if anyone deserved happiness, that woman did.

Di turned her attention back to Hawk as he continued, "They want Z, me an' Diesel to meet 'em. Told 'em that Z ain't showin' up no matter what they fuckin' want." Hawk did a chin lift toward Sophie and the baby. That motion spoke volumes. There was no way Diesel or Hawk would send the man who was not only the president of the club into danger but a new father.

"You sure they got 'im? Ain't a trap?"

"Could be a trap. Like I said, could be usin' 'im to lure us in. Could be he's on their side settin' us up. But D demanded a pic so we could use the lat an' long to find 'im like we did Jewel, but they refused. So he demanded to talk to Slade instead an' when they put the phone up to 'im he said not to come get 'im. But fuckers cut 'im off before he could say anything else."

Di's stomach churned.

She closed her eyes and tried to push aside the image of Slade being injured or worse in the hands of the Warriors. She fought down the nausea caused by the possibility that Slade might not come out of this alive. The Warriors could kill him without a second thought.

But she wondered how they got him. Why was Slade even their target? Could it be that he really was setting the DAMC up? That he truly was a Warrior like his father?

Was he on a path of revenge for his father's death?

She didn't want to believe it. And she knew that was foolish on her part, but she couldn't help it. She wanted to believe that Slade had honor and loyalty. No, she didn't *want* to believe it, she *needed* to believe it.

She needed to hold on tightly to that one thin thread of hope.

"Here's the deal," Zak said, taking over from Hawk. "Everyone's gotta stay here. Got Ace with Moose an' Rooster out at the farm watchin' some of the women. Otherwise, you're all here for the duration. Don't want 'em doin' a surprise attack when we're dealin' with this Slade shit. So, *no one's* leavin' here, got me?"

"Who's all goin' an' where do they got 'im?" Dex asked.

"Don't know yet. They're gonna text the location to us when we're ready. Told 'em we need time to gather the guns an' ammo they want. Told 'em they need to keep Slade alive while we do that or the deal's off the table."

Nash yelled out, "You really gonna go in an' work out a truce with those fuckin' bastards?"

The room got so quiet that Di could hear herself breathe.

Hawk and D's gaze met, then Hawk surveyed the room. "Ain't dealin'. Gotta plan. Gonna keep it on the D.L. for now. Like Z said, for safety's sake, everyone gotta stay here until we return... with or without Slade."

"If he's a Warrior, gonna take 'is ass out, too," Diesel grumbled loud enough that Di heard it. His eyes, cold as ice, landed on Di, slid to Jewel who still had her arm wrapped around Di's waist, then quickly moved on, his jaw tight.

"I hope Slade wasn't playing us," Jewel murmured. "He better not be luring my ol' man in there so the Warriors can take him out. I don't like D risking his life like that. He already got shot by Black Jack. He was lucky that time. He might not be so lucky this time."

"Sorry," Di murmured to her sister.

"Isn't your fault, sis."

"If he was playing me, playing all of us, I'll take him out myself," Di assured her.

Jewel gave her another squeeze, then released Di and turned to Bella. "You have to stay true, Bella. I don't need D ending up in jail or prison. Promise me you won't say anything to Axel. I can't lose him. Not now, not ever."

"I feel the same way about Axel, but... I promise," Bella said, her voice a bit shaky.

"I know you need Axel in your life, but I need D just as much. And now maybe more..."

Di studied Jewel as her sister's words drifted off. Now wasn't the time to ask twenty questions on what she meant, they had to get through this first. Hawk and Diesel, and whoever else, needed to go in and get Slade out of there alive. *They* needed to get in and get out alive, too.

Di was surprised that Diesel would not only risk his own life but his brother's for a man he never quite trusted.

Maybe there was something Diesel wasn't telling everybody. He wasn't known to be the most talkative or the most upfront.

Di's head jerked backward when Diesel called out, "Diamond, get the fuck up here."

After a quick glance at Jewel and Bella, she worked her way up to the front. It seemed as though their little speech was over, and the brothers and prospects were breaking up into groups, either heading into the kitchen for some food, grabbing a beer or beginning a game of pool or darts. They were all stuck there for the long haul and if anyone knew how to make the best of a lockdown it was the men of DAMC.

When she finally got to Zak, Diesel and Hawk, her gaze roamed over all three of them. Their faces were solemn, and she felt a niggle of fear deep in her gut. If it came down to Slade surviving or these three, she knew her choice. It would be heartbreaking but no matter how frustrating the three men in front of her were, she loved them all.

"You have to do what you have to—" she started.

"Shut up an' listen," D barked.

Di frowned and reevaluated her previous thought. Someone needed a good kick to the nads.

"Get your phone out."

She scowled at him but did as she was told even though her first instinct was to give him the finger and tell him to go to hell.

"Text 'im. Tell whoever's got his phone that you're Slade's ol' lady an' you need to see a pic of 'im for proof he's okay."

She glanced at her phone that was gripped tightly within her fingers then back up at D.

"Do it!" he shouted, making her jump.

"Jesus, D," she snapped. "Take a fucking chill pill."

"Shit's serious, woman. Ain't got time to waste."

"I didn't think you liked Slade enough to be so concerned about him."

"Ain't doin' it for me. Doin' it for you. Doin' it for your sister who'll never forgive me if your man don't come back in one piece."

Your man. Diamond looked up at him in surprise. "You said he could be a plant."

"Don't know that for sure. If he ain't, then he's a brother like the rest of us. If he is, we gotta deal with 'im. One way or another, we're goin' in to get 'im. How he comes out depends on if he's DAMC or a Warrior."

"D—"

"Text 'is phone now. No more lip."

Di glanced at Hawk, who gave her a reassuring nod, but remained quiet.

Diamond fought to keep the tremble from her fingers as she texted a message that she knew Slade probably wouldn't get, but most likely a Warrior would.

This is Slade's ol' lady. Need proof he's OK. Need 2 c a pic.

"What good is this going to do?" she asked the three of them while she waited for a response.

"Faster than pingin' his phone. Hunter knows how to get the meta... whatever from a pic. How we found Jewelee," D answered.

"Then what?"

"Then we ride," Hawk said, his voice as cold as D's eyes.

She looked at the newly engaged man. "Is Kiki okay with you doing this?"

"Women don't make decisions 'round here," Diesel reminded her.

"Right. How could I forget?" she answered him with an eye roll.

"I'm not okay with it, but do I have a choice?" Kiki said as she moved up behind her. "Honestly, do any of us have a choice if we want to get Slade back?"

"But—"

"Di, he's not a Warrior," Kiki said softly, but Di didn't miss the club's attorney giving Hawk a look that clearly said she hoped she was right.

Di's phone dinged, and after looking at it she lifted it to show Diesel. "Seems they feel the same way as you, D."

The answering text stated, *Bitches don't make demands.*

Z leaned closer, read the text then cursed while dragging a hand through his already disheveled hair.

Hawk shook his mohawked head. "Every time I think these fuckers are too stupid to breathe, they prove me wrong."

Everyone froze when Di's phone dinged again. She looked at the text. It was a photo.

Her emotions clashed. She was glad they *were* stupid enough to send a photo, but it was the photo that made her stomach drop out and her knees wobble.

"Hawk!" Kiki yelled, trying to catch her as she began to crumble.

Hawk grabbed Diamond and held her up as D grabbed her phone and studied the photo.

"Motherfuckers," D barked.

He showed the phone to Hawk and Z.

"Babe, take her," Hawk said to Kiki. "Jewel," he shouted, "get up here an' help your sister."

Jag pushed Kiki aside and hooked Di under her armpits, pulling her tight against him. "Got 'er," he grumbled. Then he exploded, "Fuck, those assholes must die."

Diamond sucked in a breath and used her brother to steady herself. She closed her eyes and a noise escaped her before she could stop it.

"Jesus, Di," Jag muttered near her ear, taking most of her weight. "Gonna sit you down somewhere."

"Not on one of those disgusting couches!" Kiki exclaimed, rushing away. Within seconds she was back with a chair from the nearby meeting room and Jag lowered her carefully into it.

Di dropped her head into her hands and wished she hadn't seen the photo. She should've handed her phone off to Diesel for him to handle.

But she didn't. And now that picture of Slade was burned into her brain.

———

Nothing like being dragged by two assholes across a concrete floor, over what felt like a paved parking lot, then picked up and tossed bodily into a vehicle. Probably a van, but Slade couldn't say for sure, since the limited vision he formerly had was now nonexistent since both of his eyes had swollen completely shut.

He struggled to take shallow breaths through his mouth to keep the pain of his cracked or possibly broken ribs to a minimum. Being a former boxer, he knew what a broken nose felt like. And there was no doubt he had one of those, too.

Besides his ribs and his face, he wasn't sure if anything else was broken, but his limbs were definitely numb from being tied up and held immobile in the same position for probably what was hours now.

As he bounced around in the back of the vehicle, he was sure this was how he would feel after taking on Diesel in the boxing ring. He was also sure the man's massive fists could be lethal.

But if it was up to Slade, he'd rather not find out.

Not being able to see made him listen more carefully while trying to figure out where they were headed. One of them mentioned "west on the Turnpike," but that was all he could gather. Sometimes he'd catch a word or two here and there from the driver and passenger of the vehicle. He assumed they were headed toward Shadow Valley.

His ears perked up when he heard one of them mention Diamond's name and in the same breath say "ol' lady."

Fuck. They thought Diamond was his ol' lady? Why the fuck would they think that?

Were they going to use him as bait to grab her? Hopefully she was smarter than that. Though, he had no idea how they knew her name unless there'd been some kind of communication between Diamond and the Warriors.

Fuck. She just needed to stay the hell out of this whole thing. Let whatever was going to happen to him just happen. She needed to stay out of it and stay safe.

After putting him on the phone earlier, he had lost consciousness again after warning Diesel not to come get him. He guessed that the Warriors didn't like what he said and was pretty sure that the sudden blackout was caused by a strategic kick to the head.

Lucky him.

He didn't know how long they drove, but it felt like an eternity. He didn't have any clue where they ended up. He couldn't even figure out if it was night or day. He knew nothing other than their journey had come to an end. Either they were going to kill him or trade him back to the DAMC. And with his father being a Warrior, he didn't know if ending up back with the Angels was a better choice. They just might end up killing him, too.

Suddenly, he was being hauled from the back of the vehicle and carried this time by his bound arms and legs, then he was airborne.

He landed on what felt like concrete, lost all the air in his lungs, his head fell forward, smacked the hard floor and everything went blissfully black once more.

———

Diamond looked at her cell phone for the millionth time. Only two minutes had passed. Two fucking minutes. She had her fingernails practically chewed down to the quick. Bella had mixed her several drinks to take the edge off, but unless she was totally trashed it wasn't going to help. And she was not getting trashed because she needed to stay sober enough to know what the hell was going on.

Hawk, Diesel, Jag and Dawg had left a couple hours ago, and no one had heard a word since then. Or if Zak had, he wasn't saying anything. Though, she'd been watching him like a hawk in case he looked at his phone. But he hadn't. It laid on the bar near where him and Sophie sat.

It was strange watching the man she'd known as a badass biker almost all his life holding his infant son over his shoulder and burping Zeke after Sophie nursed him. The contrast between father and son was glaring. His son was innocent to the ways of the world, while Z knew exactly how precarious life in an MC could be, especially after spending ten years in prison. But in another way, the two were similar. After being released, Zak had started his life again when he found Sophie, and Sophie was also the reason Zeke had come to be on this earth.

The poor kid definitely got a lot of attention from the bikers and the women alike. Who would have thought all these men had a soft spot for a baby? Though that baby would probably grow up to be a badass biker just like them.

In the beginning, Di had watched Sophie struggle to deal with the biker lifestyle since it was something unfamiliar to her. She had tried to push Z away, but he never gave up on her. He knew they were meant to be. No matter what.

Although they came from two different worlds, they had finally made it work. And produced a beautiful new life in the process.

Even though Slade came from Warrior blood and she came from DAMC, this gave her hope that they could make it work. *If* they both wanted it badly enough. She had no idea if that was what Slade would want. But she hoped so.

As long as the man hadn't betrayed them all. Because if he had, that was a whole other story. And he would need to be dealt with accordingly.

Even Diamond agreed with that.

She glanced around the crowded common area. The Iron Horse was closed to the public, the gate to the private parking lot chained shut, the exterior doors to church were locked. No one could leave or even go outside to smoke until they got word from Hawk or Diesel. However, the natives were starting to get restless.

What was worse was they allowed some of the sweet butts to come into church right before the lockdown. Diamond was relieved to see that Lola wasn't one of them. Slade had assured her that she'd be dealt with and Diamond hadn't seen her around since that night, so she could only assume Zak kicked her ass out.

Good riddance.

But there were still plenty more patch whores that hung around the club and Diamond's eyes narrowed on Tequila as she hung all over Crow like a bad blanket. She didn't doubt that the little skank was trying to convince Crow to take her upstairs.

And from where Di sat, though Crow wasn't pushing Tequila away, he certainly wasn't encouraging her, either. Maybe the man needed to be saved. And Di needed something to keep her mind off Slade.

She headed to the end of the bar where Crow sat, a half-smile on his face as he watched her approach.

"Baby doll," he greeted her with a low, soft chuckle and a shake of his head.

Di cocked a brow at Tequila since she had her big-ass fake breasts pushed into his arm and had her hips, encased in an obscenely short black leather miniskirt, smashed against his as he sat on the stool. "She bothering you?"

Tequila didn't look at Di when she said, "I'm not bothering him, Diamond. Go away."

"Baby doll, appreciate the concern, but I can handle this."

"Might have to get a penicillin shot after being that close."

Finally, the woman turned toward Di, her dark eyes and words snapping, "You're such a fucking bitch, Diamond. Mind your own damn business. I'm allowed to be here. I was invited, remember? He don't belong to you..." She waved a hand out in a "shoo" motion. "So get gone."

Di's eyes narrowed. "He doesn't have to belong to me to be concerned for his health and welfare."

"Trying to get me kicked out like you did Lola? That what you want? Coming over here to start a fight so Z bans me from the club? Are you that insecure that you need to chase us outta here?"

Di inhaled deeply, ready to give the woman a piece of her mind, but it quickly escaped her as Crow said firmly, "Tequila, give us a minute." His eyes locked on Di's.

"But—"

"Give us a minute," he said slower, emphasizing each word so it was clear that he wouldn't accept any backtalk from the sweet butt.

Tequila let out a huge dramatic huff, peeled herself from his side and stomped away in her patch whore heels.

Crow waited until she was out of earshot before saying, "Know you're upset, baby doll, but can't be chasin' all the free pussy outta the club. Know that, right?"

She frowned at him.

"Gonna make enemies if you do, an' a new one will come fill every spot you empty. Got me?"

"You're not going to lower yourself to that," she tipped her head in the direction Tequila went, "are you?"

"Fuck no. Just passin' the time. Like you said, don't need a trip to the hospital for a penicillin shot. You know I'm afraid of needles." The tattoo artist laughed at his own joke, then sighed. "Know you're worried, but this ain't a time to be pickin' fights. Gotta keep your shit together for Slade."

Diamond sucked in a breath. "What if he's a Warrior?"

Crow tilted his head as he studied her with his almost-black eyes, serious. "Then you know what'll happen."

"Yeah," she breathed.

"Yeah," he echoed her.

"Rocky killed his pop."

"Know it," he said softly.

"Even if he isn't a Warrior..." She groaned. "This is one big fucking mess."

"That it is, baby doll."

A pounding on the back door had Crow on his feet in a split second. The room got quiet as the pounding continued and a shout came through the door.

"Oh fuck," Crow mumbled as Bella rushed toward the door.

"It's just Axel," Bella yelled, holding up her phone. "He just texted me."

"Don't open that door!" Dex yelled at his sister. "I'll do it." He stepped into her path and pushed her out of the way. "Don't know who else is out there."

As soon as Dex turned the deadbolt, the door was shoved open and Axel rushed in. Dex closed the door quickly behind him and locked it once more.

"What the fuck is going on?" Axel asked loud enough that Diamond could hear him across the room. He was wearing a scowl and looked extremely unhappy. At least he wasn't there in an official capacity since he wore jeans and a T-shirt and not his uniform.

Bella grabbed his arm and said something low to him that Di couldn't hear. Axel's gaze dropped to her when he grabbed both her shoulders and turned her to face him head on. Di watched Axel's mouth moving a mile a minute as he was probably lecturing his woman on something or other. Her face remained a pale blank mask as his got darker with anger.

Finally, he stopped talking and looked up, saw everyone's eyes on them and it was hard to miss the long, deep breath he took when his chest rose and fell.

Grabbing Bella's wrist, he pulled her along with him as he approached the bar where Sophie and Zak were.

"Ah, shit," Diamond murmured.

"What the fuck is going on, Z?" Axel asked his brother. He jerked his chin toward Bella. "I'm taking her home."

"She should stay here," Z said calmly.

"Why the fuck is she on lockdown here? What the fuck's going on?" Axel looked around the room. "Where's Hawk and Diesel?"

"Ain't answerin' your questions. Bella stays here."

"No, she might be a part of this club, but she'll be safer with me. I know that even though I don't even know what the fuck's going on. So, spill it."

Zak simply said, "Club business," as if that would satisfy Axel. Which everyone knew it wouldn't. It would simply poke the angry bear.

"Club business," Axel muttered, shaking his head. His eyes fell on Zeke in his carrier, then lifted them to Sophie. "Is it Warriors?" he asked his sister-in-law.

Sophie's eyes widened slightly, but Z stepped in between the two of them. "Don't be questionin' her. She ain't gonna answer."

Sophie reached into the baby carrier, pulled Zeke into her arms and stepped around her husband. "Say hi to your nephew, Axel."

Axel stared at the baby and the anger seemed to drain from him instantly. He held his hands out and Sophie gave him Zeke. Axel cradled the baby against him, staring down into Zeke's face.

Diamond just about melted when Axel traced a finger lightly over Zeke's chubby cheeks.

He lifted his head to pin his gaze on his brother. "My nephew in danger?"

"Got it handled," Zak answered gruffly, pulling his son from his brother's arms.

"Don't think you do," Axel said, surveying the crowded room. "You want SVPD's help, Z, you need to be forthright, so we know what's going on."

"Don't need 5-o's help."

Axel snorted and shook his head before looking at Bella. "We're going home."

"Axel—"

"No, Bella, you're not staying here. If my brother wants to put his family at risk that's up to him, but I'm responsible for you, so you're coming home with me. We both could have died the night of the Christmas party when the Warriors shot up The Iron Horse." He glanced back at Zak. "Going to notify the station to up the patrols in the area."

Zak ignored him.

Axel sighed and put an arm around Bella. "Let's go, baby," he said softly.

Diamond watched Axel steer his woman through the room and out the back door. Dex locked it back up again after they left.

Diamond sighed. She wanted the same type of intense love that Axel felt for Bella. That strong need to protect her. He put up with a lot of shit from the club to be with her. And to him, she was worth every bit of it.

"Slade ain't a Warrior, then you ask his forgiveness for lyin' to 'im. He don't understand it, then move on," Crow murmured next to her, his gaze still glued to the door Bella and Axel disappeared through. "You deserve that shit, too, baby doll. All you women do."

She turned to Crow and studied his honey-colored skin, his sharp cheekbones, his dark, dark eyes and his pitch-black hair that fell down his back in a long, straight ponytail. "You do, too, Crow. We all do."

He tucked a strand of hair behind her ear. "All can't have love like that. Ain't possible."

"For once, I hope you're wrong."

CHAPTER FOURTEEN

Aspirin wasn't going to cut it when it came to easing the pounding in Slade's head. Not that anyone was offering him an aspirin or anything else for that matter. Once again, he found himself on a cold, concrete floor who knows where.

He tried his damnedest to open his eyes, but it was still impossible. However, there were voices nearby, heated and loud.

He tugged at his wrists, but the duct tape wrapped tightly around them didn't give at all. If he was going to escape, now would be the perfect time since it sounded like the Warriors were distracted with whoever they were arguing with.

Fuck!

Slade shifted his head so he could hear better. He swore he heard Hawk's voice, raised in anger.

He told Diesel not to come get him. He knew they'd be walking into a trap. But his brothers came anyway.

Why did they think he was worth it? They'd regret their decision once they found out that Slade's father was a Warrior. Probably even strip him of his colors. Possibly even carve the rockers right off the skin of his back.

"Got your fuckin' guns, got your ammo, give us Slade."

Diesel.

"Ain't done negotiatin'," one of the Warriors said. "Wanna truce."

"Why? So you can break it?" Yeah, that was clearly Hawk's voice, which was as tight as a guitar string, like he was doing his best to keep himself under control.

"Got men huntin' us?"

"Now, why would we need to hunt your asses?"

"Had a couple go rogue," one of the Warriors muttered.

Rogue. Right. No one in DAMC would believe that lie.

"You mean Black Jack an' Squirrel? Rogue as in beatin' an' rapin' our women? That kinda rogue?"

"Prez didn't approve of that."

"Right."

Shit, that last answer sounded like Dawg. Why the hell was the strip club manager here?

"Prez approve of shootin' up my fuckin' bar?" Hawk growled.

"Wanna truce or not?" one of the Warriors shouted.

"Just want Slade. Ain't gonna agree to a truce so you can come in an' hit us when we're least expectin' it."

"Well, fuck ya, then. Bastard's in there. Can't believe you want a man with Warrior blood runnin' through his veins."

"Ain't Warrior colors on 'is back."

That last came from Jag. Fuck, that meant at least four Angels had come for him. Four were putting themselves at risk by walking into a trap. Because that was what this was. The Warriors were going to use him to take out as many Angels as they could.

Slade heard several sets of heavy boots heading his direction. He tried to call out a warning for them not to approach him, but he couldn't get the words out. The only thing escaping him was a groan of pain.

"Jesus fuckin' Christ," Diesel shouted.

The sound of approaching boots quickened, then someone was on the ground next to him, and a few seconds later a knife was sawing at his bindings.

"Still breathin'?" Hawk asked.

"Yeah," Dawg said near Slade's head. "Breathin' but ain't good."

"Wanna truce when you do shit like this?" Hawk sounded outraged.

"Was askin' too many questions," one of the Warriors replied.

Slade attempted to clear his throat and tried to warn them again, "Ta...rap."

Diesel finished sawing through the Duct tape and said, "Yeah, brother, takin' you home."

Slade wondered if the club enforcer even heard him.

As D sliced at the tape binding his ankles, the big man muttered, "'Justice is for those who deserve it... *Mercy* is for those who don't.'"

Slade had no idea what the fuck D was talking about but suddenly it sounded like everyone hit the deck and someone, he thought it might have been Dawg, covered his head as some sort of flash-bomb detonated.

His heart was racing so hard the blood rushed into his ears. Either that or they were ringing from the explosion.

Suddenly, whoever had covered his head was up and away. Slade found himself free, but his limbs wouldn't cooperate since they'd been bound in one position for so long.

Fuck! He had no clue what the hell was happening. Fighting through the pain, he forced himself to sit up as best as he could and listened to the activity around him.

He wasn't sure who had the upper hand as all he could hear was shuffling, muffled grunts and what sounded like bodies falling to the floor.

It pissed him the fuck off that he couldn't do anything to help his brothers. He couldn't see, could hardly move. He was weaker than a goddamn newborn baby.

Without warning, he was grabbed by both the armpits and legs and hauled up as two people carried him out.

"Everythin's under control, brother. D didn't lie when he said we're takin' you home," Hawk assured him.

Slade tried to ask what the hell was going on. "What..."

"D's crew's here takin' care of business. All you gotta know."

Slade could tell when he was carried outside as the air became a little easier to breathe through his mouth. A deep male voice he didn't recognize said, "Found his cut in their van. Takin' the vehicle to dispose of it."

Diesel grunted an answer.

"Warriors—"

D cut off whoever was speaking, "Yeah."

"Got it, boss."

"Wonder where the fuck his sled is?" Dawg asked. He must be carrying his legs.

"Don't think any of 'em's capable of answerin' that anymore. Ain't gonna worry about that right now," Hawk said. "Gotta get 'im to the hospital."

Slade heard a vehicle door open then he was slid onto the seat and the door slammed shut.

Two people climbed into the front of whatever vehicle he was in.

"No... hospital," he got out. But just barely.

"Gotta get checked out, make sure you ain't dyin', ain't got brain damage," Hawk said from what sounded like the driver's seat.

"Doin' Diamond. Got brain damage," Diesel grunted from the passenger seat.

"Rig..."

"Ain't doin' Rig," D grumbled.

"Rig..." Slade tried again.

"She ain't doin' Rig," he shouted impatiently. "Told her to stay clear of you 'til we knew which side your loyalties were on."

What the fuck? So the Rig thing was a lie?

"Made it up, brother, tryin' to get clear of you. Gave her no choice," Hawk said over the sound of the vehicle.

Slade didn't know whether he was relieved that Diamond lied to him or pissed. He'd have to figure that out later since right now D was driving him to the hospital and that was the last place he wanted to go.

If what his brothers said was true and Diamond didn't fuck Rig... there was only one bed Slade wanted to land in tonight and it was not one at a hospital. Not knowing if he was going to live or die while in the Warrior's hands had made him do some serious thinking during that time. And even if he ended up being pissed at Di for lying to him, he knew he'd get over it quickly, that the woman was worth it.

Then it hit him that she had done what Diesel had told her... found a way to separate herself from Slade. The bigger picture was that she had *listened*. She might tend to be difficult, but she had heeded the man's direction when it really mattered. And that gave Slade hope.

Because if he was going to settle down with anyone, it was a woman who could compromise. And she proved she had it in her.

Thank fuck.

D iamond did her best not to fall to her knees as Jag and Dawg helped Slade through the door of her cabin.

She covered her mouth with her hands because she didn't need the whimper she fought back to escape.

Even after going to the hospital and getting checked out, Slade looked like total hell. Like he'd been beaten to a bloody pulp.

His eyes were puffy and discolored, a white bandage crossed over his nose, his bottom lip was split, a multi-colored bruise covered his right cheek bone and he wore a bloody shirt.

His filthy cut was gripped in Dawg's hand and he held it out to her. She rushed forward, grabbed it and draped it over one of her kitchen chairs. She'd do what she could to clean it up later, once Slade was settled comfortably in her room.

When she got the call from Hawk that they were at the hospital with Slade, she had told the club VP that under no circumstances were they taking him anywhere other than her place once he was released.

It took everything in her power not to rush to the hospital, but Hawk said Slade was getting busy getting checked by medical staff for broken bones and a concussion and there was no point in her coming there just to be a thorn in their side.

Her. A thorn. Right.

The doctors determined he had no broken bones except for a couple of ribs and he had a mild concussion, along with a broken nose and a badly bruised face. They didn't want to keep him overnight and he was complaining so badly that he wanted to leave that no one was going to force him to stay anyway. But someone needed to keep an eye on him and assist him.

And, of course, Diamond made it quite clear that she was the only one who was going to be taking care of him. Whether Slade liked it or not.

Before Dawg and Jag brought him to the cabin, she made sure to change the sheets, go to the grocery store to stock up on food and over-the-counter pain meds and whatever else she'd need to make him comfortable. She was in it for the long haul. Whatever he needed until he was up and around, she would do it for him.

She was going to make up for lying to him and kicking him out of her bed one way or another.

"Take him into my bedroom," she directed Jag and Dawg, raising an arm in the direction they needed to go.

Before they could move, she rushed past them, leading the way. At least Slade was on his own two feet. He was slow and unsteady and needed Jag and Dawg's assistance to walk, but still, it was a good sign.

She was freaking sick of the Warriors hurting her family and it needed to stop. If death to them all was one way to stop them, so be it.

As she walked into her bedroom she asked, "What happened to the Warriors who did this?"

"Dealt with," Jag muttered.

She stopped and turned to face her brother. "How?"

"Di, know I can't talk about it."

"Just tell me, do we have to worry about them coming after us again?"

Jag met Dawg's eyes then turned back to her, "No. An' that's all I'm sayin'."

Diamond gave him a sharp nod and swiped at her eyes before they started leaking in front of Dawg and her brother. She pulled back the sheet and indicated to them to help Slade into bed.

They did so after removing his boots and socks and, with a few groans, Slade was settled in. She carefully propped a couple of pillows behind him, so he could sit up comfortably. Or as comfortably as possible.

With a closer look at his swollen and discolored face, she asked, "Can you see?" The little bit of his one eyeball she could see was full of blood since a vessel had been broken. She winced.

"A little," Slade answered.

Hawk had said Slade needed some stitches and there was a bandage over his left eye.

"Do you want the TV remote?"

When he didn't answer, she tucked it near his hand and said, "I'm going to walk these guys out. I'll be right back."

Again, he didn't answer, and her heart skipped a beat. He probably hated the thought of being left behind in her care because he still believed she deceived him by cheating with Rig.

She followed Dawg and Jag out, closing the bedroom door behind her.

"Did he resist coming here?" she asked them as they headed for the front door.

"No," Jag answered, stopping by Slade's cut at the kitchen table and staring at it. He shook his head, frowning. "Fuckin' Warriors," he grumbled.

Dawg patted him on the back. "Gotta go, brother. Gotta get back to the club and get it opened up."

"Do you think it's safe enough?" Diamond asked him.

Dawg shrugged and scrubbed a hand over his beard. "Can't show those fuckers fear. We do, they win."

"Make sure you lock your door once we leave, sis."

"Yeah, I'll do that. Ace, Moose and Rooster are still up at the farmhouse, they'll stop and question anyone driving onto the farm."

"Yeah, but you're out here in the woods." Her brother lifted his chin toward her bedroom. "He ain't gonna be any protection for you right now."

"Got something you can leave behind? I don't have a gun or anything... Just in case," she added.

Jag and Dawg traded looks then her brother dug his hand under his cut into the back of his jeans and took out a compact handgun. He placed it on the kitchen table near Slade's cut.

"Careful with it," he warned her. "Know you know how to handle it, but still..."

"I'll put it on the nightstand near Slade. Again... just in case."

Jag nodded. "Any problems call me or D immediately, got me?"

"Yeah," she breathed, grateful that Jag was her brother. Even though their father was in prison for most of their lives, Jag still turned out to be a good man. She gave him a hug and he returned it, pressing his lips against the top of her head. "Do me a favor and tell Crash I won't be back at the shop until Slade can get up and around on his own, will you?"

"Yeah, sis, I'll tell 'im," he said softly and let her go. Seconds later she watched as they walked out the front door and she locked it behind them.

She turned and leaned back against the door, pressing her hands to her face. She took a couple deep shaky breaths, pushed off the door and on her way back to the bedroom, snagged the gun, checking the safety.

She pushed the bedroom door open and stopped. The last time she paused in her bedroom doorway was about a week ago when she had watched Slade sleeping in her bed before she left for work. She remembered how she felt while she studied him then...

She swallowed hard.

Now, he laid in her bed lucky to be alive. Her feelings hadn't changed one damn bit in the last week. If anything, her worrying about him made them even stronger. Those days he had disappeared without a word had eaten at her. And she hadn't realized how strongly she felt about him until he was gone.

But now he was back, and she was going to have to deal with whatever it was she was feeling. After lying to him about Rig, she knew from here on out, she had to be nothing but honest with him. That was the only way they were going to get past it.

She glanced down at the gun in her hands and closed her eyes. There were probably ten bullets in the clip. She wanted nothing more than to make ten Warriors pay for putting Slade through this. For putting her through it, too.

She had no idea how many Warriors existed since they were nomads and they seemed to be like roaches. You might see one, but you know there were many more hiding. And they kept multiplying. Take some out, more popped up in their place. There never seemed to be a shortage of new prospects and new members for that outlaw club. But the bad thing was, the new members and prospects were taking up an old beef that had affected none of them. Something they didn't even have firsthand knowledge of. And she had no idea why. It made no sense to her.

With a sigh, she moved into the room and placed the gun next to Slade on the nightstand. He watched as she did it but said nothing.

She didn't like how quiet he was. But then he was probably exhausted. She moved the remote out of the way, since he hadn't turned on the TV, and sat on the edge of the bed, placing a hand on his thigh. It reminded her that he had no spare clothes at her place and he needed to get out of his blood-stained ones.

Tomorrow she'd get a prospect to grab some stuff from his room at church. But right now she needed to talk to him and see if he'd ever forgive her. And not just for lying to him, but for what her father had done. She had no idea how he felt about that.

Hawk hadn't brought it up during their phone call and she had been too worried about Slade's physical well-being to think to ask.

She curled her fingers against his jeans and stared at his chest, watching the soft rise and fall. "I know this is probably the last place you want to be, but you can't go back to church and be on your own right now, and I'm sure you don't want any of the brothers to do it, so I'm sorry, but I'm going to take care of you."

"Princess..."

"I have a confession to make—"

His thigh muscle tightened under her fingers. "Princess..."

He couldn't interrupt her, she needed to get it out. "I didn't sleep with Rig. I'm sorry I lied to you, but I didn't have a choice at the time. I... I..."

Oh fuck. The tears were escaping faster than she could wipe them away. And soon she would start snotting and sniveling like a weak little bitch.

She bowed her head and mustered on. "I'm sorry, Slade. I'm so fucking sorry. I didn't know what to do so I said the first thing that popped into my head..." She sniffled. "I know it's no excuse. And if you wouldn't have left... you wouldn't have fallen into Warrior hands if it wasn't for me..."

She gave up and stopped wiping at her face. She just couldn't contain the tears and there was no point in trying.

She looked up when his hand cupped her cheek and his thumb brushed a tears away. "Ain't your fault," he said softly.

"Yes, it is. You left because of me. Because of what I did... or really, what I said."

"Princess... D told me why you did what you did. Told me that he found out 'bout my pop. With the shit the Warriors been pullin', don't blame him for bein' cautious."

"You didn't know your father was a Warrior?"

"Had no fuckin' clue. Been askin' 'bout him for a long time. Just had a bad photo with his name on the back."

Di decided to test the waters. "Do you know what happened to him?"

He shook his head slightly. "No. Warriors said he's dead. All I know. Not sure when or how, but they said he's dead. No reason not to believe 'em."

Diamond reached up and snagged his hand, pulling it into her lap with a squeeze. "They didn't tell you how he died?"

"No. Wasn't like we were havin' deep conversations, princess." He flipped his hand over and intertwined his fingers with hers.

"D didn't say anything?"

His fingers flexed within hers and he lifted his gaze from their hands. "Does D know?"

Oh fuck... Oh fuckity fuck.

Her mouth dropped open and the air rushed from her lungs.

She couldn't tell him yet. Not yet. Not when he needed her help to heal. Once he was up and about, she'd tell him and then he could leave if he wanted to. But not until then. She needed this time with him. Needed to make amends for what she did. She'd also made amends for what Rocky did to his father later, if necessary.

But right now, he was there, in her bed. And he needed her. She stared at their clasped hands.

"Wanted to kill Rig. Just so you know."

Diamond glanced up in surprise.

"Every time I closed my eyes, saw 'im on top of you... saw him gettin' what should only be mine, princess. That killed me, fuckin' ate at me. Had a hard time gettin' that outta my head. Couldn't. Tried to drink it away, that didn't work, either."

Diamond didn't know what to say. Her throat had closed up as he spoke and now more tears threatened to spill.

What the hell was happening to her? She was not a weak cry baby like this. She shook herself mentally.

"Have to get these clothes off of you," she finally said, clearing her throat and wishing she could clear her emotions just as easily. She reached for the bottom of his shirt. "They're filthy."

He grabbed her hand, holding it still for a moment. "Yeah, need you naked, too, princess. Need to feel you against me. Just you. Just me. Can't do more than that, but wanna feel how real you are. A reminder that I didn't die in the Warriors' hands."

She bit her bottom lip to keep from becoming a blubbering mess. "You definitely didn't die in Warrior's hands. I'm real. You're real," she whispered.

She pulled his blood-stained shirt up and over his head carefully and threw it on the floor. He unbuttoned his jeans and he slowly shimmied out of them with her help. Though, she couldn't miss the few times he sucked in a sharp breath. She peeled his boxers off next.

He needed a shower but that wasn't going to happen tonight. She gathered his dirty clothes and tossed them into the hamper she kept in her closet, then went to get a pan of warm water and a wash cloth.

When she returned he still sat up in bed naked and she let her gaze roam over his bruised body. His tattoos weren't the only colors now adorning his chest and ribs. She steeled herself and carried the pan over to the bed.

"Going to clean you up a bit, baby. Let me know if I'm hurting you." She chewed on her bottom lip as she dipped the washcloth into the water, wrung it out and began to gently wipe away the dried blood on his face and chest.

She couldn't read his expression because his face was so swollen, and his eyes were still not much more than slits. After cleaning him up as best as she could, she threw the washcloth back into the pan and sat studying him. She traced her fingertips across his collarbone and down his sternum, straightening out his dog tags before continuing down over his abs and following the line of hair that started at his navel and went south.

He grabbed her hand and held it still. "Sorry, princess. Wish I could but can't tonight."

"I know. I just needed to touch you."

"I'm real. You're real," he echoed her from earlier. "How long can you go bein' my sweet Diamond without gettin' any dick? Not capable right now. But hopin' she sticks around, anyway."

A small smile curled the corner of her lips. "I promise I'll do my best as long as you're in my bed."

"Can't go anywhere right now, princess. Even so, ain't nowhere I'd rather be."

He might rethink that after he found out the truth about her father.

"Gotta rest now so I can think straight later."

Yeah, she did, too.

CHAPTER FIFTEEN

"You said you were raised by a single mom." Diamond put her fork down and studied Slade who sat across from her at her kitchen table. He was finally feeling well enough to get around, take a shower, and sit with her at the table. She figured he'd soon be moving back to church.

Not that she wanted that to happen. But if he wanted it, she wasn't going to stop him.

Even so, it was time for her to address the issue she had put off, then if he needed to leave, he could.

"Never said she raised me. Raised in a foster home. No one wanted to step up an' claim me. My uncle was a member of an MC, so there was no fuckin' way he was raisin' an orphan like me. Distant relatives didn't want nothin' to do with me. Most of 'em couldn't afford an extra mouth, anyhow."

She pushed away her plate and picked at the label on her bottle of Iron City beer.

He glanced at her half-eaten food. "Ain't hungry, princess?"

Hell no, she wasn't hungry. She wanted to puke.

She just found out since her father killed his, he became an orphan and ended up in a foster home. That made this whole thing between their fathers even worse.

"Slade," she started, but then had to swallow the lump stuck in her throat.

He shoved a forkful of green beans into his mouth and chewed. "What?"

She closed her eyes when the room began to spin.

"What?" he asked her again, more forcefully.

"I need to tell you something..."

Her eyes popped open when his fork clattered onto his plate. His face had become dark and it was from much more than the remaining bruises on his face. "If you fuckin' tell me you fucked—"

Her eyes widened. "No!" she yelled, then took a breath and repeated, "No," more softly. "No, there's been no one but you... This is about my father."

He pushed his plate away and sat back in his chair, staring at her. "What about 'im?"

"This is about your father."

He frowned in confusion. "Diamond, what the fuck?"

She chewed on her bottom lip and looked at the man who had lived with her for the past week, the man who she'd taken care of, the one she had fallen in love with who knew when, the biker who she knew was meant to be her ol' man.

She knew it. She felt it in her bones. But that didn't mean he'd want that, especially after she told him what she was about to.

But she needed to get it out. He deserved to know. And she had asked D, Hawk and all of the others to let her be the one to tell him.

Surprisingly, they had respected her wishes.

"My dad... Rocky went to prison a long time ago..."

"Yeah, babe, know that."

"Your father was killed a long time ago..."

His head tilted as he studied her. "Don't know when he was killed. Gonna ask D to find out the details."

"Slade..."

He slammed his hand on the table which not only made the silverware jump but Diamond, too. "Diamond, where the fuck you goin' with this?"

She swallowed again then braced herself. "D already knows the details. Had Hunter dig them up."

He stared at her with his dark brown eyes intense, his brows low. "You know?"

"Yeah," she whispered. "I know."

His nostrils flared, and he didn't say a word for a long moment. "Why'd you keep it from me?"

"When I tell you what I know, I hope you'll understand why."

His jaw tightened then he demanded, "Tell me."

"My father was put in prison for killing two Warriors."

"Yeah... *oh fuck*." He shoved his chair back so hard, the legs squealed against the floor. He pushed to his feet.

"One of the Warriors was—"

"*Oh fuck*," he muttered, shaking his head.

"Buzz," she finished, closing her eyes and waiting for him to rush from the room. When he didn't move, she opened them again. He wasn't looking at her, though. He was staring at the ceiling, his hand wrapped around the back of his neck.

"Fuck," he muttered again.

She stood and rushed around the table, but he stepped back and held out a hand to stop her from coming any closer.

His dark eyes landed on her. "You tellin' me that your father killed mine?"

Diamond took a shaky breath. "Yeah, that's what I'm telling you."

"You knew for how long?"

"Since that day..."

"What day?"

"The day I lied to you about Rig."

"The day you found out my father was a Warrior an' you pushed me away."

"Yes."

"D wasn't sure of my loyalty because of that."

"Yes."

"Diamond..."

"Yeah," she breathed.

He pinned his gaze on her. "My father didn't come get me from the foster home 'cause he was probably already fuckin' dead."

Oh shit. She rubbed at her chest because suddenly she had an unbearable ache there. "Probably."

He turned away and walked into her living room. He began to pace back and forth in front of her fireplace as he scrubbed a hand over his short hair. "Might've come got me if he knew."

"Might have," she repeated, but honestly, she had no idea if a Warrior named Buzz, who couldn't bother to stick around when Slade's mother got pregnant, would have come back to claim his kid. No one would ever know if that would have happened.

He suddenly stopped his pacing and spun on his heel. He rushed up to her, grabbing her arms. "Never had your pop around because he was doin' time for killin' mine."

Diamond didn't answer. She didn't need to since she doubted that he expected an answer. He was working all of this out in his head.

"Our fathers fucked us both."

She guessed it could be looked at in that way.

He stared down into her face. "Why did Rocky kill my father?"

"I... I don't know. Just knew it had to do with revenge for another murder."

"Don't know the details?"

"Not enough."

He shook his head. "Gotta know."

"What?" she whispered, staring up at him.

He released her abruptly and stalked away to her front window, staring out. He again started running his hand over his hair. "Gotta know the details, princess. Gotta talk to Rocky." He turned suddenly. "Need to talk to your father."

Fuck. He wanted to go to the prison?

"Can't have this shit hangin' over us. We both lost our fathers for this bullshit beef that's been goin' on forever. Need to know why."

"I can understand if you feel the need to leave."

He spun around. "What?"

"I can understand if you don't want to be near me because my father murdered yours."

He blew out a breath and slowly approached her, his face unreadable. She went to step back, and he stopped her by saying, "Don't you fuckin' move."

She blinked up at him when he came toe to toe with her, staring down into her face.

"I'm sorry," she began.

"For what?"

"For my father—"

"Think you need to pay for the sins of your father?"

"Don't you?"

"Fuck no. You hate me 'cause my father was a Warrior?"

"No."

"You're not your father. I'm not mine."

"But—"

"Diamond, get that shit outta your head. You're not responsible for his actions." He reached up and brushed his thumb over her bottom lip.

"You really want to go visit Rocky at Greene?"

"Fuck yeah. When's visiting hours?"

She shook her head. "I don't know. It's been awhile since I've been there. I'll look it up. You don't want to go today, do you? It might be too late."

"Fuck no. Right now I need to take you in the bedroom an' need some of that sweet Diamond honey."

Her eyes widened. "Are you up for that?"

"Fuck yeah. Been way too long, princess. Gonna be careful. Can't get too wild, though, woman. An' know you like it rough. But need to be inside you."

"I need you inside me, t—"

He cut her off, crushing his mouth to hers. She let him in. She was relieved he hadn't run from her place, never wanting anything to do with her again. Her tongue twisted against his and a groan escaped her as he deepened the kiss.

Fuck. It *had* been too long. In the past few days, the only thing she did to take care of his needs was to give him head a couple of times. And, of course, he didn't complain about it, but it unfortunately left her wanting and on edge. She even started to take care of her own business while he watched but he stopped her. He said if he couldn't fuck her, it would be more torture for him than anything.

But now, if he thought he was ready...

He broke the kiss, almost as out of breath as she was. He pressed his forehead to hers. "Babe, would love to pick you up, carry you into the bedroom an' throw you on the bed to take you as hard as you like it, but ain't there yet. So gonna follow me into your room, gonna take your time undressin' an' then you're gonna climb onto my dick. Got me?"

"Yeah," she breathed, squeezing her thighs together as heat and wetness rushed through her. "I'm going to do just that."

He smiled, gave her a quick kiss and then pulled her into her room.

He winced when she helped him pull off his shirt. "Are you sure about this?"

"Fuck yeah, princess. Can deal with a little bit of pain. Worth it."

She finished pulling his shirt over his head and threw it aside. He unbuttoned his jeans and took his time peeling them off. Once he was naked he got on the bed and sat against the headboard.

"Now get naked... slowly. Give me a show, babe."

The impatience Slade felt was growing. He wanted to be inside Diamond more than anything, but as he leaned against her headboard, he reminded himself that he had plenty of time. *They* had plenty of time.

He was right where he belonged. In her bed. In her life. And she was right where he wanted her. Well, at the moment she was too far away but she was giving him a hell of a show. Better than any of Dawg's strippers at Heaven's Angels.

And the reason why was Diamond was his. Only his.

No other man would ever get to see this show. It was exclusively for him.

She had already stripped down to her panties and bra, so slowly that he wanted to shout at her to come over to him and climb onto his dick. But he didn't. He let her work it. She circled her hips, then would turn and bend over, wiggling her ass until those little silky black panties rode up her ass cheeks.

Fuck him. His palm itched to spank those perfect globes.

He found out weeks ago just how much she loved to be spanked. He wasn't up to it tonight but soon... Soon he'd see her cheeks red from him giving her exactly what she wanted.

He circled his dick with his fingers and squeezed.

Still bent over, she unhooked her bra, letting it fall to the floor and when she straightened, she spun around, her hands over her tits. She twisted both nipples in her fingers, her eyelids heavy, that fucking skilled mouth of hers parted.

"Holy fuck, babe. Not sure where you learned to strip, but wish I had a wad of ones."

When she laughed, it was low and throaty causing his dick to kick in his hand. She continued to caress her tits and he couldn't pull his gaze away. Not that he wanted to. He took long, slow strokes with his fingers up and down his length, the precum beading at the tip. He left it there instead of wiping it away because he was going to make her lick it clean. Oh, fucking yea, he was.

She dropped her hands and he groaned as her nipples were darker than normal from her pinching them and the tips were hard like her name. Just like diamonds.

"Wanna suck your tits."

She smiled and shook her head. "Not done with the show you wanted."

He blew out a breath. "Then hurry the fuck up. Otherwise, I might just blow my fuckin' load an' you'll have to wait until I'm ready again."

"Don't you dare," she said with a sexy pout.

His head jerked in surprise. Who the fuck was this woman?

A slow smile spread across his face. Fine, if she wanted to torture him, so be it. He was going to give her a show, too.

"Take your panties off." His voice caught, and he cleared his throat roughly. He leaned his head back against the headboard, his gaze pinned to her as she hooked her thumbs into the elastic top of her panties and teased him...

Fucking teased him by running her fingers around the edge, tugging them down just slightly so he could see just the top of her cunt where her hair began. Yeah, she had that little racing stripe that he liked to run his tongue down until he found the finish line... that little nub he liked to bite and suck until she was screaming his name.

That little button that would make her hips dance when he flicked it with the tip of his tongue, scraped it with his teeth...

Fuck.

He stroked faster, his eyelids dropping low, his breath becoming ragged.

"Lemme see how wet you are, princess."

Her cheeks were flushed, and she wasn't smiling any longer when she slowly slid those black silky panties down her luscious thighs until they dropped to her feet. She kicked out of them and on her way back up, she caressed the skin of her smooth legs as she straightened, but her hands never went higher than her pussy. He couldn't see that little racing strip of dark hair any longer since her hands were busy in that area.

A noise escaped her as she separated her folds and played with herself. Fuck, a noise escaped him, too. A deep groan he could no longer hold back.

"Lemme see how wet your fingers are, princess."

She slipped them from her pussy and even from where he sat, he could see her sweet fucking honey that he desperately wanted to taste glistening on her fingers.

"Put 'em in your mouth. Suck 'em clean."

Jesus, his balls tightened as she did just what he demanded. Her tasting herself wasn't the only thing driving him to the edge, it was the fact she was doing every damn thing he told her to.

There was nothing hotter than a woman who did what she was told.

And the naked woman standing in the middle of her bedroom was not only listening to everything he said, she was going to do whatever he wanted to please him.

Fuck. Him.

She certainly was. And, fuck him, he was going to do everything in his power to please her, too.

He might not be at his best right now, but there were plenty of ways he could make her come, make her cry out, make her want him even more.

"Get over here, babe. *Now.*"

Without even a single hesitation, she approached the bed, her curvy hips swaying, her heavy tits swinging.

Goddamn, he wished he was healed enough that he could throw her on the bed and fuck the shit out of her.

But he couldn't, so he climbed from the bed, pulled her into a deep, long, wet kiss so he could taste her for himself, then pointed to the bed.

"Hands on the bed. Ass out. Wanna see both those beautiful holes of yours."

And, goddamn, didn't she plant her hands on the mattress, bend over, and flash him just what he wanted to see. Her pussy was plump, pink and wet, ready for his dick. Her tight, puckered hole also called to him. He wanted to be deep inside her there, too.

They hadn't done that yet, but he planned to. Just not tonight. When he was one hundred percent, he was going to make Diamond his in all ways.

Because she *was* his. No one else's.

Next time they went on a club run, she was going to be on the back of his fucking sled and that's where she was going to remain.

He was going to make it his mission to keep her happy, to do whatever he needed to make sure that bitch switch stayed flipped in the off position. He was going to make it so she wanted nobody but him.

He was going to make sure his brothers, who decided that this woman wasn't worth the chase, realize they had made a mistake. She was so worth it.

But it was too late. They lost out.

Diamond was now his. And none of them would ever get a shot with her. Not if he had any say in the matter.

Grabbing her hip with one hand and his dick with the other, he pressed against her. "You ready for me, babe?"

She nodded and looked over her shoulder at him, her eyes unfocused, her cheeks flushed. "So fucking ready."

"Can see how wet you are. Can feel it, too. Want nothin' between us anymore. Got me?"

Before she could answer, he pushed forward and slid into her wet heat. He closed his eyes as she surrounded him, hot, tight, slick. He could feel nothing but Diamond surrounding his dick. Like he said, there was nothing going to be between them anymore. No wrap, nothing. He knew she was on birth control; he'd seen her take it every morning. And there was no way any other man was going to have what was his.

He started by thrusting slow, testing the pain in his ribs, but there wasn't any. He picked up the pace, pumping harder, faster, his fingers gripping her hips tightly as his skin slapped against hers. Once she started her chorus of cries, moans and whimpers, he was a complete fucking goner.

This woman never held back, was never self-conscious of what she did, what she said or the noises she made. She fucked with abandonment and that was great for him. He loved it and it turned him the fuck on. But it also took him to where he could finish way too quickly. He needed to do everything in his power to hold back, to keep from blowing his load right away. It had been a couple of weeks since he'd fucked her last and to him, it seemed like a lifetime. And the last week she'd slept by his side naked every night and he couldn't do a damn thing about it.

So now... he had a lot of catching up to do.

CHAPTER SIXTEEN

Diamond sank her teeth into Slade's neck and he twitched underneath her. He loved to be bitten. But then, so did she. Even though she didn't want to add to his bruises, she couldn't resist giving him what he craved. He blew out a breath and dug his fingers into her hair, pulling it tight.

"Fuckin' harder, princess."

His gruff demand sent a tingle down her spine.

She shifted to another spot along his neck and did what he ordered. His cock jerked deep within her. She smiled against his skin and continued to lift and lower her hips, taking him as deep as he could go.

She always preferred him on top, dominating her, taking the control, but until his ribs were healed some more, they were unable to do her favorite position. Only because when he was on top she became too demanding.

She smiled again and traced the tip of her tongue over his tattooed throat and down his chest, tugging his dog tags with her teeth.

With a circle of her hips, she ground down against him and she vocally let him know just how good he felt.

The louder she was, the more intense he got, but right now they still had to be careful with his healing body.

"Feel so good, babe. Can't get enough of you."

Yeah, she felt the same way. She nipped at one of his nipples then the other and he didn't even flinch. She skipped over his ribs, and sat up, pulling her hair from his grip. With both hands on her tits, she ground down against him again until he groaned.

"Fuck... You're killin' me."

She paused her motion. "Does it hurt?"

"Fuck no. Keep fuckin' me," and with that, he slapped her ass hard.

She laughed and savored the sharp sting as she continued to ride his cock. She was so fucking wet, and he was so damn hard.

"Fuckin' give it to me, babe."

"Yesss," she hissed.

"Wanna flip you over an' fuck you until you can't move."

She wanted that, too, and could hear the frustration mixed in with his mindless babble.

Planting her hands on both sides of his head, she leaned over and took his mouth, exploring every part of it. His tongue tangled with hers and she fought back until she groaned into his mouth.

He snagged her nipples between his fingers and twisted as hard as he could. She pulled her lips from his to cry out, her back arching, her pussy clenching hard around him.

"Gotta come soon, babe... Can't..." His eyes rolled back, and his fingers plucked at the hard tips of her nipples.

"Yeah, baby, like that," she encouraged him. "Make me come."

"Fuck, babe..." he groaned. "Gotta... Gotta... *Fuck*."

"Come inside me, baby."

"Gonna..." he grunted.

"Come with me."

"Gonna..." he grunted again. His eyes suddenly opened, and he reached up, fisting her hair, making her meet his gaze. Through gritted teeth, he demanded, "Come for me, princess."

"Coming," she cried out, riding him faster in a race to the finish line, her thumb circling her own clit to make sure she met him there. Her breath hitched, and her toes curled as the intense wave rushed through her, dragging him with her.

"Fuck!" he shouted, throwing his head back, his chest rising and falling quickly as his cock twitched deep inside her.

Seconds ticked by before they both came down from their high... He still had her hair gripped in his hands and he tilted her head down.

"Mine, princess. No one else's. Got me?"

She studied the man beneath her, and wiped a bead of sweat off his brow. "Got you."

His nostrils flared and his eyes darkened. "Crow ain't touchin' you no more. Got me?"

"Slade," she whispered.

"Ain't even a discussion. The man ain't touchin' you. You want ink, my ass is sittin' right next to you while he does it."

She sighed and carefully moved off him to settle by his side. "Baby," she started.

He shook his head then twisted it to look at her. "See 'im touchin' you, princess..." He let that warning drift off.

"He doesn't mean anything by it. That's just the way he is."

"Would you let Pierce touch you like that?"

Diamond sucked in a breath. No, she sure as hell wouldn't. "Crow isn't anything like Pierce."

"Tell me you got me. Gotta hear it."

Di closed her eyes for a heartbeat, then two. "Got you."

"He touches you an' I see it or hear 'bout it, gonna give you a spankin' you will definitely not enjoy an' then him an' I are gonna have more than words. Just sayin'."

She rolled onto her side and tucked her hand under her head, staring at him. "Are you staking your claim?"

He didn't say anything for few moments. "Ain't doin' nothin' but tellin' you how it's gonna be."

"Another rule," she stated softly. He sure as hell wanted her enough to dictate what she did and make "rules," but not enough to claim her.

"Gonna be more."

"*Jesus*. I get to make them, too, remember?"

Again, he paused for way too long. "Ain't stickin' my dick in anyone else."

"You think that's going to be the only rule?"

"Only one that counts."

She snorted and shook her head. She rolled away from him but was brought to an abrupt halt when he snagged her wrist.

Without looking at him, she snapped, "Have to go shower if we're going to head to the prison today, Slade. I can't go see my father while smelling like I'm full of your cum."

He released her and grunted, "Right."

"Since we still have no idea what happened to your sled, we're going to have to take my car."

"Right," he grunted again.

She finally turned to look at him. He remained on his back, but he was staring at the ceiling. "Guess you'll want to drive."

"Right," he mumbled.

Diamond inhaled slowly then exhaled just as deliberately to drive away the urge to throw something at him. "Right," she echoed and headed to the bathroom to wash the sex stink off her.

———

Slade stood behind Diamond as she sat in front of the thick glass waiting for her father to be escorted into the enclosed visiting room they were assigned.

They'd hardly said a word to each other on their ride to the prison, not only because she was still pissed at him from earlier but because she was a complete ball of nerves. She hated the super max prison her father was housed in. The sight of the prison alone made her sick to her stomach. She had no idea how her father survived in here.

Well, she knew. The man did what he had to do.

The door on the other side of the glass buzzed open and her father, who she hadn't seen in probably a year, stepped through wearing an outfit that reminded her of nurse's scrubs if they hadn't been an ugly orange and included his inmate number on his chest.

She'd never seen him in anything else her whole life. She couldn't even imagine what he'd look like in street clothes. She'd only seen him in something other than that godawful color in some old photos her mom had.

Pictures that showed her mother young and happy, completely unaware she would be saddled with three kids and a husband convicted of first-degree murder.

Her heart stopped and then restarted with a thump as the guard closed the door behind Rocky and the man who spent more than half of his life locked up approached the glass.

Di noticed a new tattoo on his neck, and some on the back of his fingers as he lifted his hand to press it to the window. She guessed he wanted a moment of bonding by having her press her palm against his through the thick glass. She didn't. That wasn't what she was here for.

After a few seconds, he gave up, but smiled at her anyway. After taking a seat, he ran his fingers through his long salt and pepper hair. At least he wasn't shackled like an animal during their visit.

"Diamond. It's been a while." His voice was rough and deeper than she remembered. "Missed you, baby girl."

She was not going to feel guilty about not visiting him more often. No, she wasn't. It was his fault he had been locked up for the past almost thirty years, not hers. He was the one who did something stupid and was pulled from his family, leaving her mother to raise three children on her own.

"Rocky," she answered back.

He made a disappointed face. He had more wrinkles around his blue eyes and across his forehead than he had the last time she was here. "You know better than to call me that." He tilted his head as his gaze raked over her face. "You look beautiful." His hard eyes softened, and he gave her another smile. Then his gaze lifted, got hard again as he lifted his chin toward Slade. "Who's that?"

Without bothering to look over her shoulder, she answered. "Slade."

Rocky continued to eyeball Slade when he asked more slowly, "Who is that?"

"He's DAMC, Rocky... *Dad*."

"Ain't wearing DAMC colors."

"You know he can't wear them in here. They even made him remove his wallet."

The guards wouldn't allow any wallets that had chains clipped to belt loops and that was the type most of the brothers in the club wore.

"Got 'em on his back." Rocky wasn't asking; he was demanding an answer.

"Yeah, Dad, he does."

Her father's eyes dropped to hers. "Seen 'em?"

Ah, fuck.

"Yeah, I've seen them," she answered reluctantly, knowing exactly where that question would lead.

Her father's gaze shot back up to Slade. "You fuckin' my baby girl?"

Slade put a hand on her shoulder, once again acting like he was laying claim, even though he wasn't. "Yeah, brother, I am."

Heat crept up into Di's cheeks as Rocky's body got tight. This was *not* what they came here for.

"How long you been patched in, *brother*?" her dad snarled.

Diamond raised her hand and waved it around in front of the glass to get her father's attention. "Dad, that's not why I'm... we're here. He's been an Angel for a while."

Rocky's sharp gaze dropped back to her. "What's wrong with his face?"

"Warriors."

"What about 'em?"

"A few of them fucked him up."

Rocky pursed his lips then asked, "They dead?"

Di scanned the small, divided room. They were probably being recorded or videotaped or something. She wasn't going to talk about that here.

She sighed. "Don't know, Dad."

"Get Z on that."

She rolled her eyes. "Z's not going back to jail. He already did ten years; he doesn't want to do any more."

"Your mother said he just had a baby, that true?"

"Would she lie to you?"

His lips twitched. "Nope."

"Then it's true."

His smile widened. "Fourth generation, baby girl. One of these days, you'll be bringin' some babies into the world, too. Gotta bring 'em in here so I can see 'em. Got me?"

The last thing she wanted was to bring her children, *if* she had any, to visit their grandfather who was a convicted murderer.

But she didn't have time to argue that fact with him. "Yeah, got you."

"Gonna have babies with that one?" He jerked his chin toward Slade.

Jesus. She was glad Slade was standing behind her, so he couldn't see her embarrassment.

After a moment, she answered, "Don't know, Dad."

"Don't know a lotta shit." Rocky looked up at Slade. "You gonna plant some of my grandbabies in her belly?"

Oh, Jesus! She was *not* some brood bitch.

She squeezed her eyes shut and yelled, "Dad! No! Stop it. That's not what we're here for! *Holy shit.*" When Slade started to say something, she spun around in her chair and yelled at him, too. "Don't you answer that!"

Slade smirked and lifted his hands in surrender. When she turned back around Rocky was grinning, too.

"Know what you gotta do," he ordered Slade, then gave Di an innocent, wide-eyed look.

She let out a long, *looong,* loud sigh.

Rocky lifted a hand. "Okay, sorry, I'll be good. Know you're not missin' your pops, so whataya here for?"

"I need answers."

He cocked a dark, thick brow. "'Bout what?"

"About why you're in here."

Rocky studied her for a minute. "Know why I'm in here."

"I know the general reason but not the details."

"Don't need to know the details."

"Yes, we do, Dad. It's important."

Rocky's gaze flicked from her up to Slade and back to Di. "*We?*"

"Yeah, I have to tell you something..." She felt Slade move closer, so close that his heat seared her back.

"Killed a biker named Buzz," Slade grumbled.

Rocky's jaw got tight as he glanced up at Slade. "Yeah. Warrior. No good piece of shit."

Di could feel the tension rolling off Slade's body, which made her sit on the edge of her seat.

"Why's that?" Slade asked.

"Why was he a piece of shit? Or why'd I kill 'im?"

"Probably one an' the same," Slade muttered.

Rocky's eye narrowed on Slade. "Why you care?"

"Just answer, Dad."

"It's history."

"No. It isn't. That's the problem," she said.

"What the fuck's goin' on?"

"Dad, please..."

Rocky sat back in his hard, plastic chair and crossed his arms over his chest, studying the two of them, his mouth a thin, flat line.

"The fucker killed your grandfather," he finally said.

Slade made such a sharp movement behind her that it jolted her, as well.

Di knew Bear had been killed by Warriors. She also knew her father had killed Warriors in return. But this was news... And it made their situation even more of a tangled mess. But what her father said next made her stomach drop even further.

"Two others."

She was almost afraid to ask who else, but Slade beat her to it.

"Who were the others?"

"You don't know 'em, boy."

"We need to know the whole story," Di insisted.

Rocky regarded them silently for a moment then leaned forward. "Killed another Angel, raped an' killed that brother's ol' lady. Left their kid an orphan."

Di sucked in a ragged breath and her chest tightened to the point where she almost couldn't breathe. This whole mess between the DAMC and the Warriors left at least two children, that she now knew of, orphaned. Slade and...

"Who was that?" Her question came out so quietly, she wondered if her father even heard her through the barrier. But he did.

"Brother named Coyote. You wouldn't remember him. Was killed before you were born. Had a pretty, little Indian woman as his ol' lady. Buzz an' another Warrior named Hammer ambushed Coyote, gutted 'im, then raped his woman an' slit her throat. Kid was right there, saw it all. Luckily, he was just a tot, prolly don't remember it."

Holy shit.

Di grabbed her stomach when it decided to do a couple somer-saults. "Dad, when you say Indian woman, do you mean a Native American?"

He frowned at her use of the PC term. "Same shit."

Di dropped her head in her hands and a feeling of dread washed over her. Her question was muffled when she asked it. "What was that kid's name?"

Oh, Jesus fucking Christ. She already knew the answer.

Oh, please, please, please. She didn't really want to hear the answer. She didn't want to hear that Slade's father murdered and raped...

"Crow."

...Crow's mother.

Diamond tried to swallow the lump in her throat, but it did no good. She was afraid to look behind her, to see how Slade was handling this new information. He hadn't said a word, but she could still feel him standing close behind her.

The worst part was Crow was there when it happened. He had to be a baby, but still...

"After we buried his momma an' pop, some of 'er family came an' got 'im. Didn't want us raisin' 'im in the club. Thought that takin' 'im back to his family's reservation in South Dakota was a better option. Not sure if it was, but we let 'im go. Was proud of 'im when I heard he came back to prospect. Man's got DAMC blood runnin' through his veins."

She stared at her father. "Why didn't I ever hear of this?"

"Not sure how much Crow knows. Could be he just knew his father was an Angel. He visits every so often, sits here an' hardly says a word."

"Have you told him what you just told us?"

"Hasn't asked."

Di bugged her eyes out at her father. "Don't you think he'd want to know?"

Rocky shrugged. "Wants to know, he'll ask."

Was he serious? She shook her head to clear it. "Have to ask you something, Dad..."

"Askin' a lot of questions today, Diamond."

"I need to know... Was it worth it?"

Rocky's nostrils flared, and his eyes got hard once more. "Baby doll, I'd do it again in a fuckin' second."

The hair on the back of Diamond's neck stood up when he used the same nickname Crow called her.

"The only regrets I got are bein' separated from your mother an' not bein' there to raise you kids. Knew the brotherhood would step in an' help raise you all. They did an' I'm proud you three turned out good." He sat back again, staring at Slade behind her. "Lift up that sleeve, boy."

Slade must have complied because her father nodded and said, "Marine, huh? *Oorah*. If somebody's gonna be stickin' it in my baby girl, can't complain that's he's a vet. Need more of 'em in the DAMC."

She asked Slade over her shoulder, "You heard enough?" Because she sure had.

"Yeah," was his low, tight answer.

She lowered her voice enough she hoped her father couldn't hear her. "Want to tell him?"

"Not sure that's a good idea, princess."

She agreed. It may not be the best idea. At least not now.

The door buzzed behind her father. Their time must be up.

As he got to his feet, Rocky said, "Tell your sister to come visit her old man. Tell 'er to bring that ball an' chain of 'ers, too."

Di had hoped the visit today would clear things up. Unfortunately, it just made things a whole lot messier.

———

Slade eyeballed Diamond as she sat in the passenger seat of her small sports car. His cut was draped over her lap and her fingers incessantly ran over the patches on the back. He doubted she was even aware that she was doing it.

She had cleaned his cut up as best as she could after the Warriors stomped all over it. She'd make someone a good ol' lady, just for the fact alone that she knew the life and how important his colors were to him and the club.

He looked beyond her through the passenger side window at the prison as he shoved her 370Z into first gear and released the clutch.

She'd hardly said a word to him after her little shit fit this morning and she was saying even less now that they were leaving SCI Greene.

As he drove out of the visitors parking lot, she finally whispered, "He called me baby doll."

"Yeah?"

"That's what Crow calls me."

He really wanted to tell her that Crow needed to stop calling her that, but he was already in the dog house with their conversation earlier about Crow touching her. Maybe he'd pull the brother aside and have a little conversation with him about boundaries. "So?"

"You don't think that means anything?"

"Said Crow visits 'im, maybe when your pop asks 'bout you Crow calls you baby doll."

His eyes slid to her. She stared straight out of the windshield, chewing on her bottom lip.

He bit back a sigh. Whenever she bit her bottom lip he now knew she was thinking way too hard. "Princess, your pop callin' you baby doll is the least of our problems right now."

She turned wide eyes to him. "No shit. What a fucking mess."

That it was. "Ain't gonna say nothin' to no one, got me?"

Her blue eyes got even wider. "What?"

"Gonna let it go."

"You mean not tell Crow what we know?"

"No. Might already know, anyhow." He pulled out onto the highway and pointed the car towards Shadow Valley.

"Think D knows what your father did? Not only killing Bear, but Coyote and Crow's mother? And not just killing her, raping her first."

He understood the bitterness in her voice, he was feeling it himself. "Guessin' he don't know everythin'. Otherwise, might be filetin' the colors off my back."

He heard Diamond suck in a sharp breath next to him.

"Princess, that shit happened decades ago. Not sure who all knows the details at this point. If anyone, Grizz. Maybe Ace. Possibly Pierce. An' they might not be puttin' two an' two together. Everyone knows a Warrior killed your grandpop. Everyone knows Rocky killed a Warrior for payback. An' if you never heard about Coyote an' his ol' lady, then most likely it's never talked about."

"Maybe no one talks about it to shield Crow from living that horror all over again."

"Could be. But there's plenty of times Crow ain't around an' no one's talked about the past."

"Everyone's trying to move forward, that's why. Fucking Warriors are the ones..."

As her words faded off, his jaw got tight. Rocky was right. Buzz was a piece of fucking shit. A no-good piece of dog shit. It was bad enough that Slade was DAMC and had Warrior blood in his veins, but a Warrior of the lowest kind. A bottom feeder.

"Glad he did it."

From the corner of his eye, he saw Diamond's head spin toward him. "Glad who did what?"

Slade hadn't even realized he'd said it out loud. "Glad your pop killed mine."

"Slade," she breathed, reached over and laid a warm hand on his thigh.

Releasing the shifter, he curled his fingers around hers. "No, princess. Man was a monster. Not glad you had to live without your pop your whole life. Not glad I was left on my own. Not glad Crow was left the same way. But glad Buzz ain't walkin' this earth. Glad I never knew 'im."

"You forget my father's a murderer, too."

"Know it. But did this world a favor, that's how I see it."

He had no idea what his sperm donor looked like except for that old, ratty photo he still had in his wallet. Even so, he couldn't wipe the vision of Buzz raping a woman, a young mother, and then extinguishing her life her right in front of her kid.

From what Slade knew, this whole beef started when the Shadow Warriors wanted Shadow Valley, the DAMC's territory. All that killing and violence over a town when there were plenty of others available, not only in Pennsylvania, but around the country. The nomads could've moved on and gone anywhere. They didn't. They decided they wanted what DAMC had and they weren't taking no for an answer.

So now in this car sat two people thirty-something years later affected because of a bullshit beef. One with SWMC blood, and one with DAMC blood.

Slade jerked the wheel sharply and pulled over into the lot of an abandoned business. He slammed his palms on the steering wheel, then covered his face and bellowed into his hands as his chest heaved.

He couldn't look at Diamond. He couldn't. Not until he got his shit together. He took deep breaths in an attempt to calm his racing thoughts.

It didn't help much because all that kept running through his mind was how he was tainted. "That poison runs through my veins."

"What?" she asked in a whisper, her hand squeezing his thigh.

"His toxic blood. It runs through my fuckin' veins."

"You're *nothing* like him, Slade. Don't even think like that."

"How do you know?"

He dropped his hands and she immediately grabbed one to pressed it over her heart. "Baby, I know it here."

He shook his head. She could be wrong. Maybe he'd turn out to be a monster just like his father.

He thought about why he had enjoyed boxing so much. He found nothing more satisfying than to pound the shit out of someone. To be the victor. Maybe that violent tendency was hereditary. Could it get worse?

He would never want to hurt the woman sitting in the car next to him. And he was afraid, now that he knew what he knew about his father, that it could very well happen. He could possibly snap.

"If you have toxic poison in your veins, then so do I. My father was no better."

"No, Diamond, your father evened the score for murders the Warriors did. The Warriors killed first. Doc an' Rocky an' whoever else only went after the Warriors after they tore the DAMC apart. Or tried to." He reached out and gripped her jaw, pulling her closer. Even though the car was small, and the shifter prevented them from getting too close, he leaned forward and pressed his forehead to hers before saying, "Princess, if anyone did you wrong like that, you better believe I'd be sittin' in a cell right next to those two men. Don't ever doubt that."

Because that was the fucking truth. If anyone tried to hurt a hair on her head, he would make sure that person was no longer breathing. And he would do it himself. His hands, his justice. No way would one of D's Shadows to do it for him.

No fucking way.

Nobody was touching his ol' lady and getting away with it.

CHAPTER SEVENTEEN

Slade leaned back against the bathroom counter and twisted to look over his shoulder into the mirror. He studied the large tattoo Crow had inked onto his back a few months ago.

The black and grey DAMC rockers and logo on his skin had meaning.

A purpose.

Wearing those colors on his back and on his cut created a bond with his DAMC brothers. A bond he didn't want to break. Now that he knew the truth about his father, there was no reason to keep moving, no reason to hop on his sled and move on.

None at all.

Even if he wanted to, he couldn't leave right now anyway. His Harley hadn't been found. He had no idea what the Warriors did with it, but he suspected it was either trashed or dismantled for parts.

He tried not to think about it because it made him want to go out there and join D's crew on the hunt for any remaining Warriors. That sled had been his pride and joy, his baby. It had been in his life longer than anything else or even anyone else. Even though it was metal, leather, and rubber, it meant something to him.

Whether he stayed or moved on, he needed to get another sled.

He'd have to talk to Jag to see what the man could come up with. Diamond's brother had a skill customizing bikes like no other Slade had ever seen. If he had to take more shifts at The Iron Horse to pay for it, so be it. Whatever he needed to do. He couldn't be a biker... Hell, he couldn't be a part of an MC without a sled.

He took a last glance at the tattoo. His colors didn't just represent that bond or and his membership in the DAMC, it also represented...

Home.

Family.

Even after finding out his father was a Warrior who had killed some of DAMC's own, they still came and saved his ass from the rival outlaw club.

Knowing what she knew now, Diamond didn't look at him any differently, either.

It had been a week since they visited Rocky, and she hadn't asked him to move back to church, even though he was back to work and getting around just fine. There was no reason he needed to stay in Diamond's cabin anymore. Okay, there was one...

Diamond.

This past week he'd been doing a lot of thinking. About what this club meant to him. About what Diamond meant to him. And one thing became clear...

He was here to stay.

He was now DAMC. He was now home in Shadow Valley.

He also wanted to remain in Diamond's bed.

Shutting off the light, he stepped out into the bedroom to watch her sleep. Her hair surrounded her relaxed face like a dark cloud, and she looked peaceful as her breath went softly in and out of her parted lips.

He was glad that she could sleep, because, for fuck's sake, he sure couldn't. He had too much shit on his mind.

Last week before they had gone to visit Rocky, she'd asked if he was going to claim her. He hadn't answered.

Mostly because he didn't have an answer at the time. However, during his drive back to her cabin tonight, after an exhausting shift at The Iron Horse, he realized he finally had one.

He knew what he wanted.

He knew who he wanted. In his bed. On the back of his bike. As a permanent part of his life. She knew his secrets now. She accepted them. She accepted him.

She was one badass biker bitch. Knock her down, she got right back up swinging. He loved that about her. Her tenacity, her strength.

Life had dealt them both a shitty hand. And crazy enough, instead of pulling the two of them apart, the past couple of weeks had brought them closer together.

It surprised him that he was actually thinking about claiming her at the table. Hell, making it official. Did it make his heart thump a little faster and a bead of sweat pop out on his forehead? Fuck yeah, it did.

And that wasn't the only thing he was going to ask the Executive Committee for. He didn't want to tend bar or bounce drunks for the rest of his life. If he was going to put down roots in this town, in this club, then he wanted to do it right.

He'd not only been thinking about his future with Diamond, but how he could help the club out. And it hit him how to do just that. It would not only benefit the club, but him and Diamond.

Diamond shifted, sat up, blinking at him, then ran a hand over her eyes. "What are you doing?"

"Nothin'." He moved closer to the bed.

She covered her yawn. "When did you get in?"

"A little bit ago."

She glanced over at the digital clock on her nightstand. "It's late."

Yeah, it was and he hadn't wanted to wake her. "Had to close the bar."

"Was it busy?"

With a sigh, he shoved his boxers down his legs and, when she lifted the covers, he slid in beside her. "Yeah. Probably gonna start bein' late every night. Gotta earn some extra scratch to get another sled as soon as possible."

When she didn't say anything, he turned onto his side to face her. "Can understand it if you don't want me climbin' in your bed late every night. Can move back into church."

"I didn't know you moved out of church."

"Haven't slept there in a while." Not that he needed to remind her of that. She knew quite well where he'd been sleeping.

"True, but you still have your room and most of your stuff is still there. You only keep enough clothes here to get by." She paused, then turned her soul-piercing blue eyes to him. "I don't like sleeping without you next to me."

"Me neither, princess."

"Then why don't you move in? Officially."

"Said it before, when I work late, it's hard to come all the way out here."

"We can move into town."

His head jerked back and his brows furrowed. "Why would you wanna do that?" She had turned that suggestion down when he had brought it up weeks ago about her cabin being too isolated.

"To make it easier on you."

Jesus Christ. She was willing to move out of her great cabin in the woods just to be with him. "What about you?"

She lifted a pale shoulder and let it drop. "I want what's best for both of us."

"Think livin' together would be best for us?"

"Don't you?"

"Princess, asked me a week ago 'bout claimin' you." He pulled a deep breath through his nostrils before asking, "Still want that?"

She turned on her side, so they faced each other. "Do you?" The surprise in her voice bothered him.

"Want what's best for the both of us," he echoed her. And that was damn true.

Her mouth dropped open, a little sound escaped, and he suddenly found himself tackled to the bed. She covered his body with hers and took his mouth. He chuckled, which broke the kiss, but her mouth was on him once again, her tongue dipping between his lips.

Fuck, did she taste good.

She felt good, too. She was as naked as him, the hard tips of her nipples pressing into his chest, her fingers holding his head still, and her warm, soft pussy pressed to his dick, which was now wide awake.

Slade dug his hands in her hair and pulled her head back. "Guessin' that's a yes."

She gave him a smug grin. "That's a fucking *hell yes!*"

He smiled and with a twist of his body, rolled them both over, because right now he needed to be on top of his woman. Hell, he needed to be inside her.

"Gonna fuck you."

Her grin turned into a wicked smile. "What are you waiting for?"

He lined himself up and took her hard, glad she was ready for him. But then that was his woman, that was his Diamond. Always ready and willing for him. He met his match when it came to sex, that was for damn sure.

Everything he gave her, she could give back twofold. Hell, even threefold.

He released a hiss as her cunt squeezed him so tightly that it made his body shudder. Hot silk surrounded him, making his balls pull tight. He wasn't going to last long. Not tonight. But just long enough to claim his woman.

To make Diamond his. Now. And again later in front of the club. He'd take his claim to the table, to the Executive Committee, and ask for a vote.

He couldn't imagine any of them would cast a negative one. They'd probably all sigh in relief that someone was stepping forward to keep her in line. Not that he planned on discouraging her spark. He loved that fire inside her now that he recognized it for what it was.

"Babe..."

"Yeah?" she breathed.

"Fuckin' squeeze me hard... Yeah, like that. That's it, princess."

Her nails raked down his back and she arched beneath him, driving him deeper. Her heels dug into the backs of his thighs, her legs hugged his hips tightly.

He closed his eyes when she began to make her music, the sounds that drove him crazy, drove him to the end before he was ready. She threw her head back and let out a long, loud wail as her body convulsed around his. He cursed as he tried to keep his shit together, but it was a lost cause.

He was done. Toast.

With a grunt, he thrust hard and came deep inside her.

That had to be the quickest fuck he ever had. And he sure as hell didn't want to make that a habit. But she came before he did so she couldn't bitch too much. Or at least he hoped she couldn't.

He drew in a breath to slow his pounding heart and stared down into her blue eyes. "Sorry, princess. Didn't mean to bust a nut so quickly."

He jerked forward when she slapped his ass hard. He grinned, savoring the sting.

"Don't worry, you'll make it up to me. I need to get up for work early anyway."

He fell to her side with a groan and she rolled out of bed and headed to the bathroom. His eyes tracked her as she moved across the room, naked and full of his cum.

Within minutes, she was back, crawling under the covers with him. He wrapped an arm around her and pulled her against him, sweeping her long, dark hair out of the way, so he could press his lips against her forehead.

"So, are you really going to claim me?"

"Yeah, babe, gonna claim you."

"So... does that mean..." she whispered.

He should be panicked right now, ready to roll out of her bed, out of her place. But he wasn't. An amazing sense of calm came over him instead. "Yeah, babe, it does."

A slow smile crossed her face. "I love you, too, Slade."

He grunted, pulled her tighter against him and said, "Get some sleep, princess. Mornin's gonna be here too soon."

The morning was going to bring about a busy day. He had to move the rest of his shit out of his room and go talk to Jag about getting another sled.

And have a few words with Zak about his future. Hell, *their* future.

EPILOGUE

"Was a reason I asked you to hold off on claiming Diamond," Zak announced as he sat at the head of the lacquered wood table. The one that sat in the Executive Committee meeting room. The one that had the large DAMC insignia carved into its center by one of the founders, the late brother Bear.

When Slade had approached Z about allowing him to bring the claim at one of the meetings, he'd asked Slade to hold off for a month.

A whole fucking month. Slade had no idea what that was about, Diamond acted like she didn't know, either. But she was surprisingly patient, which made him wonder if she knew what was up.

Slade eyeballed Z, the gavel laying idle by his hand, then his gaze bounced to the rest of them sitting around the large table. Ace, the treasurer. Jag, Road Captain. Hawk, VP. Dex, club secretary. And then lastly, Diesel, Sergeant at Arms. The enforcer no longer looked at him sideways with suspicion. In fact, he now looked at Slade like he was crazy for wanting to be saddled with Diamond.

He should remind the massive man he had his own spitfire to deal with. Jewel was no better than her sister. So D had no room to judge.

Diesel pushed his chair back and stood with something in his huge paw. Slade hadn't noticed it earlier when they voted to make Diamond Slade's ol' lady. It must have been hidden under the table on his lap.

He held it out and Slade, with another quick glance around the table at everyone's blank faces, approached and reached for it.

It was a black leather vest. Which made no sense. He already had earned his cut and wore it with pride. And the Warriors hadn't damaged it enough to warrant getting a new one...

He let it hang from his fingers and turned it around to look at the back. His eyes widened and his lungs emptied. The cut wasn't for him.

No, it fucking wasn't.

Holy shit.

The rockers on the back stated "Property of Slade."

The cut was for Diamond.

His gaze shot up to Diesel. "She gonna wear this?"

Not one of the ol' ladies belonging to any of the men sitting at that table wore one of those vests. Not Jewel, not Sophie, not Kiki. And Janice only wore hers on club runs.

"Gonna wear it," Diesel grunted.

He frowned. "How do you know?" Last thing he needed was to give that to Diamond and have her kick him in the damn nuts in front of his brothers. Especially since she was waiting out in the common area of church. It wasn't like he'd be able to hide it when he went out there.

"Jewelee had it made for 'er," D assured him. "Knew she'd want it."

If anyone would know what Diamond wanted, her sister would. Or he hoped so.

He fisted the vest and nodded. "Ain't settin' me up for a hurtin', right? Like to keep my eyeballs in their damn socket an' my balls in my sac."

Laughter rose from around the table.

"Afraid of your ol' lady?" Diesel asked with a smirk.

Slade cocked a brow. "Are you?" he countered.

Diesel's smirk quickly disappeared. Yeah, his ol' lady had him wrapped around that little finger of hers, all right.

Slade snorted and lifted the vest. "If I'm gonna die, gonna say right here an' now, glad you all are my brothers. Glad I finally found my home. Glad I stumbled into Shadow Valley."

Fists pounded the table and boots stomped on the floor in agreement.

Slade raised his hand, he wasn't finished. "An' I gotta thank you all for agreeing with my idea... Or our idea. Gotta give Diamond credit for it, too. Seems like she wanted it for a while but figured you assholes would say no."

A couple of the guys chuckled. But Diesel didn't.

"Probably wouldn't have agreed if you weren't in on it, too," D grumbled.

So Diamond was right. D wouldn't have wanted to back her idea of opening a gym on her own. But with Slade at her side? The man had no problem with it. None of the brothers around the table did, either. But Slade wasn't going to tell Diamond that. Fuck no. If any of the men on the Executive Committee were brave enough to, then that was on them. They could risk dealing with her wrath.

The only thing she needed to know was they were going to do what they both loved. She was going to get her gym so she could teach kickboxing and he was going to become a boxing coach. And, of course, the club would get a sweet gym for everyone to work out at... including D's "Shadows." Diesel actually almost smiled at that. And that probably ended up being the clincher to all the "yay" votes to fund the new venture and to allow Slade and Diamond to run it. But in the end, Diamond was getting her dream and that would make her happy. Which made him happy.

Today was a good fucking day.

"Got one more thing for ya, brother, but it ain't in this room," Z announced, then smacked the gavel onto the table and, as one, everyone rose to their feet and began to file out of the meeting room.

Slade followed them out and noticed not a soul was inside the common area. He had no idea where Diamond went.

They headed toward the back door to the parking lot and he followed, wondering what the fuck was going on since no one was saying a word.

All of them pushed outside into the late afternoon light. Slade inhaled the warm early spring air and just that alone made him antsy to get on a sled and take a long ride with his ol' lady clinging to his back.

He stepped around Diesel's massive body and noticed everyone who wasn't in the meeting standing in a circle. When they noticed the brothers approaching, the small crowd stepped back giving him a better view. The first thing he noticed was Diamond standing near a bike with a big smile on her face.

His heart did a flip and he glanced down at the cut in his hand. *Jesus*, his life might be over in a matter of minutes. Her gaze dropped to what he was gripping tightly and her smile didn't falter. That was a good sign.

He approached her and looked down into her beaming face. "Got somethin' for ya."

"Yeah?"

He hesitated.

"Are you going to just crush it in your hand or are you going to let me put it on?"

His eyebrows raised as her hand reached out, her fingers wiggling. "D'you know 'bout this?"

Her lips pressed together and the corners of her eyes crinkled. "Maybe."

"So you wanted it?"

She snagged the cut from his fingers and slipped it on. It fit her perfectly. "Of course I did. Jewelee had it made for me."

"Jesus, princess," he muttered.

She laughed and patted his chest. "It's all good."

"Thought I was goin' to be gutted if I gave that to you. Thought they were settin' me up."

Before she could answer, Jag stepped up next to him and waved a hand toward the Harley that Diamond stood in front of. Hell, he'd been so worried about Diamond's reaction to wearing his cut, that he ignored the beautiful sled that sat in the middle of the parking lot.

She was a beauty and he wondered who owned her. "One of yours?" he asked Diamond's brother.

Jag nodded. "Ain't a complete custom but she had good bones an' can always do more on 'er later." He bounced a set of keys in his hand. "Knew you were gonna claim Diamond today. Couldn't be a better time for this. Can't have my sister's old man not have a sled." He held out the keys to Slade.

Slade stared at Jag's hand for a moment then looked back up at him. "But you're still buildin' your own dream bike."

Jag had been riding a temporary sled while he built another custom for himself after the Warriors totaled his other one. He must have put his own project aside to put this bike together for Slade.

He realized right then and there, he'd made the right decision to patch into the DAMC. He finally felt like he belonged somewhere. That he was home.

Jesus. That was enough to make a grown man tear up.

But he didn't. He kept his shit together. Especially since they were surrounded by every club member and their women. He certainly didn't need to look like a crying pussy in front of them all.

"Don't matter," Jag continued. "Got this one done. Owner couldn't afford to finish payin' for it an' decided to hand it over since it was a complete reconstruction job. Man probably didn't pay much for the frame, anyhow. Wasn't much of a loss for him but was for the shop since we invested in all the custom parts an' shit."

Clearing the thick in his throat, he said, "Don't know what to say."

"How 'bout a thanks?" Hawk said.

Slade grinned through his emotions. "Thanks. Means a lot." He grabbed Diamond and dropped his arm around her shoulders, pulling her close. "Gonna take a ride on 'er later, yeah?"

"Yeah," she said softly, giving him a look that made his chest get tight.

"Knew 'bout this?"

She nodded, wrapping an arm around his waist and squeezing. "Can't be a proper ol' lady when I have nowhere to sit my ass."

He gave her a squeeze back. "Yeah," he agreed, softly.

She looked up at him and jerked her head to the left and whispered, "More surprises."

He glanced over to the left to where Diesel was standing, texting on his phone. Probably tending to In the Shadows Security business.

Slade's eyes were drawn to Jewel approaching her old man. They widened when he noticed what she was wearing.

A cut like Diamond's. But, of course, hers said "Property of Diesel."

Diamond jerked at him, and steered them closer as Jewel went toe to toe with the man twice her size. She grabbed his phone out of his massive fingers and Diesel's head jerked and he frowned down at his woman.

"What the fuck, woman?"

"Got something to tell you."

"Couldn't wait?" he grunted, his eyes narrowed on her.

"Nope."

It was clear when he finally noticed what she was wearing. He jerked her around and read the rockers on the back.

"When d'you decide to wear my cut?" Diesel almost shouted.

Slade couldn't tell if he was happy about it or pissed, which made him smirk, and Diamond chuckled softly next to him. "Just wait for it," she whispered to him.

"Since this." Jewel shoved something at Diesel, who had no choice but to accept whatever it was.

As his dark eyes dropped to the object in his hands, his eyes widened and his face turned sheet white. "What the—"

Before he could finish his shocked exclamation, he stumbled back and then tilted precariously forward until he fell hard to his knees on the pavement. Before anyone could catch him he landed on the ground like a fallen tree, passed out cold.

"Holy fuck!" Diamond yelled as everyone rushed over to D in concern.

Then Slade saw what the man still gripped in this fingers so tightly his knuckles where white...

The pee stick from a home pregnancy test and clearly the results showed two lines.

Diamond threw her head back and howled with laughter.

Slade's only thought was... how the mighty have fallen.

Which brother was next?

He glanced at Diamond and she gave him a wide smile.

Fuck.

Turn the page to read the first chapter of Down & Dirty: Dawg, book 7 of the Dirty Angels MC series

DOWN & DIRTY: DAWG SNEAK PEEK

Turn the page for a sneak peek of the next book in the Down &
Dirty: Dirty Angels MC series.

DOWN & DIRTY: DAWG

Chapter One

"For fuck's sake," Dawg muttered. He glanced at the digital clock that was hidden behind the bar for the tenth time.

The bitch was late.

She'd begged him for an audition, even though his stable was full.

Her soft, husky voice over the phone finally convinced him to say yes. Against his better judgement, of course. Because when he asked her if she was experienced, she beat around the fucking bush.

Which meant she wasn't. And he had no patience for amateurs or novices.

None what-so-fucking-ever.

Scrubbing a hand over his beard, he shot a glance at the front entrance, then at the clock once more.

He grabbed a cold Iron City beer from the cooler behind the bar, popped the tab on the can and lifted it to his lips.

He was done.

No bitch was worth the wait.

None.

He'd been stood up. Almost like a bad date. Though it had been a long time since he'd been on anything that was even remotely similar to one.

Well, unless fucking some random snatch until she came all over him was considered a date. Most likely it wasn't. An actual date probably included flowers, a movie and even dinner.

Or at least a shot of whiskey and a little fingering, before busting a nut.

"Fuck you, bitch. Dawg waits for no one," he muttered to the sweating beer can in his hand, then took another swallow of the ice-cold brew.

But, fuck him, if he didn't stand there and wait even longer. Again, it was that smooth as warm honey voice that made him keep his ass planted right where he was. He'd give her until he finished his beer. Then he'd head back up to his apartment, knock a quick one out with his own palm, and catch some more zzz's.

He slammed the can onto the bar, causing it to splash over his fist. With another curse, he wiped his dripping hand along his jeans.

Then he heard the door open down the front corridor and a sliver of *ass-crack-of-dawn* sunlight reflected off the wall. Suddenly a woman was standing at the end of the hall, pale as shit and eyes wide. Like a skittish doe about to be plowed down by a Mack truck.

Raking his gaze over her from top to toe, the first thing that hit him was she had sweet fucking tits. If they were real, she already had a leg up on this audition. The second was...

She was wearing a fucking high-neck blouse.

Who the fuck wore a boring beige top that covered her as much as a turtleneck to a stripper audition?

Her waist was narrow, her hips curvy, and...

She wore a skirt all the way to her fucking ankles.

And she wasn't even wearing heels!

"What the fuck," he muttered.

Maybe she was confused and was looking for a church nearby.

While there were a lot of "Oh Gods!" being said in his establishment, they were usually during private lap dances.

"Are you Dawson?"

A muscle ticked in his jaw as his teeth clenched. Dawson? He hadn't heard that name spoken out loud in a long damn time.

"Dawg," he grunted.

She blinked, but remained at the end of the corridor. He wanted to see what color those eyes of hers were and if they matched the husky tone of her voice.

"Dog? Like the woof-woof kind of dog?"

"What the fuck," he muttered once more. "No, like *Dawg*... D-A-W-G."

She tilted her head and studied him. There was another thing wrong with her... Her hair was pulled up high and tight. His customers liked his girls' hair long and loose. So they could swing it when they danced. So the men could imagine fisting it while they fantasized about one of his girls sucking them off. Or picture pulling it like the reins of a pony while fucking one of them doggy-style and slapping their ass.

Which never happened on his watch. Fuck no. His girls weren't whores. They were "exotic entertainers." They didn't put out for money. If they did, and he found out about it, they were outside looking in faster than they could say "G-string." He ran a respectable joint and certainly didn't need Shadow Valley PD breathing down his goddamn neck.

Though some of them did give it up to his brothers in the Dirty Angels MC, that was their choice and not for money. None were forced to do it. It had to be a mutual agreement between the brother and the girl.

A little reciprocal pleasure.

As he stared at the woman still hovering by the nearest escape route, he doubted this woman would give it up to any biker. She seemed way too uptight for that.

"I-I think I made a mistake."

That was an understatement. "I'd fuckin' say so."

Dawg finished off his beer, crumpled the can in his hand and whipped it into the recycle bin under the counter, then rounded the end of the bar.

Her eyes widened once again when he approached her. Which kind of, sort of, bothered him.

Yeah, he knew he could be a little intimidating. He was a big dude. He had a beard. He had a bunch of tats. He wore bulky silver rings on his thick fingers and a cut proclaiming that he was DAMC and damn proud of it. But he wasn't a man who hurt women.

Fuck no. When they screamed it was because he was licking their pussy so good that...

Fuck. Now he had half a fucking hard-on. And if he yanked on it to adjust it to a more comfortable position, she might just pee her panties. Or bloomers. Or whatever the fuck she wore under that awful shit-brown skirt.

"Don't know what you're lookin' for, but it ain't here."

He couldn't miss how hard she swallowed before taking a tentative step forward. "I called you about an audition."

Dawg eyeballed her up and down in slow motion on purpose, so she'd realize this place wasn't for her. When color flooded her cheeks, it cemented his opinion.

"What fuckin' stripper wears a goddamn shirt that don't show any cleavage an' a skirt—" he lifted a ringed finger, "—not short and leather, fuck no. One that covers her down to her ankles?"

She glanced down at herself for a second, then looked back up at him and shrugged slightly. "A kindergarten teacher."

Dawg's head jerked back. "A fuckin' what?"

She cleared her throat and pulled her shoulders back. *Which* he just happened to notice emphasized those big-ass tits. "A kindergarten teacher."

He blinked and let what she said sink in. "You wanna role play when you strip? My clientele might like that. Kinda like a sexy librarian. Or a sexy teacher who knows how to use a wooden ruler in a good way, but you gotta drop the 'kindergarten' shit. That might be a turnoff."

She shook her head and bravely took another step forward. Now she was only a few feet from him, causing his nostrils to flare when he caught a whiff of her scent. Flowers. Or something light. Nothing heavy and clingy like his girls wore.

And from where he stood, he didn't think she had a stitch of makeup on.

"No. I'm a real teacher. I teach kindergarten. You know, with children?"

He frowned. If she was a teacher, what the fuck was she doing in his club? Dawg waved his arm around Heaven's Angels Gentlemen's Club. "Does this look like a fuckin' kiddie school to you?"

Her head lifted slightly higher when she answered, "No."

He studied her for a second and decided he needed a better look. "Step under the light so I can see you better," he ordered. In no way was this woman here for any kind of audition. He pointed to the recessed light in the ceiling that was closest to him.

After a slight hesitation she did it. She bit her bottom lip and held it between her teeth as he checked her out once more. The lip thing was pushing the blood into his dick at an alarming rate. Which was surprising since the way she was dressed did nothing for him.

He took a step closer and her body wavered slightly, but she didn't back up even though she barely came up to his chin.

"Look up," he demanded. And when she did, he finally saw how blue her big eyes were.

Even though she held his gaze, she was nervous, and he could see the determination in her. She had a fire in her belly. He liked that. The woman was here for a reason and that reason was important, whatever it was.

Her blonde hair looked like her real color. Not all bleached out like some of his girls. He hated that shit and yelled at them all the time for it. He wanted his girls to look as natural as possible, but it was a losing battle.

But all that blonde hair was pulled back tight at the back of her head in a bun or whatever they were called. Similar to how Bella wore her hair when she was working in the bakery to keep it out of the cupcakes and icing and shit.

Her face was, just as he thought, clean of any makeup, naturally pretty, even wholesome looking. A perfect example of the *girl-next-door*.

But something about her was definitely not *girl-next-door* if she was here for a job.

"If you're a kindergarten teacher, you already got a job," he murmured, fighting to keep from reaching out and running a knuckle along her cheek to test how soft her flawless ivory skin felt.

"I need the money," she whispered back, not breaking his gaze. A spark had flared in her eyes when she admitted that.

Being a stripper wasn't one of her career goals. Fuck no. Probably wasn't even on her bucket list. She needed cold, hard cash. That was the real reason she was standing before him, trying desperately to hide her fear of him. She thought that flashing her tits would be a windfall, would get her out of whatever financial jam she was in.

"For what?"

She dropped her gaze and shook her head. "That's personal."

This woman was here for the wrong reasons.

Suddenly, he was feeling generous. "Look, if you need some scratch... a loan..."

Her eyes flicked back up to him. "No, no loan. I'm already in debt because of..."

"'Cause of what?"

She swallowed hard. "Nothing."

"Ain't nothin'."

She sucked in a breath. "Just forget it. I'm sure there are other clubs in the area who will give me a chance."

Though he needed fresh faces and fresh bodies to bring in new clientele, and to keep the regulars coming back, he didn't need any right now and he was sure he would regret his next decision.

When she turned to leave, he grabbed her wrist. "Hold up."

She stared at where he held her, her wrist looking tiny in his hand. He loosened his grip slightly since he didn't want the bulky rings on his fingers to bruise her, but not enough where she could slip away.

"What's your name?"

"What?"

"Your name. What's your name?" Dawg barked.

"E-Emma."

He already knew her real name; she had told him it on the phone. "No. Your stage name."

The confusion on her face was another telling sign that she didn't belong in his club, or even on a stage. And certainly not naked in front of a crowd of men, for fuck's sake.

"Em..." She hesitated. Then with a look of understanding, she began again, "Em... Ember!"

Ember. Fitting for that flame inside her. "Better. Can't have a kiddie-garden teacher named Emma on my fuckin' stage."

Her eyes widened in surprise. "You're going to give me a shot?"

Fuck. His big dumb ass was going to regret this. "Gonna give you an audition. Nothin' more 'til I see what you can do."

Relief crossed her face, and it made him shake his head.

He was such a fucking sucker.

He released her wrist. "Got an outfit you need to change into?" He jerked his chin toward the back of the club. "Dressin' room's in the back."

She glanced down at what she was wearing *again*. As if she didn't find anything wrong with that shit she covered herself up with from neck to toe. She could be going door to door, preaching religious shit and handing out pamphlets, dressed like that.

"I'm wearing it."

His lips twitched. Sure she was. "Got you. Wearin' it underneath that getup."

Her mouth opened, then it snapped shut. *Right*.

"I-I have to dance for my audition?"

His eyebrows shot up his forehead. "No, you're gonna hand me your fuckin' resume an' I'm gonna look it over... Of fuckin' course you gotta dance. Jesus fuckin' Christ." He turned on his heels and ducked behind the bar.

Normally on busy nights he had a DJ playing. During the day and on slow nights, he just used the high-tech sound system that was wired throughout the club. Each VIP room had their own smaller system, so the girls could pick whatever music they wanted for private dances. Then there was also a room off the main stage area for private parties, VIPs and special traveling entertainment troupes. It was a smaller version of the main club area, with its own stage and a bar.

He had to admit that his club was the shit and the nicest in the greater Pittsburgh area, if he said so himself.

He glanced at the woman who remained frozen in place near the entrance. "What music?"

"What do you mean?"

"What do you wanna dance to?"

She blinked at him.

"Ah, fuck. You don't have a routine ready an' a song picked out?" Of course not. All the red flags in his head were whipping in the wind.

"Should I have?"

This whole thing was going to be a disaster. He should just chase her out of there and stop wasting both of their time.

But he couldn't. He was dying to see what was underneath that virgin-like outfit of hers. If she had potential, he could get one of his seasoned dancers to give her a few pointers.

Yep, that's what he told himself. Had nothing to do with him wanting to check her out for himself. Fuck no. She didn't make him curious at all.

"Rock? Country? R&B? What?" he prodded.

When she didn't answer, he scrolled through his music and found a song that worked well to get his girls moving on stage. He set up the track and, grabbing the remote, headed down the long, narrow stage that was dead center in the main club area. It had a pole, from stage to ceiling, on each end and the bar was attached to the end closest to the entrance.

He settled his bulk into one of the low, vinyl club chairs that sat directly in front of one of the poles. He wanted a good seat and a very clear view.

He glanced her way. "Need help gettin' up on stage?" He jerked his chin toward the steps. "Stairs are down on this end."

She unfroze herself, shook her head and moved toward the back of the club where the three steps led to the lighted stage.

"Might wanna take those things off your fuckin' feet first," he suggested. He wasn't sure what they were called, but they were the most unsexy shoes he'd ever seen on a woman. Besides Crocs. Those gave him limp dick. Her shoes were a close second. Some kind of brown pleather shit.

She got to the end of the stage, bent over to unstrap her shoes, then kicked them off. Straightening her spine, she blew out a breath and climbed onto the stage.

Dawg leaned back in his chair and crossed his arms over his chest. "Lemme know when you're ready, *Ember*. I'll hit the music."

She nodded and eyeballed the pole.

"Poles are clean," he reassured her. "Cleaning crew just left 'bout an hour ago."

With a little nod, she wrapped a hand around it. He really wanted her to fist that hot little hand around his dick instead.

He sighed. "Gotta plan, right?"

Her gaze dropped to him. "Yes. Get naked."

Well, damn. "Normally gotta keep your bottoms on. Ain't legal to take 'em off when we're open to the public. But since the club's closed, leavin' that up to you. Sometimes I give private parties for my VIPs an' the girls go totally naked. They really rake in the tips those nights."

"I'll keep that in mind."

"You do that," Dawg said and then snorted, shaking his head.

"Okay," she said softly, staring up at the pole.

He cocked an eyebrow at her. "Okay, what?"

"I'm ready."

Dawg pinned his lips together. "Sure?"

She nodded, a determined look on her face.

Dawg shrugged and hit *play* on the remote. Ginuwine's *Pony* began to blast through the hidden speakers.

Her body jerked at the sound. "What's this?"

"Music. Just go with it."

She bit her bottom lip again, and that went straight to his dick.

Then she began to move...

He was hoping he'd been wrong, and she was a secret little slut with hot moves that would make him want to bust a nut. But fuck no, she wasn't. Her hips moved in a wooden circular motion as she held a death grip onto the pole with one hand.

Dawg groaned. This was going to be worse than he thought. As she tried to match the rhythm of the song, she threw her head back and closed her eyes, letting the music move through her.

Dawg sat forward in his chair. Maybe this wouldn't be so bad...

She reached up to pull her hair clip out, and her golden hair cascaded down around her.

Holy fuck.

All that blonde hair and her natural looks...

He lost his breath as she continued to shift around awkwardly but reached for the top button of her blouse. Which was promising...

With visibly shaking hands, she worked the buttons out of their holes one by one, and as the fabric gaped, he caught glimpses of a black bra underneath.

He attempted to swallow the lump in his throat and he willed her fingers to move faster.

The little he saw was no grandma panty set. Fuck no, it wasn't. He swore he got a glimpse of see-through lace.

She stopped unbuttoning when she got to her waist and reached around to the back of her skirt. Suddenly it shifted when it became loose and she caught his gaze as she began to push it down her hips.

The "suggestive" wink she gave him looked more like an eye twitch.

Even though this woman had the seduction skills of an eighty-year-old virgin, Dawg's breath caught.

She stopped moving around the stage as she rolled the long skirt down her thighs. But he couldn't see shit since her baggy blouse covered the V of her legs. He wouldn't be surprised if the woman had a huge untrimmed bush trying to escape her panties.

Finally, the skirt dropped to her feet and she stepped out of it, almost tripping herself. He jerked forward as if he could catch her, but she caught her own balance and then stood there unsure, wearing just her blouse partially unbuttoned.

His eyes slid from her face down to her legs. What the fuck?

She was wearing thigh-high stockings!

Maybe she wasn't lying about wearing an "outfit" under her conservative clothing.

But she just stood there, staring at him!

"You done?"

She shook her head. And, fuck him, she bit that bottom lip of hers again. That was going to be her signature move. She could do some sort of naughty teacher routine, and bite her bottom lip, while giving his customers an *I-need-to-be-fucked* look.

They'd be throwing twenties at her. Fuck, maybe even fifties.

She had no idea just how dick-hardening sexy she appeared with all that blonde hair loose, wearing thigh-highs and that half-open blouse. Like her brains had just been fucked out, and she was in a sex coma.

Jesus. He needed to see the rest of her. But not up on that stage. That was too impersonal, and he wanted to get so much more personal.

"Maybe that big stage's makin' you nervous. How 'bout makin' this dance a little more personal."

Her brows furrowed. "How?"

"Gotta show me somethin'. Some kinda skill. Right now, you ain't showin' me nothin' I wanna see."

For the most part anyway. Nothing a strip club manager would want to see. Dawg, the man? Fuck yeah. That was different.

He pushed to his feet and came around to the steps, holding out his hand. She stayed where she was on the stage, her skirt pooled at her feet, her blouse hanging crooked. She stared at his hand as if it was going to bite her.

"All my girls gotta do private dances... you know, lap dances. Get up close an' personal with my customers. Makes both of us some extra scratch. Better than the tips you'll make on stage. The stage is just used to entice these fuckers into the VIP rooms. Got me? It's the tease. Gotta get 'em droolin' for you, get 'em rock hard. Make 'em think they got a shot with you. They pay big money for that personal time. That's where you make most of your scratch. You act like they're special to you, not just any regular Joe, an' they'll become regulars. The regulars are the best. They'll even ask you out. You always say no, got me? No datin' the customers. No fuckin' 'em, either."

"Am I hired?" she asked, surprise clearly in her voice.

No shit. He was just as surprised that he was wasting time on this woman who had no fucking clue what she was getting herself into.

"Nope. Ain't hirin' you yet. Gotta convince me to. Just like you gotta convince the customers to throw those dollar bills on that stage. Right now, you've only convinced me that you're lost."

"What do you mean?"

"That you don't belong here. This ain't for you."

She nodded. "You're right. That's exactly what I am. I'm lost."

Well, damn. He hadn't expected for her to agree.

Dawg dragged a hand through his hair that needed a damn cut and shook his head. "Woman, you're crazy for bein' here. This ain't you. Anyone can see it."

"No. I'm not crazy. I'm... I'm desperate. I need this... this job."

"Strippin' ain't a job, it's a career." One that could be lucrative for the right woman. Only she wasn't the right woman.

"What do I need to do to get this job?"

The desperation in her voice, in her eyes, killed him, twisted his gut.

"Like I said. Money's in the lap dance. Gotta sell yourself. Right now, you ain't sellin' nothin' 'cept that you're an uptight teacher up there. C'mon down." He held out his hand again. She grabbed her skirt and approached the end of the stage, but avoided his assistance. She took two steps down until her gaze was level with his.

"I need this," she whispered.

He wanted to close his eyes and savor that honeyed voice of hers. But he didn't. He had to remind himself that this was business. "Why?"

"I-I have to make a lot of money and make it fast." The desperation was thick in her voice. And that bugged him.

"Why?"

Instead of answering him, she shook her head.

"Girls ain't got no secrets from me."

"So you think."

Damn. She was probably right. But when they were down on their luck, and they needed help, he was always there for them. He took care of his girls, made sure they didn't want for anything, and in turn, they took care of him. They came to work with a good attitude, and that spilled out on stage.

Happy strippers made the club money, ones with problems didn't. It was difficult to shake off a bad attitude when you were in the spotlight swinging around a pole only wearing a thong. There was nothing to hide up there.

He knew it. The clientele knew it. So he kept his girls happy.

"I'm going to ask again. What do I need to do to get this job?"

Learn more about *Down & Dirty: Dawg* here:
www.books2read.com/Dawg

IF YOU ENJOYED THIS BOOK

Thank you for reading Down & Dirty: Slade. If you enjoyed Slade and Diamond's story, please consider leaving a review at your favorite retailer and/or Goodreads to let other readers know. Reviews are always appreciated and just a few words can help an independent author like me tremendously!

Want to read a sample of my work? Download a sampler book here: BookHip.com/MTQQKK

BEAR'S FAMILY TREE

BEAR Jamison
DAMC Founder
Murdered 1986

MITCH Jamison
Blue Avengers MC
b. 1967

ROCKY Jamison
DAMC
b. 1964

ZAK Jamison
DAMC (President)

AXEL Jamison
Blue Avengers MC

JAYDE Jamison

JEWEL Jamison

DIAMOND Jamison

JAG Jamison
DAMC (Road Captain)

DOC'S FAMILY TREE

		DIESEL Dougherty DAMC (Enforcer)
	ACE Dougherty DAMC (Treasurer) b. 1963	
		HAWK Dougherty DAMC (Vice President)
		DEX Dougherty DAMC (Secretary)
DOC Dougherty DAMC Founder b. 1943		
		IVY Doughtery
	ALLIE Dougherty b. 1968	
		ISABELLA McBride
	ANNIE Dougherty b. 1971	**KELSEA Dougherty**

ALSO BY JEANNE ST. JAMES

* Available in Audiobook

Made Maleen: A Modern Twist on a Fairy Tale *

Damaged *

Rip Cord: The Complete Trilogy *

Brothers in Blue Series:

(Can be read as standalones)

Brothers in Blue: Max *

Brothers in Blue: Marc *

Brothers in Blue: Matt *

Teddy: A Brothers in Blue Novelette *

Brothers in Blue: A Bryson Family Christmas

The Dare Ménage Series:

(Can be read as standalones)

Double Dare *

Daring Proposal *

Dare to Be Three *

A Daring Desire *

Dare to Surrender *

A Daring Journey *

The Obsessed Novellas:

(All the novellas in this series are standalones)

Forever Him *

Only Him *

Needing Him *

Loving Her *

Temping Him *

Down & Dirty: Dirty Angels MC Series®

Down & Dirty: Zak *

Down & Dirty: Jag *

Down & Dirty: Hawk *

Down & Dirty: Diesel *

Down & Dirty: Axel *

Down & Dirty: Slade *

Down & Dirty: Dawg *

Down & Dirty: Dex *

Down & Dirty: Linc *

Down & Dirty: Crow *

Crossing the Line (A DAMC/Blue Avengers Crossover) *

Magnum: A Dark Knights MC/Dirty Angels MC Crossover

Guts & Glory Series

(In the Shadows Security)

Guts & Glory: Mercy *

Guts & Glory: Ryder *

Guts & Glory: Hunter *

Guts & Glory: Walker *

Guts & Glory: Steel *

Guts & Glory: Brick *

Blood & Bones: Blood Fury MC®

Blood & Bones: Trip

Blood & Bones: Sig

COMING SOON!

ABOUT THE AUTHOR

JEANNE ST. JAMES is a USA Today bestselling erotic romance author who loves an alpha male (or two). She was only thirteen when she started writing and her first paid published piece was an erotic story in Playgirl magazine. Her first erotic romance novel, Banged Up, was published in 2009. She is happily owned by farting French bulldogs. She writes M/F, M/M, and M/M/F ménages.

Want to read a sample of her work? Download a sampler book here: BookHip.com/MTQQKK

To keep up with her busy release schedule check her website at www.jeannestjames.com or sign up for her newsletter: http://www.jeannestjames.com/newslettersignup

www.jeannestjames.com
jeanne@jeannestjames.com

Blog: http://jeannestjames.blogspot.com
Newsletter: http://www.jeannestjames.com/newslettersignup
Jeanne's Down & Dirty Book Crew: https://www.facebook.com/groups/JeannesReviewCrew/

f facebook.com/JeanneStJamesAuthor

twitter.com/JeanneStJames

a amazon.com/author/jeannestjames

instagram.com/JeanneStJames

BB bookbub.com/authors/jeanne-st-james

g goodreads.com/JeanneStJames

pinterest.com/JeanneStJames

Get a FREE Erotic Romance Sampler Book

This book contains the first chapter of a variety of my books. This will give you a taste of the type of books I write and if you enjoy the first chapter, I hope you'll be interested in reading the rest of the book.

Each book I list in the sampler will include the description of the book, the genre, and the first chapter, along with links to find out more. I hope you find a book you will enjoy curling up with!

Get it here: BookHip.com/MTQQKK

Made in the USA
Coppell, TX
01 August 2021

59830492R00146